THE ICE DAGGER

A CAVAN OLTBLOOD NOVEL

STEFON MEARS

Thousand Faces Publishing

Also by Stefon Mears

Cavan Oltblood Series
Half a Wizard
The Ice Dagger
Spells of Undeath

Spells for Hire
Devil's Shoestring
Zombie Powder
Spirit Trap
Dragon's Blood (coming December 2019)

The Rise of Magic
Magician's Choice
Sleight of Mind
Lunar Alchemy
Three Fae Monte
The Sphinx Principle

The Telepath Trilogy
Surviving Telepathy
Immoral Telepathy
Targeting Telepathy

Edge of Humanity
Caught Between Monsters
Hunting Monsters

Power City Tales
Not Quite Bulletproof
No Money in Heroism

Devil's Night
Portal-Land, Oregon
Stealing from Pirates
Fade to Gold
With a Broken Sword
Twice Against the Dragon
The House on Cedar Street
Sudden Death
On the Edge of Faerie
Confronting Legends (Spells & Swords Vol. 1)
Uncle Stone Teeth and Other Macabre Poems
The Patreon Collection, Vol. 1-4 (Vol. 5, coming soon)

Published by Thousand Faces Publishing, Portland, Oregon

http://1kfaces.com

Front cover image © Mdorottya | Dreamstime.com

ISBN: 978-1-948490-05-4

THE ICE DAGGER

A Cavan Oltblood novel

PROLOGUE

ONE MONTH AGO...

Everything about this smithy screamed *human*. Starting with the outer walls. There weren't any. Only stone posts holding up the tiled roof. The same blue-gray stone that was used for the floor and the worktables.

Rechaxo shook his head at those missing walls.

True, this smithy was inside the tall, strong walls of this baronial manor. Walls patrolled day and night by guards with crossbows and spears, so the risk of thieves and spies was small, but still.

No outer walls...

Criminal, to let so much lovely heat escape.

But then, humans had no tolerance for proper levels of heat.

The stone seemed solid and reliable enough though. Quarried from those nearby mountains, no doubt. At least they'd chosen chunks that didn't glitter the way the mountains did. An interesting visual phenomenon, but the high crystal content would have made the stone too rough to be regular.

Good stonemasonry had gone into the worktables. The tops of those tables had been hewn from single slabs each. Thick enough to withstand impact, and well supported.

Rechaxo knelt and ran his hand along the thick edge of a table. Cold. He would have to see how well they held heat. That could make the difference, in the finer work.

They looked perfectly level though. So whoever had built this smithy had known their business. At least, as well as any human might.

Rechaxo sniffed that table. He could smell the work that had been done here over the weeks before his arrival. Nothing too recent, but he could still detect three types of iron, and two of steel, underneath the smells of coal and beeswax. Beyond that, only the smell of human sweat.

Human sweat always smelled sour to Rechaxo. Dwarvish sweat smelled ... well, almost like pig iron. As though dwarves had spent so many generations working metal that they were nearly half iron themselves.

Dune elves had worked with metals at least as long as dwarves. Probably longer. But dune elf sweat had a proper, spicy tang to it.

Rechaxo shook his head. He would have to get used to the smell of human sweat if he stayed here. Or likely anywhere else in the north.

He wasn't in Xel-nachde anymore.

Slowly, listening to the acoustics of the smithy — they echoed too much because of the lack of walls, but that might aid the music of his hammers — he inspected the three anvils. They were in good shape, and three was a decent number. Not as good as four, but humans did not worship Indaxia, goddess of smiths.

And a fourth anvil could be installed easily enough.

He moved to the one, inner wall next. This wall had a door. No doubt leading to storage space, and perhaps accommodations for the master smith.

On that wall were the tools of the trade. A good selection of hammers and chisels, tongs and fullers, plates and mandrels and more. All showing plenty of use. Competent tools. More signs that this smithy had been used by a good, if human, smith.

Still, Rechaxo was glad that he was carrying his own tools in the knapsack over beside the majordomo, who was watching Rechaxo examine the smithy.

Finally, Rechaxo moved to the center of the smithy to inspect the furnace. It burned low, now, smelling of old coal and only slightly of new coal. Just enough to keep it burning during inspection, no doubt. He inhaled deeper. Five heavy, bready smells, and two sweeter. So five types of iron, but only two of steel and no other, subtler scents.

Did the humans not work their gold, silver and copper here? Did they leave *everything* to their "jewelers?"

Rechaxo shook his head at the thought and again at what he saw. This furnace would have to go, if he stayed on here. He would need to replace it with a proper dune elf furnace. One that would burn twice as hot and focus the heat more efficiently.

Not to mention driving away some of this northern chill.

And this was the height of summer. Rechaxo could only *imagine* how cold it got here during the winter.

But that was not a concern for today.

The furnace was a concern for today. But it was manageable. Rechaxo knew the spells to make up the deficiencies of the furnace. Impractical in the long term, but in the short term, they would suffice.

So he stood tall and visibly nodded.

He turned back to face the old majordomo. Blinked a moment to remember the human's name. Olivart. Bent like an olive tree, he was, though he held the brown stick he carried more like a scepter than a cane. Gold for the handle and the tip, completing the image.

He had a long gray beard, and much of the hair on his head was gone. His wrinkled skin had a soft, pale look, as though he were near death, but his hazel eyes sparkled with life.

And those eyes were waiting.

Rechaxo nodded again. "The smithy will suffice. For this task, at least."

"I understand that it's not up to dune elf standards," Olivart said. While he spoke, the old man's eyes flitted along Rechaxo's deep red skin, where it could be seen on his face and neck, as well as over the ochres and blood reds of his sandsilk clothes. As though Olivart had never seen a dune elf before.

"If I take a position here," Rechaxo said, "I'd need funds to improve it. Recast the furnace. Perhaps resurface the worktables. Put walls around the outside. How you let so much heat escape—"

"Our people ... have not the tolerance for heat that your people do." Olivart smiled, and Rechaxo had to admit that the man had a charming smile. Must have come with the job. "But outside walls might prove a problem for any human journeymen and apprentices—"

"We haven't discussed journeymen and apprentices."

"We haven't discussed many things about this post." Olivart raised an eyebrow. Rechaxo tried to remember what that human gesture meant, while Olivart continued, "To be honest, I didn't expect you to be interested in staying on. I mentioned the post only because I would have been remiss to not at least *try*..."

Olivart's sentence drifted away as Rechaxo turned. Looked over the smithy again. Could he pass dune elf secrets on to human apprentices? The journeymen, they would be too set in their ways to learn. But apprentices were another matter...

Still. The spells sung to the three oils? The tricks of extracting deepsand from regular sand? Of working deepsand into steel to create true dune elf *licha*?

Passing those secrets on to humans, that might be betraying his entire race.

"No journeymen," he said, his voice high and firm. "No apprentices. Someday perhaps, but not anytime soon."

Olivart tapped the gold handle of his cane against his palm.

"What of those who want to learn the craft?"

"I smelled at least three human smithies on my way here through town," Rechaxo said. "Let aspirants go to them."

More taps.

"Is it reluctance to work with humans? Is that it?"

"Not the way you mean it," Rechaxo said. "But I am a master of my craft, and privy to secrets that have never been taught to any outside my race. I—"

"I see," Olivart said, holding up one hand in that way that Rechaxo knew humans did when they wanted him to stop talking. "I am not trying to steal your secrets. I'm only concerned about the time it would take you to do your work, without the aid of apprentices and journeymen."

Rechaxo laughed like the whipping the desert wind he missed.

"I assure you," he said. "Speed is not at issue. You will see when I make this sword of yours."

"Not of mine," Olivart said, moving his stick back and forth as though he could erase those words. "This sword is for the future Baron Juno. Cavan Oltblood."

"As you say," Rechaxo said with a nod.

Human politics. Could anything be duller?

But Olivart may have misunderstood Rechaxo's tone, because he continued, "And this sword must be the finest work you can craft. Only a masterwork will suffice." Almost as an afterthought, he bowed his head and added, "Given the limitations of the smithy."

"I assure you," Rechaxo said. "You will not be disappointed."

1

———

CAVAN SAT CROSS-LEGGED ON THE COLD STONE FLOOR OF HIS PRIVATE room in the inn, clad only in his brown riding breeches. Dim light emanated from a single beeswax candle, in one of the two sconces by the door. The window shutters, shut and barred. The large, red-and-yellow woven rug that had taken up the center of the room lay bunched up near the bed.

The feather bed. The *big* feather bed. Wide enough that even a man as tall as Cavan could lay across it any direction he chose, without letting his feet dangle off the edge. And he knew that, because he'd tested it the moment he was alone.

Just the kind of feather bed Cavan loved. Slept in as often as he could manage it.

Preferably while sharing it with a lithesome lass. Like that serving wench. Kristiana. With her golden hair, and coquettish glances.

Cavan shook his head. He'd been at his spells too long again, if he was having longing thoughts about his bed and...

He rolled his tight shoulders and neck. He could hear the faint strains of music and laughter, through the solid oak door that led into the hall. His friends were all out there right now, in the main room of the inn. Amra, enjoying her ale and no-doubt teasing the serving men. Ehren, with his perpetual smile. And Qalas, the newest member of their little group. Probably restraining himself still as he studied the dynamics of Cavan and his friends, while pretending that wasn't what he was doing.

Cavan shook his head again.

He drew three slow breaths through his nose. Let them out just as slowly.

Three fast breaths then. Out just as fast.

Finally, one long breath, taking as long as he could possibly take to bring it in, filling his lungs and diaphragm near to bursting before he let that breath out again, every bit as slowly, until his insides felt empty and he sagged forward over his cupped hands and their precious contents.

Cavan closed his eyes. Breathing back to normal now as he sat straight once again, in the pose of consideration that Master Powys had spent so many days teaching him. Back before Cavan had failed his apprenticeship as a wizard.

Failed. But retained those skills. Honed them as he could in the years since.

And today his skills were more than equal to the task before him.

He hoped.

Five days he'd been at this now, with breaks only for meals and sleep. Five days, and he'd learned little more about the crystals than he knew before taking this room.

Cavan opened his eyes. Focused them on the three rare crystals in his hands.

One pale as first light. One royal as the summer sky. One dark as coming night. All three shades of blue, and clear as a fine mountain spring.

Not just crystals. Gemstones.

Three gemstones, mined from the depths of the Ice Dagger, mightiest of the Blue Mountains.

Three gemstones, containing more concentrated magic than Cavan had ever found before in a single place.

But what kind of magic? And how could Cavan access it?

He had tried many spells to unlock their secrets. Spells that could have opened his mind to the ways of rock and tree, to water and fire, to nearly anything he might find.

None of them had worked for these gemstones.

But then, Cavan was likely the first human trained in magic to even hold these gemstones, much less study them. The miners in Juno had found them. Kent, Cavan's foster father and a master jeweler — and steward of Juno in the name of King Draven — had recognized their beauty and rarity.

Falstaff, Cavan's uncle on his father's side and the duke of Nolarr — the duchy within whose borders lay the Redoubt Inn, in which Cavan now sat — had seen them, but not gotten his hands on him.

Cavan had seen to that.

And now Cavan had the gemstones.

He had only one last idea of how to unlock their secrets. Risky, but risk was part of life.

"*Zu nil, aha ne sakanis,*" he said slowly, breathing power over the gems along with words that twisted a spell he already knew. A spell that would extend his own perceptions of magic further than they went on their own. Twisting those words to sharpen them. To direct them.

To open them.

If this spell worked the way he expected, Cavan should synchronize his senses with the pulse of the magic inside those gemstones. Bend his perceptions in ways that might finally, *finally* bring the secrets of that magic into the light.

If the spell failed ... well ... Cavan wasn't quite sure. He had never attempted anything like this before.

This was why he needed so much stone around him, instead of one of the cheaper, wooden rooms upstairs. Stone — thick, normal stone — would cut away the risk of his senses locking onto anything other than the gemstones in his hands.

Of course, if it all went wrong, the stone would also do more to absorb the random flailings of a half-trained wizard than anything else.

Or at the very least, stone was rarely flammable.

Cavan repeated those words again, breathing yet more power with each word.

The gemstones began to glow, each a gentle haze that matched its color.

His spell was working.

Swallowing his excitement through a quick focusing exercise, Cavan steadied his breathing and heart rate, and breathed those words of power across the gemstones one more time.

The three distinct glows spread, became a single, royal blue brightness.

And sucked Cavan inside.

YEARS AGO, BEFORE HE EVER MET EHREN OR AMRA — TO SAY NOTHING of Qalas — Cavan had attempted to scale the mightiest peak of the Dragon Spike Mountains, way to the north. The Dragon's Tooth itself, stretching into the sky so high that the local orc tribes swore that even rocs did not nest in its highest peaks.

Those orcs claimed that their highest god, Great Tilnak, kept a throne at the tip of the Dragon's Tooth, and that when Great Tilnak returned to his throne, he would call together every living orc, then raise up every orc who had fallen in battle, and finally lead the mightiest horde of orcs ever assembled in a sweep across the known lands.

This was how orcs believed the world would end. A great sweep of orcs, conquering all, burning everything in their wake until Great Tilnak carried the survivors triumphantly back to his hall in the sky.

Cavan never made it past the rocs' nests. True, he'd climbed higher than even the local orcs had managed, but still, it had felt like one more failure in Cavan's life. He'd failed to become a warrior. He'd failed to become a wizard. He'd failed at his brief flirtation with thievery — though that had more to do with scruples than skills — and he'd failed to mount the peak of the Dragon's Tooth.

But it was at the highest height he had achieved — miles above the valley below — that Cavan had experienced the worst freezing cold of his life. And not just from the ice and snow on the mountain itself, though those were bad enough even at the height of summer. No, more than that, the wind bore daggers of cold that pierced Cavan's thick layers of clothing straight to his core. Turning his skin blue. Forcing him to stutteringly chant such spells as he could manage to keep his poor, abused body from freezing solid.

One great gust almost did him in.

He had only just managed to prevent himself from falling. Held himself together long enough to reach an outjutting below where he could gather himself to abandon his foolish assault and make his way back down.

Cavan experienced that cold once again as he got sucked inside the three gemstones in his hands — *had been* in his hands?

So cold his body could not shiver. So cold his lungs refused to breathe, so that he could not even see white plumes of breath to assure him that he yet lived.

So cold that...

Wait.

Cavan *had* been seated. But now he stood, if frozen still. The gemstones *had* been in Cavan's cupped hands. But Cavan's hands were empty now, hanging at his sides.

Cavan *had* been in his room in the inn.

Now Cavan stood inside a solid block of ice. Ice three shades of blue: pale, royal and twilight...

No. Not ice.

Gemstones.

Cavan *was* inside the gemstones. That had not been a trick of his spell.

But what did that mean? Was his body...

No.

Wrong question.

This spell twisted Cavan's perceptions. Not his body. Cavan's *mind* was inside the gemstones. Not his body. That was why he could not see past the stones themselves, when the candlelight should have flickered by now. Should have shown him the gray stone floor, and walls, and ceiling.

Stop.

Distractions. The biggest danger of this kind of magic.

Already Cavan had lost time worrying about details, when he needed to focus on his goal. How much time had already passed? How much longer could he remain here?

Or was he trapped now? Frozen forever inside the magic of the gemstones?

More distractions.

Cavan attempted his focusing exercises, but most of them oriented around his body. His heart rate, his breathing, the feel of his muscles.

He could sense none of those things. Only the frozen solidity inside the gemstones...

Ice.

They were ice magic. Had to be.

Good. That was a step in the right direction.

And then, without the lips to voice them or the lungs to blow power, Cavan focused on the words of his spell. Repeated it three more times in his mind, here inside the gemstones.

With the third repetition, Cavan's perceptions went deeper still.

Power crashed on him like a tidal wave. Shattered the feel of the cold, while deepening Cavan's sense of the cold itself.

Cavan's mind swam...

Cavan, six years old, sitting on the back cobblestones of Kent's house in Tradeton. Sitting at the feet of the traveling wizard whose name he never learned. A smiling man, with snow white hair and beard a stark contrast to the deep black of his southern skin.

Kent, with his proud belly and fine clothes, stood beside the wizard. The wizard was talking.

"Yes, the boy has talent. There's no denying it. The question is, does he possess the discipline required for the art? That will be his failing. At least, in my opinion. Despite his touch of the gift, I suggest that you try his hand at war. Then, one day, perhaps..."

The scene shifted.

A memory?

Cavan, an infant. Held so warm against the naked bosom of ... his mother? Her skin feverish and sweat-soaked. Her limbs shaking, but clinging tightly to Cavan's tiny form. The room around him, blurry, like the dozen voices talking at once. Worried female voices, angry male voices, angry female voices...

Too many. Too many to understand. Too many to pick apart. And infant Cavan could not understand their words.

Trapped, amid a tumult of emotions.

All infant Cavan could do was cry.

Another shift.

Cavan, ten years old. Holding a training sword and a round shield that was too heavy for him. Five other trainees in the melee, three boys and two girls. All of them older than Cavan. Stronger than Cavan. He spun this way and that. Leading with his shield, which took a constant stream of blows. As though all the others were going to eliminate him before turning on each other.

Young Cavan's heart pounded faster than their strikes. His shaky arm tried to lash out. To strike back. But too slow. Nothing connected. His feet frozen in place. Only able to spin in place. Only able to present himself as a target.

Nothing he could do. Nothing he could...

Wait.

That wasn't how it happened.

Cavan remembered that day. The others were larger and stronger, yes, but Cavan had always been quick. He had thrown his shield at the Tarry boy and brought the blunted blade across the larger boy's thighs. Had turned and dove past a pair of strikes, before...

He had lost. True. But he had not frozen...

Frozen.

Of course.

Cavan studied the scene the gemstones showed him. Not as a memory or self-blame, but for what it was.

Magic.

SOMETIME LATER, CAVAN STUMBLED INTO THE MAIN ROOM OF THE INN. His teeth chattered, and he huddled for the warmth of his shaking arms. If his skin wasn't blue, it felt as though it should have been.

The cacophony of the early evening had died down by now. Of the six bench tables, only two were still occupied. One in the far corner, where traders negotiated in harsh, quiet voices while their guards diced.

Not the table Cavan wanted.

He aimed his unsteady feet at the other table. His friends were at this table. Amra, eyes closed, juggled a dagger with one hand while she drank from a clay tankard. Ehren and Qalas watched her. The latter, slack-jawed in amazement at the speed of her twirling dagger, while Ehren, in a low voice, was likely explaining exactly how many times he'd seen her do this particular trick.

But Cavan bypassed his friends just then. Their table sat next to the fire, and even across the room from it, that fire had felt as warm and welcoming as a bath in a hot spring.

Good, but not enough right now.

He plunked himself down on the warm stones beside the fire and brought his hands so close the flames that Ehren called out to him in a sharp tone.

"Cavan!"

Cavan didn't look away from the dancing orange and red heat that restored prickly feeling to his numb, shaking hands and fingers. Not when he heard Kristiana's sweet voice ask if he was all right. Not even when he felt Ehren's steadying hand on his shoulder.

Cavan focused on drawing that wonderful heat from the fire into himself, beginning with his hands, and spreading it up his arms. From there it would reach his torso...

"Cavan," Amra said from where she sat, "will you reassure these two mother hens before they yank you up and drag you off to bed or something."

In a more thoughtful tone she added, "Though you'd probably like that if only the wench did it."

Cavan uttered something. A grunt, most likely. He kept his focus on that delicious heat. Spreading it through his torso, then up his neck and into his head before sending it down, down to the very tips of his toes. Driving out the clinging chill that those gems had spread throughout him.

Finally, when Cavan felt warm enough to be human again — or at least as warm as a human might have been outside on a cool, late summer evening like tonight — he turned to face his friends.

Ehren, still crouched and ready. Ehren, with his long, sun-blond hair, fair skin, and spotless white clothing — marks of a favored priest of Zatafa the Sun — from his linen shirt and breeches to his low, doeskin boots.

Worry in Ehren's clear blue eyes.

Amra, watching from the table, her tankard and dagger still in her hands. Amra, with her tanned skin and curly black hair. "Short but deadly" as Ehren liked to call her, all in black leathers that tapered to show off both her curves and her muscles — and she had plenty of each — with the hilt of her wyrding greatsword jutting up above her shoulder.

Laughter in her green-and-gold eyes.

Qalas, with his ebon skin and his black hair shorn tight against his scalp. He still wore the brown, studded leather armor he'd worn as one of the duke's top hunters. Before leaving Nolarr's service.

Qalas' deep blue eyes looked uncertain. Torn between Ehren's concern and Amra's amusement.

Yes, his friends were all watching.

As was Kristiana, apparently, who stood over Ehren's shoulder, where the priest knelt beside Cavan. Kristiana's beautiful face looked as worried as Ehren did.

Cavan smiled at her.

Ehren's hand dropped away. He shook his head in smiling disbelief. "He's fine."

Ehren went back to his place at the table.

Cavan stood up, still smiling at Kristiana. Her golden hair was hanging straight down past her shoulders, tickling the skin exposed by the enticingly low neckline of her blue bodice. The white shirt underneath, with its poofy sleeves, teased at the softness of her arms, but her long green skirt hid the rest of her in a way Cavan found tantalizing.

Kristiana wasn't looking Cavan in the eye though. She was staring him straight in the chest.

The bare chest. Cavan was still clad in nothing but his brown riding breeches, with belt pouches for his spells and the gemstones. Most of his swarthy skin on display. He ran his fingers through his soft brown hair to show off a few lean muscles.

He was all ready to say something charming when...

"What do you think?" Amra asked, voice just shy of laughter. "Is she counting his scars?"

"Not likely," Ehren said. "He only has the three, though the one just below his collarbone is somewhat impressive."

"I think she's just returning the favor," Qalas ventured. "After all, he's been staring her in the chest since we got here days ago. Perhaps she thinks it's a sign of respect, where he comes from."

"Food, my lord?" Kristiana asked, meeting his eyes now, with a wink.

Cavan's stomach rumbled louder than the crackling of the fire.

His friends all laughed.

"I'll take that as a yes," Kristiana said, and swept away.

"Ale too, if you'd please," Cavan called after her.

"Did you hear that?" Ehren said. "Please. I think he likes this one."

"He likes all of them," Amra said.

"So how can you tell the special ones then?" Qalas asked.

"Now?" Cavan interrupted, taking a seat beside Ehren, across from Qalas, and choosing not to point out that "please" was not a rare word in their company. "You finally decide to join in the jokes, and you wait until they're at my expense?"

"Seemed safest," Qalas said with a smile. "After all, if I made the others angry, Ehren might deny me healing or Amra might beat me senseless. You, I'm pretty sure I could take."

The others laughed louder now, and Amra clapped Qalas on the shoulder.

"Today, you are truly part of the group," she said.

"Does that mean you'll tell me the story behind that sword of yours?"

The greatsword, whose hilt jutted above Amra's shoulder. The weapon she was never without. Its blade as black as night, and harder than steel.

"Not yet," Amra said mysteriously. "Have to save *some* stories for those long nights on the road."

Cavan's stomach rumbled again.

"Better hurry up with that food," Amra called.

"Please!" all three of Cavan's friends added.

Cavan shook his head, but knew better than to defend himself from their teasing. Still, as his eyes took in Qalas' studded leathers again, he did interrupt their fun.

"Are you happy in those? If you'd like a change of armor—"

"Armor's armor," Qalas said with a shrug. "Not heavy enough to slow me down, and not noisy enough to bother me. Does the job."

Kristiana returned then, carrying a platter featuring a big bowl of lamb stew with beets and carrots, a heel of bread — buttered even — and another round of ale for the table.

"Have to keep your strength up," she said.

Cavan was about to reply, but Ehren said loudly, "*Thank* you, Kristiana. And I promise, we won't keep him long. But we do need him for a few minutes."

Kristiana's cheeks pinked at that, but she smiled as she turned away.

"'rying 'o 'uin it 'or 'e?" Cavan asked around a mouthful of delicious dark bread. Not as good as Oltoss rye, but still tasty.

"I wasn't trying to ruin anything," Ehren insisted.

"Honestly," Amra said, "if you don't invite that girl to your room soon, she's likely to show up on her own."

Qalas drew breath to add something while Cavan bolted down a third of his bowl of wonderful, spiced stew, but Ehren held up a restraining hand.

In a low voice, Ehren asked, "You've stumbled in here exhausted before, but not like that. Not frozen half to death. What did you learn?"

Cavan patted a pouch at his belt.

"They're ice magic. Powerful stuff, with more flexibility than I would have thought. Tricky though. They feel..." — Cavan pondered that while he finished his stew, and the others let him, for a change — "they feel almost as though ice, through them, is like a true element. Not an aspect of water and air, as taught by Master—"

"We don't need the history," Amra said, always eager to cut off a potential lecture, though Ehren was worse about that than Cavan ever was. Or at least Cavan thought so. Amra finished, "What do they *do*?"

"A lot." Cavan shook his head. "Too much. As they are it would be like ... like..." — Cavan's eyes settled on the hearth — "like trying to pick up fire by a lick of flame."

"So we need to find you a brand," Qalas said.

"Yes," Cavan said, surprised that those words had come from Qalas instead of Ehren, for a change. Perhaps Qalas truly *was* feeling more a part of the group now. "Exactly."

"So," Ehren said, "you need a staff then? Or a wand?"

"Where does one buy such a thing?" Amra sounded as though she wanted to hurry this along.

Cavan furrowed his eyebrows at her.

She puffed out an impatient sigh.

"I can't be the only one listening to gossip here," she said. "Not as though we've had much else to do, apart from training up Qalas' horse."

"I've been listening too," Qalas said. "Troop movements. The duke put out the cry. He's rallying forces."

Ehren's eyebrows rose. He turned to Cavan.

"He can't move against you or Kent directly, not without breaking his oath. And Zatafa won't let him break that oath. I saw to it. Could he declare war on Juno?"

"The king would never allow it," Cavan said with a firm shake of his head. "It's *his* land right now. He'd send in the royal army, close off the pass and trap Falstaff's forces here in Nolarr. And then Falstaff's real problems would start."

"Only if the king gets word in time," Qalas said. He was leaning forward now. Intent.

"The mine," Amra said. "Where those crystals of yours came from. The duke knows about them, even if he doesn't know what they do. If he moves fast, he could invade. Take the mine and who knows how many crystals before King Draven could kick him out again."

"She's right," Ehren added. "And if the stones are as powerful as you say, we need to get into those mines. Find out how many there might be. If they fall into the duke's hands..."

"I've learned all I can here. And I'm not going to try to stop and *make* a staff," — Cavan directed those words at Amra, to answer her query — "not until we're back in Juno."

"But the *mine*," Ehren said.

Cavan knew where Ehren was saying. The mine was in section of the Blue Mountains that formed the border between the duchy of Nolarr on one side and the barony of Juno on the other. Going far enough into Juno to find staff wood meant going away from the mine.

So Cavan spoke over his friend.

"*Can wait* until I have these things in a staff." Cavan patted the belt pouch again. "I need a focus for these gems if I'm going to figure out how to control them. They may even help us find more of their kind. Figure out how many we're dealing with, potentially."

"Where then?" Qalas asked.

"Juno proper," Cavan said, another bite of bread so close to his mouth he could taste the butter. "Olivart will rally the troops if I tell him it's necessary. Wouldn't be enough to stop the duke, but it should slow him down, at the least. Plus, the baronial manor has plenty of fruit trees, and I think lemon would be perfect for working with these gemstones."

Amara opened her mouth to say something, but Cavan hurried to finish his thought.

"*Besides*, I want to leave Kent's family sword with Olivart. I can pick up another one there. This one should really go to Reed or Alec. They're his *actual* sons—"

"So we're leaving in the morning?" Amra said. "Finally?"

"Can we afford to wait 'til morning?" Qalas said. "The moon's waning, but there should still be enough light to take the Royal Road."

"Beginning at dawn will give us the blessing of Zatafa," Ehren said. "Plus, we're going to want one more night on real beds. No way to know when we'll see one again."

Kristiana swept past, refilling their mugs of ale, but pausing long enough to give Cavan a saucy look before she checked on the table full of merchants and guards.

Yes, leaving in the morning sounded much better than riding right now.

And then he turned his full attention to his food.

OF ALL THE WAYS TO AWAKEN IN THE MORNING, NAKED IN A FEATHERBED, with a beautiful woman — also naked, and curled against him — was Cavan's favorite.

He was *warm*. Deliciously toasted, after feeling as though he'd never be warm again.

He was happy, too.

Oh, the fears of last night had not abated. He was worried about what Duke Falstaff was doing and he was worried about the people of Juno who might get hurt in the process.

But Cavan's life had taught him to savor little bits of happiness wherever he could.

And he wanted to enjoy this one just a moment longer.

Nothing like celebrating the successful application of a magical twist of his own invention. To say nothing of the knowledge he'd gained by it.

And that Kristiana had been more than willing to celebrate with him — even if she didn't understand what they were celebrating — well, that just made life all the sweeter.

She stirred slightly. Shifted against him with a small sound that he took as protest against the onset of morning.

It was a quarter hour to sunrise, precisely, when Cavan's eyes had opened. Exactly as he'd planned. Sunrise, sunset, midday and midnight, those times were all a wizard's for the asking. Any wizard worth his pouch of spells could feel them, no matter where he was. Could set little alerts for himself when they neared or occurred.

Even a half-trained wizard like Cavan could do it. But that might have been because his tutelage had been under the great Master Powys, and Master Powys emphasized details like time.

Right now, that emphasis meant two things. One, that Cavan was awake in time to get dressed before Amra came banging on his door to wake him up.

And two, it meant that the day had finally come to leave the Redoubt Inn. It meant he would spend no more nights flirting with Kristiana. Worse, it would mean only the one night in her embrace.

But Cavan had to admit that he relished the little thrill of adventure fluttering in his belly. On the road again. Facing soldiers, and who knew what in the bowels of that giant mountain, the Ice Dagger.

Cavan reached down and stroked Kristiana's bare side. Perhaps he had time to awaken her. Perhaps even to have a little more fun before—

"Oh, I'm sure he's smart enough to get out here soon," Amra's voice said loudly from somewhere down the hall...

Somewhere outside Cavan's thick door...

Hells. She was right outside his room, wasn't she?

And here Kristiana lay, still smelling of honey and bread, as she had last night...

Grumbling, Cavan dragged himself out of bed as gently as he could. No point in awakening Kristiana before he had to.

He dressed in the slivers of pre-dawn that fell in around the cracks of his closed shutters. Not much light, but operating in the gloom was not new to Cavan.

He slipped into his riding breeches, a green tunic, and his calf-high leather boots. Belted on his spells, his gemstones, and his foster father's family sword. Finally, he draped his light, loose-woven gray wool cloak over his shoulders and fixed it into place with its gold clasp, featuring a blue mountain emblem. The baronial sigil of Juno.

Cavan checked his pack. Made sure everything else he needed was in order.

Finally, he returned to the soft mattress of the bed. Ran his eyes longingly over Kristiana's frame once more, but contented his hand with her shoulder.

A gentle nudge.

Another.

"Sweet Kristiana," he whispered.

Then again until she stirred. Smiled up at him through her sleep-mussed golden hair.

"Must you leave so soon, my lord?" she asked. She'd seemed to relish calling Cavan "my lord" instead of his proper name. Even though she knew full well he wasn't a lord yet. "I'm not due in the kitchen until midday."

Cavan drew breath to answer, but she shook her head. Smiled a little wider.

"I'm teasing," she said. "I heard your friends. Amra, especially, can't wait to leave."

"I'd stay longer if I could," Cavan said.

"Sweet of you to say," she said.

And then he kissed her, and with a final goodbye, he left her to enjoy the feather bed for as long as she could.

He closed the door softly behind him as he stepped out into the hall.

"Good," Qalas said. He stood only just outside knocking range, leaning on his halberd. A wicked weapon, it was. Taller than Qalas himself, with a spike and axe at one end, and a steel-wrapped handle at the other. And Cavan knew Qalas was just as good with either end of it. "Another few minutes and I was supposed to get you."

"Ehren's idea?"

Qalas nodded.

"Thanks," Cavan said, clapping him on the shoulder, and leading him back into the main room. "How long have you three been awake?"

"A good hour," Amra said from the same table where they'd been sitting the night before. "I *thought* we were supposed to hit the road early."

"Dawn should be early enough for any man," Ehren managed through a yawn. He never looked quite awake before the sun rose. Still, Ehren could even smile when he yawned.

"Not a man," Amra said, fluttering her eyelashes.

Qalas joined them at the table then, while serving men distributed tankards of fresh water and bowls of lamb-and-beet porridge. Likely made from the remains of last night's stew.

"No flirting with the serving men?" Cavan asked, blinking his eyes at Amra.

"Too scrawny," she said. "I'd break them in half."

And then they broke their fast. Cavan had to admit, the innkeep had done a splendid job of turning the leftover stew into porridge. Where the stew had been spicier, the porridge was heartier. More than enough to see them through midday.

As they ate, dawn broke. Even without his wizardly training, Cavan would have known the instant it did, merely by watching Ehren.

Ehren, just before the dawn — yawning, sagging, eyes drooping, nearly forcing himself to eat.

Ehren, as the sun rose, even though it did not shine on him directly — back straightening, smile widening, eyes alert once more. Life filled his voice as he uttered a quick prayer to Zatafa in the tongue of ancient, lost Penthix.

Qalas paused his eating while Ehren prayed. Cavan and Amra did not.

When Ehren finished, Qalas said, "We should get food for the road. Better here than—"

Ehren held up that wondrous backpack of his. Cavan was more than used to the way Ehren could pull a seemingly endless array of foods and necessities from inside it, but apparently it was still too knew to Qalas.

The ex-hunter shook his head. "Are there *any* limits to that thing?"

"Not so far," Ehren said, setting it back down. "But then, I only come to it with need, not greed."

"Don't tell me it cares about your intentions," Amra scoffed.

"It's old magic," Cavan said. "And beyond anything *I* understand. It may well."

"Where did you get it?" Qalas asked.

"Another time for that," Amra said, tone all business, and her words quite clear despite her mouth full of porridge. "We're ready to go as soon as we're done here, yes? No final trysts?"

Cavan shook his head. To Qalas he said, "Replaced your bow?"

"No," Qalas said, disgusted. "The best weapons around here have been shipped away for the duke's troops."

"We'll find you another in Juno." Cavan turned to Amra and Ehren. "The horses ready?"

"Checked on them myself," Amra said. "And Qalas' Ondiq took to our command training readily. A good horse."

"A rouncey, remember," Qalas said. "Not a hobby like you three have. Sprint too fast and you'll leave us behind."

"Don't worry," Ehren said. "We'll keep that in mind."

Cavan pushed his empty bowl forward.

"Let's go."

2

———————

KAETHE HAD ONCE BEEN TOLD THAT ALL DWARVISH MUSIC EMULATED the sounds of mining. On mornings like this one, she could understand why.

She stood at the mouth of the mine. A great gash in the side of the mighty Ice Dagger itself, tallest and broadest of the Blue Mountains. Or at least, the highest peak here in Juno.

She stood within that yawning chasm, a naturally occurring cave that had formed the very beginning of the mine, back when tin was first discovered.

She stood at the outer edge of the cave, and she listened.

Clinks and pings, smacks and thumps, all coming in a steady rhythm that told her that her workers were doing their level best to meet the day's quota.

They were good men and women, these miners. Kaethe almost never had to come down on them. At least, not here at work. Their antics in town just after payday were another matter...

But this was not that day. This was a beautiful late summer day, when the skies seemed to carry on their pale blue from the peak of the Ice Dagger high above. As though the great mountain were but a spike in a dam, and if some giant plucked it forth, the skies would open up in a torrent that would wash the world away.

Kathe looked back down across the lush, verdant land of Juno.

No sign of that giant coming today.

To work then.

She began smelling stone dust no more than three steps in. A pleasant, familiar smell. Like chalk, the others said, but Kaethe always detected a smokier undersmell, as though the act of mining had given the dust a tang.

The dust was not thick enough here that she would need a kerchief for her face, but she donned it anyway, before she descended. She knew the miners down below all had their kerchiefs on.

Rules were rules, and Kaethe enforced them all equally. When they had to arrive, when they took their breaks, when they stopped for the day, and how they did their work. How many torches they were allotted, and how many paces between each.

Every rule had to be followed. Safety — and productivity — demanded it.

Kaethe had been overseer of this mine for more than twenty years now. Her eyes were not as sharp as they once were, but her hearing was still good enough that she could pick out which miners were swearing when there was a break in the steady rhythm of their work.

And her back was as straight as it ever had been. A point of pride to her that, despite the graying of her short hair and the wrinkles on her weathered face, she had yet to bow before the weight of her years like her own boss, Olivart.

She eschewed the finer clothes that were the right of her position, as well. She dressed as the other miners did. Rough, strong breeches and tunics, with simple undyed shirts beneath. A belt for tools, and flint and tinder in case any of the torches guttered out.

Kaethe paced quickly through the yawning cavern and started down into the mine, following the wooden rails that could carry carts of tin back to the surface and down to where her assistants could log the haul before the teamsters transported them on.

Here the mine was still wide enough for a dozen miners to walk abreast, even while a cart came the other direction. It wouldn't narrow until farther down.

Under her arm, she carried her checklist. She had to make sure her workers were hitting their marks, with their lunch break so near.

If they were ever going to slack off, they did it when they felt that lunch, or day's end, was approaching.

Thus, Kaethe made it her habit to randomly come down for a check close to those times. Just so they never knew when she would be watching.

The mere thought of them hustling back to their picks made her smile.

But the music of their mining was steady, and she was sure she'd come back with every box ticked.

That thought made her smile wider.

Down and down she went, following the gentle slope of the mine, which curved wherever the tin vein required it to. Not often, fortunately, though Kaethe could pick out three spots along her route where the shimmering crystals took on a different hue in the torchlight coming from the sconces, placed every dozen strides.

In those places of different hues, Kaethe was sure a branch might find something else worth mining. Iron, perhaps, or silver...

Perhaps even gold.

Oh, that would be a wonder. To oversee a gold mine.

That thought brought back the familiar itch. That little nagging feeling at the back of her mind. She had it whenever she felt that an opportunity was going wasted.

And the truth she tried to hide from herself, every day, was that an opportunity was going wasted in that mine right this minute. And would, until the order finally came...

Kaethe gritted her teeth, and kept about her rounds. Tried not to think about that opportunity.

She passed the first squad on clean-up detail. They had the small hammers and picks, checking a place where the vein seemed dry up, to make sure no tiny sliver remained. And then smoothing the walls again, and testing in case they needed to be fortified.

Kaethe had never seen a mine that did not need fortification. Not before she came to Juno.

Most mines required buttresses in key places, sometimes all along their length. Critical, they were, to ensure that the mine did not collapse. This mine, it seemed, did not. Not even near the chasm, which spanned far enough that building a solid wooden bridge had been some trick.

Even there, though, the mine needed no supports.

The stonemasons here in Juno had laughed when Kaethe had asked about buttressing. Told her how many generations had quarried stone before tin had ever been discovered here. How they swore up and down that this was the hardest stone they'd ever worked with, and insisted —*insisted* — that it would not cave in unless the miners did something colossally stupid.

Kaethe had to stare down a whole room full of proud stonemasons who were asking, without asking, if Kaethe were colossally stupid.

The townspeople still talked about the tongue lashing she gave those arrogant pricks.

A thought that brought the smile back to Kaethe's face.

Two more squads on clean up or finishing detail before Kaethe reached the proper day's work. Four carts scattered among three more squads of miners, ten miners to a squad, plus a foreman.

Kaethe checked each cart first, measuring to make sure it reached the minimum level etched into the sides.

Then she watched the workers for a few minutes. Watched their techniques, correcting one or two who were using their arms too much and their backs too little. Common problem, especially among big men. But fixing that habit now would mean an easier life for them in their later years.

Finally, she checked with the foreman for problems. None reported. Everything moving along smoothly.

That was to be expected. Truth was that there might have been a dozen little problems that morning, from tardiness to laziness or worse. But if the foreman handled it and resolved it, then officially he could report that there was no problem. That way Kaethe didn't have to get involved, which might mean a firing. If the offense was bad enough.

Mining was the sort of work that always had little problems. It was rough and demanding, and, often, so were the people who did it. So anything that could be resolved without becoming official, was better resolved that way.

No problems reported, which meant that everyone was happy so far.

As was Kaethe, even as she crossed that chasm and went deeper still until she reached the current end of the mine.

Then the itch came back, and her smile went away.

The main branch of the mine ended in stone, of course, and would until the nearby veins were tapped and the miners had to proceed deeper.

A small, exploratory side channel had been opened up to the right of the ending, near where the vein appeared to be thickest.

And it was the right call. The vein did continue at the same thickness, down that passage.

However, they'd found something else down that passage.

Gemstones.

Kaethe was no jeweler. She'd thought they were sapphires, and reported as much to Olivart, when she'd handed over the small handful of samples she'd brought back.

Then Olivart got the steward involved.

The steward was a jeweler.

Apparently, these gemstones weren't sapphires.

Apparently, they were a lot more rare and valuable than sapphires.

Rare enough, and valuable enough, that the steward had immediately suspended mining activities down that branch until further notice. He'd even had the branch boarded up, to cut off the risk of any miners attempting to take off with any jewels. Even instituted a new rule that each miner be searched at the day's end, just to make sure that hadn't happened.

Kaethe hated it, but she did it.

Rules were rules, and she enforced them all.

But what bothered her most was that it wasn't some great vein. There weren't even enough of the gemstones to fill a third of a cart. Maybe not even a fourth.

Kaethe pulled a torch down off the wall, told a foreman what she was going to do (rules again, because now Kaethe herself would have to be searched), and slipped past the wooden barricade and into that little channel.

Here the sounds were muted by the wood. Here the single torch guttered from the lack of breeze.

It wasn't a long passage. She couldn't afford to stay in here for much time, not with the torch eating her air.

But she wanted to see them again.

Oh, how they glittered in the torchlight. A dozen shades of blue, at least. And so few of them. She'd forgotten. Unless that vein reached deeper than it looked, there might not even be enough to fill a sack.

But beautiful they were. And their shape, there along the wall, as of the back of some kind of lizard that had been frozen in place by the years. She could even make out the shape of its legs. She held the torch closer, to watch the thousand thousand reflections within the countless facets.

She brought the torch even closer.

What was that rumble?

Kaethe had been deep inside this mine more times than she could count over the years, and never had she heard a sound like it down here before.

But she had heard it elsewhere.

She ran back past the barricade before her mind could finish ordering her body to do it.

"Out!" she bellowed. "Everyone out! Now!"

But these miners, they'd never done this work anywhere else.

They didn't understand what a sound like that meant, deep within the bowels of a mountain. If they didn't get at least across the chasm in time...

"Quake!" she bellowed, throwing every once of command into her voice that she could muster. "Everyone out now!"

Screams and panic now. Not enough time spent practicing this sort of evacuation. The locals never believed it necessary. Kaethe should have insisted. She knew better, even if they didn't.

Kaethe started ushering the stragglers out herself, wondering when it would begin. When the shaking would start. When the dust would come down from above, just before the tunnel collapsed and tons of mountain would rain down and crush them all.

Still she heard that rumble, faint within the ground beneath her. But still the shaking did not start.

Kaethe yelled for them all to hurry. To get the hell out of there.

At least the foremen understood the urgency. They organized the flight as well as they could, though the tunnel was now littered with tools.

Better tools than bodies.

Still, though, no shaking.

Kaethe couldn't understand it. The others had fled almost out of sight. Only Warren, the oldest of the foremen — a widower who'd actually flirted with Kaethe from time to time — lingered behind, yelling back that she had to flee too.

But Kaethe turned about. The lack of shaking and dust was too puzzling. It itched at her mind worse than even the wasted time not mining those gemstones.

It had been loudest down that newest passage.

Kaethe worried at her lip. She still held the torch in one hand...

"C'mon!" Warren yelled. "You too, Kaethe."

Must've been worried to be calling her by her proper name, when they were at the mine.

But the shaking hadn't started. Only that odd rumble.

Kaethe held up a hand to acknowledge Warren, but tell him to get moving.

She stepped carefully over the that new passage. To the wooden barricade.

Kaethe pulled it back.

She saw a lizard-like face, and way too many sharp teeth.

And then she never saw anything else.

3

By mid-day, Cavan and his friends rode as three little groups instead of one large group.

Ehren was in the lead, as usual, on his blond chestnut, Highsun. Ehren rode alone right now, because he was so happy to be on the road that he'd been singing songs to Zatafa all morning.

All. Morning.

Cavan had been the first to drop back, reining his blue roan, Dzink, to a slow trot to let Ehren have a lead and give his own ears a bit of a rest.

Ehren ... had more enthusiasm than bardic talent. A fine baritone voice, but not one he knew how to use melodically.

Or maybe Cavan was just tired of hearing his friend sing.

Anyway, Cavan had dropped back first, and farthest.

Amra and Qalas had dropped back a short while later, her on her bay, Chestnut, and him on his buckskin, Ondiq. They rode side-by-side, but Cavan didn't think for a moment that they were flirting or swapping stories.

Oh, Amra wasn't above flirting — and Qalas certainly had the kind of muscled physique she favored — but he could tell from the way they spoke and the way they gestured that they could be discussing only one thing.

Troop movements.

Odd, that the duke's troops were not on the Royal Road. The Royal Road was dirt so hard-packed as to be dust free. As though it were brick, not dirt. Or maybe that was due to the spells that had been laid on it in ancient times. This road, and all roads like it, went back to the days when the kingdom of Rentiss stretched sea to sea.

Certainly, the Royal Road eased the way to travelers. Took less effort for even casual speed, and had an almost springy quality to it. As though riding or walking it were more like traversing thick grass than hard dirt.

Perfect for troops and horses. And yet, the duke's troops were well off the road.

Maybe the troop movements had nothing to do with Juno?

Natural features did a good deal to isolate Nolarr and keep its borders secure. The Blue Mountains to the west. The landlocked sea of Tormyr to the south. And the tall Cliffs of Evermourn formed most of its eastern and northeastern border overlooking the kingdom of Surta. To attack Nolarr from Surta, Surtan troops would have to come up over the sloping hills near Surta's western border — and the rest of Nolarr's northern border — shared with the kingdom of Holst.

Surta and Holst had the kind of bloody history that meant neither could bring troops near Nolarr without a response from the other.

So it was *unlikely* that either Holst or Surta would invade. But if Cavan were duke of Nolarr, he'd made sure both Surta and Holst knew Nolarr had an army ready to defend itself.

Perhaps the troop movements were as simple as that? A matter of security?

Perhaps.

And yet, by midday, Cavan had seen less traffic than he expected. Local farmers and tradesmen and salesmen, certainly, but where were the caravans? There should have been at least two caravans by now, heading for the Blue Mountains ahead of them to the west, but Cavan had not seen even one.

Still, it was a fine, beautiful day. The larks were singing (not quite drowned out by Ehren), and Cavan could smell corn and peas on the air, even above the grasses.

And the view from the Royal Road through this part of Nolarr was lovely. Rolling hills of farms, small towns in the distance...

...and troops.

No great army gathered, not that Cavan could see yet. In fact, what he saw looked no larger than squads on maneuvers. Cavan would almost have thought that this was to fool the locals into thinking nothing was happening.

Except that there were no caravans.

Finally, when Ehren gave his vocal cords a break to toss lunchtime apples and cheese back to his friends, Cavan voiced the question that had started nagging at him more and more over the past hour.

"Where are the caravans?"

"Gone, of course," Amra said, as though it were the most obvious thing in the world.

Worse, Qalas was nodding as though he found it just as obvious.

"But, we're past midsummer. There should be at least one more round of caravans before the harvest. Not to mention that some run year-round."

"And all of them hurried their asses out of Nolarr a week or two ago," Amra said, as all four friends moved their horses to ride side-by-side now. And the Royal Road was more than wide enough for them to do so comfortably.

"Of course," Qalas said. "The minute the traders caught wind of troop movements, they sped everything up. Wanted to get their caravans through the pass before it got closed."

"You think it will come to that?" Cavan said. "The troops might be heading for maneuvers near the northern borders."

Qalas shook his head. "No one in the inn was talking about Surta or Holst."

"Besides," Amra said. "If you traded for a living, would you take the gamble?"

"No," Cavan said with a slight head shake. Then asked, "And what have your two military minds concluded?"

Ehren's smile faded as he caught up to Cavan's implications. Truly the man had no idea what his friends got up to while he was singing.

"The duke's forces are heading west," Amra said. "Not north."

"Which means trouble for us," Qalas said. "No reason to keep their troops off the Royal Road, not unless they're trying to hide something."

"But obviously everyone knows—" Cavan started, but Amra interrupted him.

"Every local in *Nolarr* knows. Every one of them has either lived here long enough to see the signs and know what they mean, or was told by someone who has. No, those troop movements are being hidden from *us*."

"We can see them," Cavan said.

"No," Qalas said, face as grim as his voice. "We can see that they have squads watching us as we ride out of Nolarr."

Cavan blinked as he absorbed that.

"Why?" Ehren asked. "There's no need. It's not as though they can attack."

"Provoke them and they can defend themselves," Amra said. "I'm willing to bet that somewhere between here and the pass we'll find ourselves provoking them. One way or another."

"No," Cavan said. Normally wouldn't consider contradicting Amra when she was willing to wager. Her record was too good. But in this case he didn't see the logic. "I mean what would be the point? Falstaff knows we can carve through his soldiers, if we have to."

"A couple of dozen, sure," Qalas said. "But what if he has fifty waiting for us? Or a hundred? Or just a company of archers?" Qalas shook his head. "I don't know about you guys, but I don't fight so well with a few dozen arrows in me."

"You know this from experience?" Amra asked.

Her tone sounded serious enough, but Cavan knew better. Before he could answer, though, Qalas did.

"Six was plenty," he said, voice quiet. "Punched right through the rings of mail I had for a hauberk." He glanced over at Ehren. "Didn't have a priest of Zatafa with us. Nilasah either. When I fell, I didn't think I'd ever get back up."

"Who saved you?" Amra asked.

Qalas gave her an evil grin. The first Cavan had seen from the ex-hunter.

"That's a tale for another time," he said. Then to Cavan he added, "Right now I'm more worried about the duke's soldiers."

Their logic seemed sound enough to Cavan, but the more he thought about it, the more something about the situation bothered him. Something he couldn't quite name.

"That they're keeping an eye on us I believe," Cavan said. "And that they're reporting our movements, I don't doubt. We lingered here, when Falstaff would have expected us to run for the border first thing."

"Why didn't we again?" Qalas asked.

"The gemstones," Amra said. "Cavan needed to play wizard."

"Couldn't that have waited until—"

"Cavan didn't want to carry power he didn't understand," Cavan said.

"They didn't cause problems for the miners," Qalas said with a shrug. "And they didn't cause Kent any problems when he rode with them."

"One," Cavan said, "we don't know that for certain. Two, Kent's not even half a wizard, and Juno mines without magic. I had no way of knowing how the gemstones would respond if I cast a spell near them."

"I, for one," Ehren said, "am glad Cavan chose not to put the countryside at risk."

Cavan couldn't have been the only one to hear the words "for a change" implicit in that sentence. Before he could reply, though, Amra nodded and spoke.

"Fair enough."

That ended the debate.

"So," Qalas said. "What are the chances that the duke knows you understand the gemstones now? Tries to use that against us?"

"I wouldn't say I *understand* them," Cavan said, shaking his head once sharply. "Only that I've covered the basics. And I don't see how he'd use *that* against us."

"We'll find out by nightfall," Ehren said. "Unless we push, we won't make it through the pass today."

Ehren kept talking for a moment, but Cavan wasn't listening. Qalas' question. Something about it chimed with that niggling itch in the back of Cavan's mind. That sense that he was missing something...

Cavan sat up straight in his saddle. Whistled the halt. All four horses stopped.

Amra's hand went to her sword's hilt. Qalas grabbed the handle of his halberd, ready to slide it from its sling on the side of his saddle-bags. Ehren made no move. Merely looked curiously at Cavan, who was shaking his head.

"The duke has been distracting us with mundane threats. Threats we could easily see. He has something else watching us. Something he conjured. I'm sure of it."

Amra's sword was in her hand before Cavan finished his sentence. Qalas held his halberd only a moment later. Ehren took up his goldenwood staff only a moment after that.

Cavan placed his hands over his eyes as he spoke words of power that would enhance his wizard sight. Show him anything that might be hidden nearby. Or at least difficult to see.

"*Neela asa.*"

He drew his hands away and looked about.

The skies above were clear, which made Cavan puff out a breath. He'd half-convinced himself that Falstaff had managed to conjure up a manticore, or something even worse, and managed to hide it.

The road ahead was clear as well. Nothing more than a handful of riders in the distance, none with any magic to them.

The sides of the road showed Cavan nothing unexpected, save a twist in the world atop a hill nearby. Not one of conjuring, but the sort of natural spot the common folk called "faerie rings" where even those with no magic could not pass the day or night without getting more than they bargained for.

And behind...

What was that in that patch of amber grass just beside the road?

"A snake," Cavan said. "Red and yellow stripes."

"I see it," Amra said. "Tiny thing. Not just a snake?"

"There's magic to it. I'm positive. It has an orange glow that fades in and out..."

There *was* more to it than that. Which meant an active spell was involved, hiding its true form. If only he could remember the exact spell needed to reveal it.

It was from a derivative branch of detection magic that Cavan used all too little. What was the second declension of the verb *Neel* again? Cavan started running through the grammar of magic in his head...

Qalas trotted over on his horse, halberd already swinging.

"Wait!" Cavan yelled, hands up as though he could stop the strike.

Qalas' blade hit the small serpent.

And suddenly it was no longer tiny.

CAVAN ONCE WRESTLED WITH A TREE PYTHON THAT WAS BIGGER AROUND than his biceps, and longer than he was tall.

And one time, with Ehren and Amra beside him, Cavan had fought down a great, gray-green snake that had to have been twenty feet long, and wider around than Cavan's chest.

But when the axe blade of Qalas' halberd struck that seemingly tiny, red-and-yellow serpent in the tall, amber grass beside the Royal Road that day, it became the largest snake Cavan had ever seen.

So large that, for a moment, the word *dragon* flashed through his mind.

But this snake had no legs, nor wings.

It had the size, though.

This great beast of a snake was now thirty or forty feet long, and thicker through its body than a horse.

It reared up high, and a membranous hood flared around its head. Thin enough that Cavan was sure he could see sunlight coming through it. Or maybe it was just a golden shade on its own.

Qalas' horse reared, but Qalas kept his saddle.

Amra leapt down from hers, as did Cavan and Ehren.

The giant serpent hissed and from its mouth billowed a sickly green cloud.

Ehren thrust his staff in the air and yelled out words in ancient Penthix.

A shaft of sunlight flared from Ehren's goldenwood staff, meeting the billowing green gas and dispersing it.

Qalas, barely in control of his horse, still managed to hack one-handed with his halberd. No easy feat, and the strike was not as strong as it might have been.

The axe blade bounced harmlessly off the creature's skin.

Then Amra was there.

Her great dark sword opened a gash in the creature's flesh. A gash that spewed steaming blood all over her. Drove her back a pace.

The snake bellowed in rage.

Bellowed?

What kind of snake bellowed?

The answer to that question mattered. Cavan knew it. Tried to remember as he charged toward the snake, by reflex whistling the command for the horses to flee the fight.

"Hey!" Qalas yelled, as his newly trained horse carried him away from the fight.

Amra was down, but moving. Covered in red gore that yet steamed in the warm late summer sunlight.

The serpent's jaws came down at her.

Cavan leapt forward, slashing.

His blade hit the serpent. Forced the creature to miss its strike and slam the ground instead. But the blade, like Qalas' halberd, did no harm.

Even blinded, Amra took advantage of the opportunity to slash through the creature's hood and into its neck.

But its nose struck Amra. Knocked her to the ground.

Ehren continued praying in rapid-fire Penthix.

A great golden dome appeared over the battle. Trapping the snake inside, but also trapping Amra, Ehren, and Cavan.

Then Qalas was there, rushing forward and shouting a war cry.

Amra somersaulted backwards to her feet, eyes clear of blood and full of rage. Sprang forward, sword high.

Cavan spent another useless strike on the beast's hide while he tried to remember just what kind of giant snake could bellow instead of hiss.

The creature reared. Slammed its head on the dome, which rang like a deep bell.

Cavan, Qalas and Amra all struck as one.

Only her blade cut into the creature, and not deep enough to stop it.

Worse, it was healing from the cut its had suffered already.

Wait. Healing. Poison breath. Bellow. Cavan remembered these signs from his studies with Master Powys. Some kind of creature not of this world, but not of the elemental realms either.

No, this was a thing from one of the various tangential worlds that bordered this reality.

And it was called a "varmthras."

How did one kill a varmthras?

"Varmthras," Cavan yelled, both to identify it and to see if the creature would respond.

It did.

It attacked him.

Its head, coming down faster than a charging destrier on the battlefield. Jaws open wide enough that Cavan could see just how long those fangs were.

They made his sword feel inadequate.

That was all he had time to think before it struck.

Pain.

Searing pain.

All through Cavan's guts. Sharp pain. Red pain. Spreading out from the places those fangs now held him.

Worse, Cavan was airborne. The varmthras had lifted him.

It banged its head on the golden dome again. That ringing sound was even louder close up, and Cavan was struggling for breath. His heart rate was slowing instead of speeding. That was bad.

He had a sword in his hand, but his arm wasn't responding to his orders to stab the creature.

That was worse.

Down below he could see Amra and Qalas striking for all they were worth. Qalas was striking at wounds Amra had already opened, which made his strikes more effective, but even with the distant clarity of deep pain and the certainty of impending death, Cavan could tell that those strikes wouldn't be enough.

No, nor would whatever prayers Ehren was calling forth to battle this creature.

The varmthras came from a different world. A sunless world, where the power of Zatafa could not touch it. It was blind, Cavan remembered, and it tracked its foes only truly by their taste in the air.

And ... and there was something else...

The time of year was important. More powerful during this season. It was a summer creature. From a summer land...

The world was beginning to go black around Cavan, starting out from the edges and creeping in faster than he would have believed. Shouldn't it have come slowly? With his heart down to so few beats a minute.

For that matter, shouldn't the pain have abated some by now? Instead of staying so sharp and clear that Cavan could feel it down into the very core of who he was.

Hot pain now.

So very hot.

No good. It was all no good. The lessons about this summer creature were too distant. Cavan could not remember the truths of the varmthras, nor how to beat it. Not with the beat of his own heart so slow. Not with the world going as dark as the sunless land that bore this thing.

Sunless...

But a summer creature...

And the pain pulsing through Cavan was so very hot...

He needed cool. He needed ice. He needed...

...the gemstones.

Cavan reached within himself, even as part of him reached out to the gemstones in his pocket.

His lips mouthed words he could no longer hear over the slow roar of his own blood. The battle cries of his friends down below him.

Cavan pulled on power he could not sense. Not past the searing pain in his guts.

Cavan felt himself make contact with something deep inside those gemstones. Something cold. Primally cold.

If there was a time before the creation of the sun, it might have been as cold as the core of these gemstones.

With everything that he had left, Cavan mouthed words of power, took that cold in the grip of his will, and thrust it through the jaws of the varmthras and deep inside the creature.

And then, his dark world went silent.

CAVAN AWOKE SOME TIME LATER, ON THE BANKS OF A WIDE RIVER. HE lay under the shade of an oak tree, on a patch of thick green grass, just outside a brambling bush that didn't even have the decency to offer any berries.

Something foul and herbal. That was all Cavan could think of the smell that dominated this beautiful summer afternoon. Only one of Ehren's poultices could smell so foul, and even then only the ones he considered the most potent.

Cavan's mouth was so dry he was sure his tongue had cracked.

And nothing in this, or any other world, sounded better to him just then than the thought of fresh berries, bursting on his tongue. Blackberries, like he picked in his youth in the hills outside of Tradeton. During the long and lazy summer days, after his chores were finished, and he had nothing to do but look toward the sky and dream as he snacked on wild blackberries.

This was not quite like those days, though.

The sun was hotter, for one. And his skin was shaky and wet. His lips felt like slabs of steak. His neck didn't seem to want to lift his head. Nor did any of his limbs want to move.

Dull, throbbing pain all through Cavan's torso. He ached all over, but the worst pain centered just below his ribs, and fanned out from there.

His ears seemed to choose that moment to wake up.

A moment ago, Cavan realized, the world had been silent. But now, suddenly, he could hear the rushing of the river. The cries of water birds as they fished.

The conversation of Ehren and Qalas.

"...have to do something. I can't go through that again. Almost didn't make it back to the fight before you threw up that dome."

"You'll have to learn to dismount faster. We don't often fight from horseback."

"Why in the hells not? You'd give up that advantage?"

Cavan tried to speak. All that came out was a vague, raspy croak.

They didn't hear him.

"We have some of the finest horses any of us have ever ridden. We told you before, we consider them every bit as much friends and part of the group as we consider each other."

"Then they'll behave all the better in battle. I've never seen horses so well-trained as your three."

Cavan tried again. No better results.

Worse, he couldn't turn his head. He could only stare up at the sky — darkening slowly in the late afternoon — and the branches of the oak tree above him.

He made one attempt to bend at the waist, but the riotous rebellion from his stomach region quashed that quickly.

Just the effort made him cold, and dizzy. And he was sure he was sweating more than he'd been a moment ago.

"And the first time an enemy cuts one of them out from under us?" Ehren paused, and Cavan could almost picture the way his friend must have been shaking his head. "No. Horses are targets in battle. Only people who consider their horses expendable take risks with them."

Cavan tried to speak again. Managed a croak that came out louder than a whisper.

And just like the Ehren was beside him, smiling down at him.

"Awake? Good." Ehren poured a little water into Cavan's mouth. "I'll need to change your poultice soon anyway."

Pleasure. The taste and feel of that clear, clean water in Cavan's mouth and throat was the kind of pleasure some people could only pay for.

Ehren held up a handful of blackberries.

"I'll feed them to you one at a time, if you can open your mouth."

How did he always know?

A short time later, Cavan was sitting up against that oak tree, with Ehren sitting on one side, and Qalas on the other. Their horses were hobbled in a patch of grass not twenty feet away.

Cavan could move his arms and neck, and his hands weren't shaking so badly now. He'd gotten a look at the wound in his belly when Ehren changed the poultice.

He wished he hadn't. It looked foul and sickly, and smelled worse than the poultice Ehren placed over it, while praying.

Only the one puncture mark though. According to Ehren, Cavan was only alive because he'd managed to twist at the last second and get caught by only one of the varmthras' fangs.

Cavan looked over at where Amra lay sleeping, beside the river.

"How is she?" Cavan asked.

"Nothing that I can't take care of by the first light of day tomorrow." Still, he shook his head. "Have to say, though, that the blood of that thing — what did you call it?"

"A varmthras."

"The blood of that varmthras had some qualities that reminded me of acid. But the treatments for acid weren't any good."

"What did you do?"

"Zatafa has many blessings," Ehren said with a broad smile. "And I know most of them."

Cavan shook his head.

"Questions," Qalas said, his tone so businesslike that Cavan almost felt as though he'd offended the ex-hunter.

Cavan nodded, though.

"You'd sounded dismissive of the duke's skills before. Magic, I mean. But he conjured *that thing*?"

"It's..." Cavan shrugged. "It's like this. There are two kinds of wizards."

"Trained and half trained," Amra said, sitting up and turning to face them.

She looked to have deep burns all over her face, and every bit of skin Cavan could see. Her black leathers held together, but they'd lost their shine, and were more brown than black now. They looked more like something had chewed them up and spit them out before she'd donned them.

"Amra," Ehren said in his lecturing voice, "you need to lie back down and rest."

"The half-trained ones like Cavan and the duke," Amra continued, as though she hadn't heard Ehren, "are the more dangerous. Because they have only half an idea of what they're doing."

Her smile looked grisly through all those burns, but Cavan couldn't help smiling back at her.

"Down," Ehren said, pointing at the grass. "Stay awake if you must, but *lie down*."

"So," she said, stretching out on the grass, "it took you only three years to try to get me on my back. I'd wondered how long it would take."

"Amra," Cavan chided her.

"Hey," she said, shrugging one shoulder and grinning with her teasing. "*You* still haven't tried."

"Wizards," Qalas prompted Cavan, his tone still businesslike.

"Tower wizards and field wizards," Cavan said, happy to distract the conversation that he didn't think any of them wanted to have. Amra didn't desire Cavan or Ehren any more than either of them wanted her, but when she was hurt badly enough, she couldn't help teasing.

"And that means..." Qalas said.

Amra closed her eyes and faked snoring, in protest to the lecture she must have felt coming.

"Well," Cavan said, "it's about what you'd think. Tower wizards stay home and study their grimoires and experiment with magic in controlled conditions. Field wizards study too, but" — Cavan grinned — "we don't have the luxury of controlled conditions when we experiment. They're better at some things, we're better at others."

"Plus," Ehren said, "Cavan was getting into the duke's head."

"Some," Cavan admitted, "but honestly, I could tell he was a tower wizard trying to act like a field wizard. That gave me all the advantage. Give Falstaff time, and he can summon and send out something pretty nasty. But pressure him and he can't hold up."

Cavan frowned. "How exactly did we beat the varmthras, anyway?"

"You froze it solid," Amra said, "and it shattered on my next blow."

"That worked?" Cavan said, astonished. "Cold shouldn't have been enough. Not for a creature from that sunless world."

"If it came from a sunless world," Ehren said, "Zatafa's presence, through me, should have defeated it."

"No," Cavan said, shaking his head. "The sun is too ... alien. Too far removed from its world. The traditional method of killing a varmthras is shadow magic."

"That doesn't make any sense at all," Ehren insisted. "If it's from a world of darkness, how could shadow hurt it?"

"Shadow isn't darkness," Cavan said. "It's a blend of darkness and light. Enough dark to open the way for the light to touch the creature. That would kill it. To kill it with cold would have required a tremendous amount of power."

"That," Ehren said to Qalas, "is why we're better off that Cavan didn't take those gemstones anywhere without studying them first."

Qalas nodded, then frowned.

"Let me get this straight. Instead of killing that bastard duke when you had the chance to do it legally, you chose to spare his life, but piss him off. Then you went away, thus ensuring that he had all the time in the world to choose how and when he wanted to attack you?"

"Does sound bad when you say it that way," Amra said in a sing-song voice.

"He spared a life," Ehren said. "It was the right call then and it will be the right call in the long run. You'll see."

"Besides," Cavan said. "Amra was right about one thing."

Cavan waited until she'd opened her eyes and was looking over before he finished his thought.

"The duke sent an observer that couldn't attack until it had to defend itself."

Cavan didn't look at Qalas then. Neither did Amra. Ehren began digging into his brown leather backpack.

"I'm sorry," Qalas said, and he sounded worse than Cavan liked.

Recognition of a mistake was one thing, but Qalas was saying something a lot more. Enough that Cavan had to bite down his instinctive reply to give the man a chance to finish.

"I shouldn't have attacked first. Amra'd even mentioned it might come to that. And then I almost ran myself out of the fight by not dismounting." He shook his head. "Maybe I'm not good enough to ride with—"

Cavan, Ehren and Amra all shouted him down at once. Cavan wasn't sure what his friends said, but Cavan knew Kent wouldn't have wanted to hear Cavan say the word he'd used in protest.

Between the three of them, their outburst managed to stop Qalas' line of reasoning.

Cavan started to speak before anyone else could.

"Look," Cavan said. "This is the first real fight you've had with us since we got out of the duke's keep. Not to mention the first that started on horseback. And what did you do?"

Cavan let the word hang for just the barest moment. Just long enough that he could see the wrong answer on Qalas' lips. *Then* Cavan continued.

"You leapt into the fray against a monster that could have made an entire regiment flee in terror. And when your weapon failed to harm the beast, you kept at it. Then you found a way you *could* hurt it."

Cavan let that thought hang for a moment, to make sure Qalas absorbed it. Both Amra and Ehren were watching Cavan now, content to let him take the lead here.

"You risked your life right alongside ours. *For* ours." Cavan smiled at the ex-hunter. "I'd ask nothing more of you than that."

"Nor I," Ehren said, smiling once more.

"I might," Amra said, though she was smiling too. "I might ask that you dismount *before* your horse flees the next fight."

To his credit, Qalas joined in the laughter then.

But only for a moment. His face turned serious again. Worried, almost, as he turned to Cavan.

"You asked me about armor last night. But what about you? You're not even wearing leather."

"Never has," Amra said. "I assumed it was a wizard thing. Like Ehren and his whites."

"It's not," Cavan admitted. "Not really." Then he sighed. "One of the last things Ser Dreng said to me before he failed me as a warrior was, 'Boy, if you insist on fighting, forget armor. You're useless in it.'"

Amra stared at him for a moment.

"Cavan," she said, voice as irritated as her expression. "Are you twelve years old still?"

Cavan didn't bother answering that.

Amra repeated it. More slowly.

"No, Amra, I'm not."

"Then maybe you could realize you've learned a thing or two since then?"

Cavan blinked at her.

Ehren started laughing. Qalas joined only a moment later, and Amra a moment after that.

Finally, Cavan joined in the laughter too, until the pain in his guts made him stop.

Finally, panting for breath, he agreed that he'd try some armor when they reached Juno.

* * *

THAT NIGHT WAS ROUGH.

Cavan's belly seemed to grow worse as the time approached to change his poultices — which Ehren did more often than any of them liked — and only abated again when fresh poultices were in place.

And when it was exposed to air, that wound didn't smell good. It smelled — and Cavan tried not to think too hard about this — as though whatever poison had been in the cloud the varmthras had breathed, had been in the creature's mouth when it bit him.

And Cavan could almost feel that corruption inside him. Spreading slowly, and burning where it spread.

The pain left him writhing more and more, over time, until Ehren returned to pray over him again, and replace his poultice.

And then the cycle started again.

Only one thing kept Cavan calm during this struggle with his wound: Ehren.

Ehren's calm smile never broke. Not when he changed the poultice. Not when he washed the wound. And certainly not when he prayed, nor when he explained to Qalas about how the golden dome had been his insurance that we would not send a wounded monster off to eat farmers while it licked its wounds.

Amra seemed more or less settled on the grass near the rushing river, where the spray helped keep her burnt skin cool.

Dinner that night was something Cavan would rather forget. Ehren had spoon-fed him some kind of mush made from nuts and berries that tasted good enough, but caused a series of cramps through his guts as he digested.

Ehren's prayers and poultices helped only so much, it seemed.

Worse, sometime after dusk, soldiers spotted their campfire. Came and tried to roust them.

Qalas had stood, halberd ready, but Ehren had stayed him with a hand on the shoulder. Still smiling, Ehren explained to them how he could not move his patients. And how the duke would not want to see his nephew die of wounds caused in *his* duchy.

The soldiers hadn't cared. Tried to roust them anyway.

Qalas had hefted his halberd, but Ehren stepped in front again, still smiling.

He informed them in gentle terms that they were not going to move unless forced. And that forcing them would be *certain* to damage Cavan.

The look on the soldiers' faces had been exactly what Amra had predicted.

They'd wanted to Cavan and his friends to give them an excuse to fight. But they could not act to harm Cavan. Not unless offered violence.

They left then. Which was some small consolation to Cavan, who hadn't realized he was so near death that he couldn't be moved.

That gave him something unpleasant to worry about through his sleepless, painful night. A night spent fitfully tossing and turning, trying not to moan, as he slipped into and out of a series of visions that had to have been fever dreams. Some of them pleasant, involving women who'd been only too happy to take Cavan to their beds.

Others involved some of the worst failures of Cavan's life, trotted back in front of his eyes to remind him that — in the eyes of the world — he was still just a bastard by-blow his mother never wanted, who'd failed at being either a proper wizard or a proper warrior.

But when Cavan sensed the dawn approach, hope flared in his chest.

Salvation.

He wiped his sweaty brow. Licked his dry lips with an equally dry tongue. Tried to sit up again against the oak tree, but no good. His body wasn't obeying him again. Sometimes it did, sometimes it didn't.

But that wouldn't matter for long.

Ehren was already kneeling, facing the east. Prayers already moving his lips, in the tongue of ancient Penthix.

He stood, goldenwood staff in both hands, held high above his head.

His prayers grew louder, until his words were almost shouted into the morning breeze.

Cavan could pick out only one word among the many: Zatafa. The people of Penthix, whoever they'd been, had been the first to revere Zatafa, and it was their prayers that lived on long after their people and countries had been lost to time.

The first shaft of sunlight flared high in the sky, aimed as though entirely at that tall, blond priest in his spotless white clothing.

That one ray lit Ehren with a golden halo. As though he were a shaft of sunlight himself.

He reached to his right, where Qalas knelt in the thick, dewy grass, also facing east, eyes lowered in what might have been prayer, or simple reverence. Cavan didn't really know.

The tip of Ehren's staff touched Qalas at the base of his neck. The golden glow spread to encase Qalas' body. He drew himself straighter. Eyes open now. Lips smiling. The name of Zatafa on his lips.

The countryside around them all began to lighten, as more sunlight came along with the breaking dawn.

But Ehren had handled only the most minor of his healing so far. Healing that might not have needed the sun's first light, but Cavan would never question the priest's decisions. Not on matters of his goddess.

Amra's turn came next.

Ehren stepped to where she lay, beside the river, looking up at him with a grimace. Her own night could not have been much better than Cavan's from the sweat that soaked her hair.

But then Ehren's staff touched her as he prayed. The golden sunlight of his halo spread to encompass her as well.

And Amra's burns faded as though they'd never been there in the first place.

And that was not all. Her armor. Her treasured black leathers. They mended as well. The brown mottling turning to glossy black once more. Even the sweat and grime from her face and hair evaporated like morning fog on a hot day.

Amra sprang to her feet with a delighted cry.

Cavan sat, shaking, as he awaited his turn.

Ehren, smiling, came to him then. Prayers still moving his smiling lips in nearly silent devotion.

Ehren touched the staff to Cavan's forehead.

Bliss. Pure, warm bliss spread through Cavan. Relaxing every worn and tired muscle. Rejuvenating him. Mending his flesh, as well as his spirit. Reminding him that he had value, and friends, even as his flesh knitted and grew whole.

Finally, Cavan sagged in relief. Hale and hearty and clean once more, and ready for breakfast.

Cavan noted, with a wry smile, that though Zatafa had chosen to restore Amra's leathers to their proper state, his own good green linen shirt was ruined.

Still, before he stood, he offered his own small prayer of thanks to Zatafa.

After all, a shirt, he could replace.

4

———————

As seneschal to the duke of Nolarr, Inari had two offices.

Her primary office, her official office, was right across the hall from the office that the duke kept himself. A place of prominence. Well known, and even better appointed.

There were people waiting for her at that office at this very moment, she was quite sure.

Well, they could wait.

Right now, Inari had pressing business to deal with. Secret business. Business she could not even let the duke know about. Not after that damned fool had let a priest of Zatafa seal an oath.

At least he'd been smart enough to tell her about the oath, and its particulars. Unlike his predecessor, that damned fool Duchess Kanda. She'd thought keeping secrets from her seneschal was a bright idea.

More the fool she, but then, that was why Kanda was dead, and her line with her, while her title went to the king's younger brother.

Inari didn't care much who sat in the duke's chair. So long as they let her do her business.

But Falstaff, she liked. He was bright. Capable. Foolish in his pride, yes, but that just meant he was more willing to let his seneschal do her work than some of the lords she'd known over the years.

Sixty years Inari had been in this world. Forty years since she'd risen from her sad position as the unmarried third daughter of a minor noble to become seneschal for the ruler of the largest duchy in Oltoss.

Of course, Oltoss was hardly a large country. But better to serve the most important duke in a small country, than the least duke in a great country.

Especially when that duke had the will and resources to make himself king. Perhaps even to expand the borders into Surta and Holst as that fool King Draven should have done ages ago.

But as matters stood, Falstaff could not accomplish any of those things. Not with Draven's by-blow standing in his way. And Falstaff had committed himself to not going after the whelp, any more than he could go after the whelp's foster father. That jeweler.

Well, the duke's oath was not binding on the seneschal. Not if the duke never learned what the seneschal had done, until it was too late. No doubt Falstaff would smile on her work then.

Royal Seneschal Inari Flintblack. She rather liked the sound of it.

It was in service to this cause that Inari was not seated in her big, beautiful, official office, but in her *other* office. The office the duke did not even know about. Not unless he had spies that Inari had not found.

And she doubted that. Falstaff was good, but he was not so subtle as he liked to think.

Honestly, ordering his soldiers to harry the whelp, but not to strike the first blow.

What a waste of manpower.

Inari inhaled rose oil from the handkerchief that she kept up the sleeve of her beautiful blue robe. It helped keep at bay the odor of dust and disuse that did an excellent job of making sure that anyone who stumbled on this little room would think it a forgotten closet. Inari never left the room unlocked, but just in case another key existed, the room had to look forgotten.

Low ceiling. Gray stone with no whitewashing or wood paneling. Only the one sconce for a smokeless torch, the kind the duke was so fond of. And even that smokeless torch was only there because Inari brought it in with her.

The office did have a desk. Small, and apparently of cheap, worn soft woods, exactly as she'd had it built, along with its matching uncomfortable chair. Inari was careful not to set anything on that desk, so she never disturbed its layer of dust.

What she kept hidden away in secret compartments within that desk's drawers, however, was another matter.

A tiny little cupboard of an office, tucked away under a little used set of stairs, near the sally port into the duke's grand, blue-enameled castle.

The perfect place for Inari to meet with those who should never be seen entering the castle. Or at least, never seen meeting with the seneschal.

Right now, the first of two people she'd meet here today was standing and trying very hard not to fidget.

He was a messenger for the duke's army. He'd already brought his report. He'd been on his way back out to the stables when one of Inari's agents stopped him. Brought him here.

The boy — and he could not yet have been old enough to shave — looked too skinny to swing a sword well. Too skinny for anything but messenger duty, perhaps. And goodness knew that no horse would object to his inconsequential weight.

"I said, *report*, boy."

"But—"

"Boy, do you know who I am?"

She gave him the eye then. Oh, not the way she did it in her youth, when she might have found his brown hair pretty and his brown eyes prettier, before she'd decided that such pursuits were a distraction.

No, this was what she thought of as the *seneschal's eye*. It was a look calculated to make merchants think twice about their prices, and diplomats reconsider their positions.

The boy squirmed well.

"I..." he swallowed. "I know. Ma'am."

"My lady," she corrected him.

"M'lady," he said quickly.

"Good," she said, and clapped her wrinkled hands together once. "Now that we've established that you're not a complete fool, why don't you give me the report I asked for before I change my mind and have you whipped?"

"Nothing to report, ma'am. M'lady. I mean, nothing's happened."

She raised her eyebrow a fraction. "And that's what you told the duke?"

"Yes, m'lady ma'am." The boy nodded so fast Inari thought his head might fly off.

"And did the duke ask any questions?"

"Yes, ma'am." The boy grimaced. "*M'lady*. He asked—"

"*It's obvious what he asked, you fool.*" She drew a deep breath, and let the boy squirm while she let it out. "He asked if Cavan and his friends had made it to the Street of Death."

Damned fool name for a mountain pass. Yes, good for scaring one's enemies, but it hardly invited traders and tourists, now did it?

"Yes, m'lady."

"And you said..."

"No, m'lady. They stopped a half-day shy."

"And did Cavan and his friends have any encounters with our soldiers?"

The boy gave a quick, stuttering report that did, indeed, amount to nothing. At least, in the boy's eyes. The duke's eyes too, no doubt. But that was only because Falstaff could not likely see the significance of it.

Cavan and his friends had outmaneuvered Falstaff again. Determined the little trick he'd tried to play with his soldiers, and not fallen for it.

Exactly as Inari wanted.

She smiled.

The boy squirmed again.

"You've done well," she said, and the honey in her voice made the boy squirm almost as much as the seneschal's eye had done. Might have been smarter than he looked. "And you must have a long, thirsty ride ahead of you."

She reached into a desk drawer for a small, undecorated brown ceramic cup, filled with water. Oh, it had a few drops of something else in it, but nothing that would cloud the look or taste of the water.

She held the cup forward.

"Drink," she said.

The boy looked like he wanted to argue, but knew better.

"I'm the seneschal to Duke Falstaff of Nolarr," Inari said, professional levels of impatience in her voice. "If I wanted to do away with a messenger, I'd hardly waste poison on you."

The boy took the cup. Downed the water in a single gulp. Smiled, and nodded his thanks as he handed back the cup.

"Now be off with you," she said. "I've work to do."

The boy hurried out of the room as though fleeing his death.

The drops of memory bane would kick in slowly over the next hour, Inari knew. Soon, the meeting itself would be nothing more than a half-remembered dream, and of the office where they'd met, he'd remember nothing.

Inari had made good use of memory bane over the years.

She couldn't use it on her next guest, no, but the Order of the False Dawn were as well known for their professional discretion as for their skill at assassination.

No. Cavan would not be interfering with Falstaff's plans much longer.

5

———

It might have been Cavan's imagination, but it seemed to him that the sun was always brighter and clearer on a day he'd received a major healing. And he had experienced enough of them now to have noticed the pattern.

There were streaks of white clouds up above in the otherwise clear sky, but they did not dare come near the sun. Not today.

Today, the sun shone down warmer than yesterday. But it was a comforting warmth. A happy warmth. Not the kind of heat that might make a day's ride a chore for rider and horse. No, this was the sunlight of hope.

Sunlight that make Cavan believe he would reach the mine before the duke. Retrieve the gemstones before they fell into the wrong hands.

Maybe even make peace with the duke along the way.

The day was just that uplifting.

Gentle summer smells coming from wheat fields, not far from the Royal Road on either side. Birds singing in harmony with Ehren — the surest sign to Cavan that Zatafa's healing had a leftover cheering effect. Qalas joined in a verse from time to time. His voice was higher than Ehren's, and he had a better idea of what a melody should sound like.

But Qalas did not sing too often that morning. The four of them were riding too hard for that, and Qalas had not received a major healing. The ex-hunter kept his eyes as sharp and moving as Amra did.

Even as good as just being alive felt to Cavan than morning, the four of them knew what was at stake.

Those soldiers were coming. The duke was after as many gemstones as he could pluck from that mine. And Cavan needed to keep that from happening.

By noon, the worries of his cause had begun to erode that leftover sense of general wellbeing.

Just in time to reach the mighty Blue Mountains.

They glittered in the bright summer sun as though they were made of sapphires. Not an aftereffect of healing, either, but the result of crystal deposits that ran all through those mountains. Crystals that had an odd, dampening effect on sound, and resonated strangely with magic.

Those outer crystals carried no true power themselves. Cavan had tested them many times in his youth, and he knew that he was far from the only one to do so. It was more that they almost seemed to sing when magic was used too close to them.

In fact, Cavan had heard of some wizards purchasing the crystals to use in their wards, to aid in sensing hostile magic.

Those wizards no doubt lamented their purchase, when they discovered that those crystals would chime nonstop in a wizard's house.

But Cavan could not give too much attention to those crystals right now, even beautiful as they were in the midday sun.

Instead, he had to focus on the scores of soldiers, standing in ranks, between Cavan and the Street of Death.

They all wore chainmail hauberks, covering them from head and neck down to about mid-thigh. Underneath they wore leathers, protecting not only their bodies from the mail, but their legs and arms from enemy weapons.

All of them bore the duke's sigil — crossed black spears on a field of yellow — on their left breasts. And most of the soldiers Cavan could see were armed with spears and small, round shields, though a few also carried swords.

Did that mark them as officers? Sergeants, perhaps?

Amra whistled the halt, which Cavan knew meant she'd stopped them just outside arrow range. Important, because he could now see squads of archers along the periphery.

"Hail," she called, picking an officer out of the crowd fast enough that Cavan felt blind for not having spotted him. The one she addressed rode a horse. "Whom do I have the honor of addressing?"

"I am Count Urlich of Yula, vassal to the duke of Nolarr." The man speaking rode a black stallion, and wore finer armor than any of his men. Plate armor, enameled in white, a stark contrast to his steed. His white helmet had eagle's wings, and the visor was up to show off both the scar filling most of his right cheek, and a drooping brown mustache. He carried a lance and shield, but also wore a spiked mace at his side.

"I am Amra, and these are Cavan, Ehren and Qalas. Why do you block the Royal Road, my lord?"

"I know who you are," Count Urlich said. "And our business is the duke's."

"And that business is..." Cavan said.

"Not yours for the asking, bastard."

And up 'til now this had been such a friendly discussion.

Worse, the count had to go and sneer, which made his long mustache look ridiculous, and didn't do kind things for his voice as he added an unpleasantry.

"In fact, perhaps I should kill you for your insolence."

Cavan could feel the tension of his group ratchet up at the count's words. No one had moved for weapons yet, which was definitely a good thing, but weapons were closer to being drawn than Cavan would have liked.

So he laughed.

He was forcing it, at first, but real laughter didn't take long. It helped that he thought about how ridiculous the whole situation was. A company of soldiers, led by the duke's chief vassal, all standing between Cavan and the only pass through this part of the Blue Mountains.

He kept laughing until the count's horse fidgeted, and the count frowned.

Only then did Cavan speak.

"Of course I'm a bastard. My name is *Oltblood*. Hardly a revelation, my lord. However, my friends and I need to continue down the *Royal Road* into Juno. You know. Down the *king's* road, to the barony this bastard will *inherit* one day?"

"One day, perhaps, but not today."

"Enough of this farce! We both know that you're not allowed to attack me. So let us stop playing games, my lord. Give us room to pass."

Cavan had seen more than a few smiles in his day. Most of them friendly.

The smile on the count's face now was not friendly.

In fact, Cavan could only think of it as "slimy."

"You," he said, pointing at Cavan with an armored hand, "may indeed pass unmolested, unless you're foolish enough to engage us. Your friends, however, are another matter..."

Any lingering sense of cheer from the morning's healing faded with those cold words.

In fact, the cold of those words seemed to seep through Cavan, starting at his ears, and running down his spine as a chill that reached all the way to his boots.

No. Falstaff wouldn't go that far. This had to be a bluff.

"A moment, my lord," Ehren said.

And it was a good thing he spoke just then, because Cavan had been ready to dip into his pouch of spells.

Ehren trotted Highsun forward a few paces, then stopped again when Amra cleared her throat, signaling that any closer meant the risk of arrow attack.

"My lord," Ehren said, and Cavan could hear the smile on his friend's lips, "there is no need for any of this. Cavan here is unquestionably a citizen of Oltoss. And as such, by law, he and his companions are allowed to travel the Royal Road unmolested. I understand that your liege has placed on you the onus of impeding us, but that does not mean you must fulfill his orders, especially when they are of dubious legality at best."

"The Royal Road is the king's road," Count Urlich said. "That is true. But here within Nolarr, its control and maintenance is in the duke's hands. He has the power to close it as he sees fit, if—"

"*Enough!*" Amra said, more steel in her voice than on the count.

She trotted up beside Ehren. Cavan and Qalas closed ranks behind her, just in case.

"You claimed to know who I am, *my lord*," she said. "And that means you know I've been a been a *commander*, as well as a soldier."

"I do," Count Urlich said, and from the grimace on his face, he saw where Amra was going with this.

Cavan wished that he could.

"Then since your force is blocking mine," Amra continued, "and since we are not currently at war, I invoke my right as a commander."

Count Urlich's grimace deepened until Cavan thought the man's mustache might touch his pauldrons.

"I'm not sure that applies—"

"You block my path. You threaten violence. And yet, we are not at war."

"You are not *their* commander," Count Urlich insisted, that slimy smile back in place.

"Yes, she is," Ehren said.

"It's true," Cavan said. "I lead us well enough in peacetime, but it's Amra who directs our tactics and strategies. She is definitely our battle commander."

"Unquestionably," Qalas said with a nod. "I'd charge your ranks right now if she gave the order."

Count Urlich grimaced again.

"And you wish to invoke the commander's right?"

"I do," Amra said, voice as certain as the nod that accompanied it. "You certainly can't claim my company is too big for it to apply."

"No," Count Urlich said with a sigh. "I suppose I can't. Very well." He turned back to ... someone in the ranks. Cavan couldn't tell who. But to that person, Urlich said, "Fetch the company champion."

A spearman from the south end of the line turned and ran back deeper into the assemblage.

"Don't have the nerve to face me yourself?" Amra taunted.

"My wife is with child," Count Urlich said. "And as you said, I know who you are."

Amra dismounted then. Cavan and the others followed suit.

WELL, IF AMRA HAD TO FIGHT A DUEL, AT LEAST CAVAN WAS SURE SHE couldn't complain about the conditions. The Royal Road was the best ground anyone could hope to fight on — level, dust-free, and downright easy on the legs. The skies above were clear, the sun bright, and the summer breeze was little more than a suggestion.

Plus, she had quite an audience of assembled soldiers. Cavan was sure that little fact would please her. That most of the audience would support her opponent probably pleased her all the more.

The company champion himself was one of the biggest human men Cavan had ever seen. Big enough that Cavan would have been surprised if the man had no orc blood. Or perhaps a trace of ogre or giant blood.

First, he was tall. Now, Cavan was a tall man, but this champion looked to stand a head-and-a-half taller than Cavan. And he was broad enough, and muscled enough, that Cavan would have pitied any horse stuck with carrying him.

The champion's hair had been shaved down to black fuzz against his deeply tanned scalp. So deeply tanned that if not for the man's size, Cavan might have wondered if he had forest elf blood. He kept his short black beard oiled, and tapered to a point.

He wore a chain hauberk and leathers, like all the other soldiers, and he carried a spear and round shield the same as they did. But he carried a sword as well. A sword of war, by the look of it, designed to be wielded with two hands.

At least, Cavan would have needed two hands to wield it. Probably Qalas would as well.

But this champion pulled it from its scabbard with one hand, after tossing his spear aside.

He threw the blade, spinning, into the air as though he'd planned to take down a low-flying bird.

He caught the sword by the handle, an inverted grip, and swung it through a series of movements that might have been intended to intimidate an opponent, or might have been a way to loosen up his muscles before the fight. Most one handed, but some with both hands. And if the small, round shield on his left arm did anything to slow him down, Cavan couldn't tell.

Amra did nothing of the sort.

Well, not quite *nothing.* She rolled her neck and shoulders.

That was about the extent of it. Apart from watching the big man go through his warm-up routine. Typical for Amra, really.

"Big," Qalas said, standing beside Amra. "Moves well too."

"He does," she said, a little longing in her voice. "Pity I may have to kill him. We might have had fun together."

"You don't *have* to kill him, do you?" Ehren asked, quietly. He stood beside Cavan, with the horses, but Cavan knew Amra heard him.

She shrugged. "Depends."

Finally, the champion finished his routine, a light sheen of sweat glistening on his face. He smiled. Looked Qalas up and down.

"Never fought a Southerner," he said. "You any good with that halberd?"

"Very," Qalas said, and Cavan could hear the smile in his voice. "But I'm not the one you're fighting."

"No," the champion said, and Cavan thought the astonishment in his voice was faked. "Not that little beauty beside you."

Qalas held up one hand as though surrendering, and stepped back to join Ehren and Cavan.

Cavan couldn't see Amra's face, but he would have bet his horse that Amra was fluttering her eyelashes just then.

"Me," she said. "Is that a problem for you?"

"Well," the champion said, waving his hand at her chest, "might not be easy to reach your heart through all that. Might need a longer sword."

"Wrong thing to say," Cavan muttered to Ehren, who nodded.

Oh, Amra's chest was ... plentiful. No one could deny that. Went well with the rest of her curves.

But reducing her to her chest? The man had just guaranteed himself some pain before this was all over.

And Cavan was certain not only that he knew what the outcome of this little fight would be, he was just as certain that it would last only as long as Amra wanted it to.

This champion, he was a big man. And he was fast.

But Amra, well, was Amra.

She drew her sword, and the champion looked away from her chest for the first time. His eyes flicked up and down the black metal blade that any observer could tell was not truly steel.

"What ... is ... that?" he said.

"Doom," Amra said. "Ready?"

The champion nodded, but he looked a little less certain now.

"Begin," Amra said.

The man leapt forward, leading with his shield. His sword held high in one hand.

Amra held her stance, sword out of line.

The man came down swinging, and Amra wasn't there. She was already past him.

He spun faster than Cavan could have believed. Got his shield in the way of her strike.

Metal screeched as she carved a gash in that shield.

The champion nodded and tossed it aside. Took his sword of war in both hands.

Him on the attack then. Short, quick cuts. High. High. Low. Low. High. Mid.

Amra ducked the high strikes. Parried the rest.

The champion had reach on her. Used it to keep her sword at bay while he continued his assault. Slowly pressing her back toward the tall, amber grass at the side of the road. Where the footing would be less regular. Give him an advantage.

High cut again. Low now. High…

When the champion cut high that time, Amra dove under his blade. Somersaulted behind him. Came up swinging.

Amra on the attack now. Slow, for her. Still testing him perhaps. Or maybe she was just proving a point. Trying not to kill him.

The champion was stronger. She couldn't press him back under the weight of her strikes.

But by all the gods did his sword protest each parry. It screeched and complained. Sparked, and dinged, and notched. All the while her sword looked as pristine as ever.

He wasn't smiling now.

The champion threw all his strength behind a parry. Knocked her blade out of line. Turned the move into a low attack, cutting for her legs.

Amra parried, spun and slashed the back of his left thigh. Cut through his leathers like they weren't there.

Blood gushed from the wound. The champion went down to one knee.

"Do you submit?" Amra said, circling his lame side.

"No," the champion said through gritted teeth.

Amra knocked his blade aside. Sliced his left shoulder. Not deep, but she proved her point, cutting through the chainmail hauberk with no more effort than for the leather. Meanwhile, Ehren hissed at the amount of blood dripping from the champion's wounded thigh.

"Do. You. Submit?"

"Never!" he bellowed. "I'll never submit to a woman. I'll—"

"He submits," Count Urlich called, tossing a dagger onto the road beside him. A white kerchief had been tied to the dagger's handle.

"No!" the champion called, while Amra picked up the dagger, her token of victory. "I'm undefeated. I'm—"

"You lost," Count Urlich said, coming over, facing his man. He leaned in closer and said. "She beat you. Accept this, or perhaps I'll let her kill you."

"Kill him yourself," Amra said, voice irritated. She yanked the kerchief from the dagger and handed the former back to him. "You submitted on his behalf. Your right as the represented. The only reason I'd kill him now is that he couldn't admit he was beaten by a woman."

Amra slid her sword back into its scabbard. She didn't bother to clean it, of course. In all the time Cavan had known her, no substance had ever stuck to that sword. She slipped the naked dagger into her belt.

Amra dusted her hands as though she'd finished something unsatisfying.

"Honestly," she said. "They don't make champions well here in Nolarr. Over in Martinsford, it might have taken me five minutes to best their champion. And afterwards, I would have respected him enough to enjoy bedding him. This was just…"

She shook her head.

Ehren stepped forward, poultice already in hand to help the champion.

"Let's go," Cavan said.

Ehren turned, clearly about to argue.

"They'll have healers," Qalas said. "Every company of the duke's has at least two."

"Let's. Go," Cavan said again.

Amra agreed, and Ehren was outvoted. He tossed the champion the poultice and turned back to his horse.

The four friends mounted their horses, ready to ride past the soldiers before the count could think of any other reason to detain them.

Cavan never enjoyed riding down the Street of Death. Not just because of the name. Not even because he'd traveled the side passes used by the military, and knew full well exactly how many soldiers could be up there, watching from unseen posts. Ready to drop rocks, arrows, boiling oil, or a host of other nasty things.

No, for Cavan, the real disquiet of the Street of Death came from everything else about it.

Yes, it was still the Royal Road. Just as wide and easy to ride here as it was everywhere else that the Rentissi built their roads (and Cavan assumed the Rentissi did it, though he knew that some in more scholarly circles debated this).

But the Blue Mountains themselves, and their countless ridges of crystal deposits. The way they sucked in sound always left Cavan feeling uneasy.

And here, in the pass, it seemed worse than anywhere else.

First, because the sun had moved enough now that the pass was in shadow, after Cavan had gotten used to the sun on his back. With the sheer walls and mighty peaks on either side, riding down the Street of Death always seemed unsafe. As though one of the mountains on either side might simple decide to move and crush anyone foolish enough to ride here.

A ridiculous notion. Cavan knew that. But the image had occurred to him on his first trip down the road between Juno and Nolarr, when he'd seen a mere five summers in this world, and only just learned to ride a horse.

Young Cavan had been certain that these silent mountains could move. That they were holding their breath, which was why no sound could carry here. They could just slide themselves a few feet when no one was ready for it. And if they crushed someone in the process, well, such huge mountains might not even notice, much less care.

So many years since then. About a score. And yet, that image stayed with Cavan.

Second, the lack of echoes. It was intimidating, even beyond the size of the peaks themselves. So odd, to hear his friends' voices, their horses hooves, and yet, to have those sounds so unfinished. Lessened, by the unnatural presence of those crystals.

And that day, riding down the Street of Death, yet one more thing disquieted Cavan.

The gemstones in his pouch.

(He knew they might not be proper gemstones. Not the way Kent would have defined them. But still, in Cavan's mind, such valuable crystals could not be properly called anything else.)

Those gemstones, they seemed to hum without noise, as Cavan rode. And it definitely wasn't noise. He'd realized that after only a few hundred yards. Nor were they truly vibrating — it wasn't that sensation he felt against his side.

It took him halfway through the pass before he realized just what it was.

Resonance. Magical resonance.

They resonated, here between the mountains themselves. As though all the crystals of the great Blue Mountains were singing a song of magic, and the gemstones in Cavan's pouch conducted the tune. Perhaps led with their voices, as much as their direction.

It was enough to make Cavan wonder — when he could spare attention for watching for the ambush that he did not trust Falstaff not to order — if the mountains themselves were part of some great spell. And if perhaps the gemstones were keystones to that spell.

Worse, the only thing Cavan could think of that the spell might be, had to do with the story of Juno in the first place. Back when the Dunaian people yet lived in these lands.

That that deep within the bowels of the mountains lay a cave that led to the Underworld, home to an ancient destroyer god of the Dunaian people.

How did that story end? Ehren had spoken only of the plight of the poor human woman, Juno, who'd fallen in love with the destroyer god. Even Ehren hadn't known what became of that gateway.

A gateway to the *Dunaian* Underworld. And the *Dunaian* destroyer god. Yeenach.

Dunaian magic?

Was that their deepest secret? Were these gemstones the keys to some ancient spell? Perhaps a lock that sealed that gateway to the Underworld? Perhaps that held that destroyer god in place? Had that lock already been weakened by the removal of just these three gems?

Ehren had once pointed out that, before their people were lost to history, the Dunaians had interbred with some of the human royal and noble lines in the region that was now Oltoss.

Ehren had suggested that Cavan himself might have Dunaian blood.

If some god had been trapped in the mountains by Dunaian magic, could that be why Cavan sensed the crystalline deposits — and the gemstones — so strongly?

Was it a sign of his heritage?

No.

Ridiculous.

Cavan told himself so at least a dozen times as he rode. The whole idea was preposterous. The mine was still active. All the gems might have been plucked from it by now.

If some gateway to the Underworld was sealed deep within the Blue Mountains, with gemstones as his key, then creatures from that Underworld would already be loose on the world once more.

Perhaps even this Yeenach himself.

Cavan took the existence of the duke's soldiers, not so far behind him at the Nolarr end of the Street of Death, as proof that this had not happened.

He reminded himself of that proof every so often, until the worry faded from his mind, and he chatted with Amra and Qalas about the duke's disposition of forces and what it meant. Each had ideas. Qalas, having served the duke, felt he had a better idea of how the man commanded.

Amra, for her part, had more faith in her own knowledge of tactics and strategy.

Cavan, for his part, would trust Amra's view. Not that he bothered expressing this.

All told, the distractions helped, and they made it through the Street of Death with no further attempts to bar their way.

6

———————

The sun was halfway to the Dwarfmarches in the west, by the time Cavan and his friends made it into Juno proper.

Here the wild grasses were greener, but that was because during the first half of the year, most storms either blew northwest from the landlocked Sea of Tormyr — and stayed west of the Blue Mountains — or blew north from Nyar.

The rains meant there were more evergreen trees as well. Pines and spruces, as well as others, such as oaks and beeches.

Here, Cavan knew the farms, if not the farmers. He'd passed them all so many times in his youth, he could guess which would grow beans and which beets, which peas and which corn.

His guesses were off a great deal, but that was likely because thoughts of the farms distracted Cavan with thoughts of the farmers.

All the farms between the mountains and Juno proper, all the vineyards as well. All of them would be ruined if the duke marched through them. They might not be ravaged and burnt, but they'd be raided for food to feed the army, at the very least. Food that those farmers — that the whole barony — relied on.

And so, Cavan pushed for more speed. Despite the bumpy, less even roads they traveled now that they had to leave the Royal Road behind.

And by the time they reached the township that had sprung up around the baronial manor of Juno, Cavan was sure of two things.

One, he was saddle-sore as he hadn't been in a while. Clearly he'd been pushing Dzint too hard through the last stages of the day.

Two, Juno was going to have to start keeping up better patrols. At least for so long as Duke Falstaff maintained his ... imperialist tendencies. If Juno had any scouts of patrols between the baronial seat and its northern border, Cavan hadn't seen them. And he didn't think Amra had either.

The township of Juno was nothing compared to some of the bustling cities Cavan had seen. Nothing even to the capital city of Oltoss itself.

No cobblestones on the roads here. No oil lamps or enchantments at the street corners, to light the evening once the sun was gone for the day. Most buildings were only a story tall, and most were made of wood, albeit in ways that guaranteed comfort, if not extravagance.

Still, Cavan had to admit that there were more two-story buildings than he remembered. More windows had glass now as well, instead of simple wooden shutters. And that was just from what he could see, riding swiftly along the outskirts on his way to the manor itself.

Business in Juno had to be good.

The barony was prospering under Kent and Olivart.

Cavan would have to make sure the duke didn't ruin that.

Soon enough the walls of the baronial manor were in sight. Tall, strong walls, of course. Built around huge blocks of stone from the nearby mountains. Tall enough that the manor itself seemed to vanish behind them as Cavan approached the wrought iron gate.

Only wrought iron. Never enough for a siege. And the manor might have a wall, but what of the township? If war came, where were the people supposed to take refuge?

No, this would not do. Not once Cavan became baron here.

His friends began to rein in as they approached the gates. Ehren was already waving the spearmen standing guard. Or perhaps to the crossbowmen on the walls.

Cavan rode right past them, hailing them only as he went.

He'd been here recently enough. He knew they'd know him on sight. Especially wearing the cloak Olivart had given him, with the baronial sigil for the clasp.

Sure enough, the guards hailed him, and word preceded him up the well-kept road, between the well-trimmed lawns, and the even better maintained groves of fruit trees.

But Cavan did not leap from his saddle until he reached the front door of the four-story mansion where most of the barony's business — and the official business of the township as well — was conducted.

A page in the baronial livery was sputtering and pulling open the door for him...

...or perhaps for Olivart, who was standing in the doorway.

Olivart looked just as Cavan always remembered him. Bent and graybearded, but with sparkling, youthful eyes and energy, and carrying that walking stick he never used to support himself. More of an affectation, or an excuse to carry a weapon — albeit a weapon with gold at the handle and tip, instead of steel.

"My future lord," Olivart greeted Cavan with the phrase he always favored. "I'd only barely heard you were coming before you arrived. What brings you—"

"Soldiers," Cavan said, breathlessly. He'd intended to go inside first. He'd intended to sit with Olivart in the old majordomo's office and go over the details with him.

But hours on the road had been hard on Cavan's patience. And riding past the homes and lives of those he would one day govern had driven the last of that patience away.

"The duke is mustering and on the march. You need to send word to the king, put out the call and send troops to the mine."

"The mine? Not the Street of Death?"

"If you can muster by the morning, the Street of—"

"The Street of Death is fine," Amra said. She, Ehren and Qalas were rushing up to stand beside Cavan. "I've already told your sergeant that the call is going out. Wave and he'll know you agree."

This was all happening too fast for Olivart. Cavan could tell by the way the man's lips shook. Olivart was a careful man. A man who did not believe in risks he didn't have to take. Especially not with the lives of his people.

And Cavan did not doubt that Olivart thought of the residents of Juno as *his* people. He was right, too. They were his in a way they might never be Cavan's. Not even if he ruled here for a hundred years.

Olivart had been born and raised here. Lived here all his life. Cavan had not. It was that simple.

Olivart looked at Cavan. Cavan looked at Amra.

"The Street of Death," she confirmed. "Let them meet him there, or as close as possible."

"While we head for the mines ourselves?" Cavan nodded. Turned to Olivart. "She's right. But send the word — do not engage. Not unless the Nolarrites attack first."

Cavan frowned and added, "And do *not* let the invaders *forage*."

That word lit a fire in Olivart's eyes. Made him understand exactly how serious this situation was.

Olivart gave the wave Amra directed, then turned to that page, who was still shaking. Poor kid. Couldn't have seen more than a dozen summers, all of them peaceful. Just the thought of war coming to Juno was enough to drive the blood from his face, get him sweating, and to start his legs and arms shaking.

Olivart gave the boy a smile, and Cavan wished he knew the secret of that smile. It seemed to give the boy heart. Settled the tremor in his legs. Stiffened his lip, and straightened his posture.

"Fetch Ranus," Olivart said, "and have him meet me in my office. And make sure he brings his armor."

No sooner was that page gone, then Olivart had called three

others, and sent them off with orders. News to the farmsteads nearest the danger zone, as well as orders within the manor itself.

Cavan was just starting to itch for action when Olivart turned back to him.

"Now, Cavan," Olivart said, without a trace of the usual quaver in his voice. "Tell me everything while you eat."

"We don't have time," Cavan started, but Olivart didn't let him finish.

"You're not going off for the mines without food and information."

Cavan gnashed his teeth, but nodded.

Olivart led Cavan and his friends into the mansion itself.

The interior of the house had been paneled in dark yellow wood, with tapestries showing major events in the history of the barony. Starting, it seemed, with the legend of Juno herself. Cavan barely had time to take in the fine, but functional furnishings as Olivart led him through the large assembly room and straight down the long, central hall.

More wood paneling down this hall, lit by candles in mirrored sconces every five steps. Between the candles were portraits of all past barons Juno, beginning with the current baron, King Draven.

Cavan expected to turn at the first hallway, which would have led to the dining room in one direction, and the baron's meeting hall in the other.

Olivart didn't turn. And for a bent-backed old man, he set a swift pace the rest of the way down that hall and into the kitchen.

The kitchen was large, but it had to be. Not only did it cook all the food for the mansion and all who worked here, but also for any major events that were held in the barony.

It was a kitchen large enough to feed an army. Cavan could only hope it never had to.

Olivart finally sat at a small table to one side of the kitchen, "guarded" by a gray-whiskered old black dog, who lay beside the door to the outside.

Cavan remembered that dog.

"Ollie?" Cavan said.

The dog looked pained getting to his feet, but he wagged his tail and ambled to Cavan as he sat.

Cavan stroked his old friend, and petted his ears while he and his friends caught Olivart up on everything they knew about the duke's troop movements and his reasons.

By the time they finished — and that did not take long — servants had brought over roast chickens, with corn, beets and peas, along with plenty of fresh water to drink.

Cavan slipped some of the chicken to Ollie, for old time's sake.

"Now," Olivart said when Cavan was clearly finished with his side of the telling. "You need to know about the mine."

The tone in Olivart's voice as he said those words was almost enough to sour the taste of the excellent chicken, which had just the right amount of rosemary.

"Kent ordered us to halt all mining of those special crystals as soon as he had a sample. The ones he gave you."

"Why would—"

"He wanted time to assess their value before letting miners do their work. After all, blue crystals coming out of those mountains don't *sound* impressive. He wanted to make sure they'd merit the cost of extra precautions, otherwise—"

"I understand," Cavan said.

Kent was always the best at wringing profit out of a situation. Naturally he wouldn't want to spend more on the mining process than he had to, and if he needed to spend more, he'd want to know exactly how much more before he acted.

Still, Cavan remembered his speculations of the afternoon. Dunaian magic, and the idea of those gemstones locking the gate to the underworld.

In fact, he got so caught in his own speculations — as he gnawed on a chicken leg — that he almost missed what Olivart said next.

"Just as well," Olivart said, voice both sad and angry. "I've had to order the mine closed until I could reach Kent. There's been a death."

Cavan dropped the chicken leg.

Ollie snatched it right up off the floor, but Cavan couldn't spare a smile for the moment.

"Tell me," he said.

"The way I was told," Olivart said slowly, "there was a rumble in the mine. The overseer, Kaethe, feared a cave-in and ordered everyone out."

"Sounds sensible," Ehren said.

"Only there was no cave-in. Warren, one of the team foremen, saw Kaethe go into the restricted area near the special crystal deposits. Then the rumbling started. Then she came back out and ordered everyone out."

Olivart shook his head. "The ground wasn't shaking though. Just that rumble. And she went back to look into the restricted area again."

Olivart kissed his fingertips and touched them behind his right ear. An old tribute to the dead.

"Something snatched her through. She never even had time to scream. Warren said ... Warren said he could hear something eating her."

"He ran, I hope," Amra said.

"He did," Olivart said with a nod. "Ordered the crew home, posted guards at the mine, then and took the story straight to me."

Cavan looked at his friends. Saw the same look of fierce determination in their eyes that he felt in his own.

They would go into those mines, and they would kill whatever devoured Kaethe.

"We'll leave at once," Cavan said, standing up.

"Not quite yet," Olivart said. "I have something for you."

OLIVART WENT TO FETCH THE PRESENT PERSONALLY, AND CAVAN LED HIS friends back out front while they waited. Already they were making plans.

"The horses won't stand up to speed," Amra said.

"Then we change them for horses that will," Qalas said.

"We'd still be leaving horses at the mine when we go in," Ehren said.

Cavan was only half-listening. Striding quickly as he could down the hall. Throwing the front door open himself.

He'd wanted to change his sword while he was here, but there wouldn't be time. He'd have to hope Kent wouldn't mind his family sword defending the lands he held as steward.

The moment the four friends were out front, Cavan whirled on Amra.

"Check the horses," he said. "We need to be sure."

"I *am* sure," she said.

"We need speed, and they won't have anything—"

He broke off as the front door opened again. Olivart hurried out...

...carrying a sword.

Oh, he was carrying his "walking" stick too, under his arm, but Cavan was more interested in the sword in Olivart's hands.

A longsword, by the look of it. Good length for Cavan. Pretty close to what he was used to. It had a fine leather scabbard, embossed with images of Juno, with the baronial seal itself near the opening.

"I know you weren't comfortable carrying Kent's family sword," Olivart said, with a smile Cavan hadn't expected. Even smiling, the old majordomo looked worried, but the pleasure of giving this gift was still evident in his posture, the reverent way he held the sword.

"Well," Cavan said, unsure what else he could say. "I had been planning to change blades here, but I hadn't expected... Thank you, Olivart."

"Draw it," Olivart said, that smile widening just a hair.

Cavan frowned with curiosity, and did.

The sword was beautiful. Long and smooth and sharp. But more than that, it was a reddish-yellow color. The steel itself. Cavan had never seen anything like that. It wasn't enameling. No one would enamel a sword. And it wasn't any kind of dye. Dyes never held well on blades that saw any real use.

No, this blade had to actually be made from some kind of reddish-yellow steel.

Cavan had never heard of such a thing.

And that wasn't all.

There was magic to it. No spells, as such, but Cavan could feel enchantment woven into the blade, from the forging process.

The hilt was fashioned from the same steel as the blade. Reddish-yellow, and worked into grooves and filigrees that looked not only beautiful, but seemed to cling to his hand as he took it in his grip. The sword was deceptively light, and perfectly balanced.

Amra whistled admiration.

Cavan tested with a couple of cuts through the air, and the blade practically sang.

"*Licha*," Qalas said, reverently.

"What?" Cavan asked.

"True, dune elf steel, you mean?" Ehren asked, as though reducing this work of art to a matter of intellectual curiosity.

Amra nodded, her eyes still moving over the blade.

"I've read about it," Ehren said, "but I've never seen any before."

"I wouldn't think you would," Qalas said, eyes still wide. "Not this far north. *Licha's* not a naturally occurring metal, but something dune elves fashion out of regular steel, by techniques known only to them." He shook his head. "Even dwarves can't work *licha*."

Qalas turned to Olivart. "Where did you *get* it?"

"Question for another time," Olivart said.

"Well," Amra said with a teasing smile. She clapped Cavan on the shoulder. "Now you don't have to envy mine. Though yours is a *touch* small for me."

To prove her point, she drew her own wyrd black blade, which was wider, as well as longer. And the magic woven into her own steel seemed to resonate with that of Cavan's new blade. Not quite in harmony, but not quite clashing either.

Cavan didn't rise to her joke about size, and he didn't worry about the contrast in magics. Not right then. He was still studying what had to be the finest sword he'd ever held. He turned it this way and that, marveling at the way the late afternoon sunlight seemed to swim along the steel, bringing out highlights in different shades all along its length.

But then he noticed, the sword was unfinished.

On each side of the hilt, and at the base of the pommel, were places for adornment. The way Cavan had seen some swords adorned with rubies and sapphires...

Three places...

He glanced over at Olivart, who smiled and nodded indulgently. "Kent sent me word that he'd given them to you. That they were magic."

Cavan quickly dug the three blue, crystal gemstones from his pouch.

It was the work of only a few minutes to affix them to the sword. Cavan used a modified version of the spell he knew for fashioning staves. No time for weaving further spells. Just the basic enchantments to make the jeweled sword a conduit.

And the magic of the sword seemed to welcome the gemstones. As though the sword itself had been waiting for something, and Cavan had brought just the right thing.

The darkest blue he attached to the base of the pommel, with the other two centering the narrow crossbar on each side.

"Will it work as well?" Ehren said, and Cavan knew he meant as compared to a staff for controlling the gemstones.

"I doubt there's any way that sword is inferior," Qalas said, voice still reverent as he answered the wrong question.

Cavan only nodded. He needed to change his scabbard. He knew that. He now had more than enough replacement for Kent's family sword, and certainly no reason to carry both.

Still. He was loath to sheath his beautiful new sword. It felt so good in his hand. So natural. He felt himself smile grimly at the thought of getting to test it for the first time on the creature that had slain Kaethe.

That thought snapped Cavan out of his reverie.

Cavan had never met this Kaethe, but he didn't have to. She was an innocent, slaughtered for being in the wrong place at the wrong time. And that she was a citizen of Juno just made him all the more eager to avenge her.

"Right," he said, sheathing the marvelous blade.

Remembering his manners, he quickly gave his thanks to Olivart, but Olivart dismissed the effort just as quickly, telling him that the best thanks would be to slay the thing in the mines.

Cavan changed scabbards, handing Kent's sword to Olivart. Only then did Cavan turn back to his friends once more.

"Right," he said again. "Let's go."

"But the horses," Amra said.

"We won't need them," Cavan said, grim smile on his face. "I have an idea."

LATE AFTERNOON NOW. THE SUN BEHIND CAVAN WAS THROWING THEIR shadows well up the road to the mines. Still a fair distance to travel, but they were making good time. They sped along past small camps for traveling salesmen and their guards. Past smaller and larger farms, and ranches. Copses and small forests of pines and firs.

They sped along in a heavy wooden cart. The kind usually used to haul tin down from the mine. Thick, heavy slats of wood. Six, huge wheels.

The kind of cart usually pulled by a team of horses.

At the moment it was propelled by something else. In a way that no one had ever done before. Or at least, not to Cavan's knowledge.

Cavan stood astride the bench seat at the front, facing wind that smelled of the mine. Like tin, already. Even though he could have been smelling the trees and the farms, if they'd been going slower.

Right now, though, they were traveling at least as fast as Dzint could gallop. And Cavan could only smell the cool wind. He might not have even smelled the tin. He might have been imagining it.

But he couldn't spare attention to wonder. He needed to keep his focus on his spells.

Amra sat below him on the seat, face forward to the wind. Whooping every so often, as though this were the best way to travel that she could imagine.

Qalas and Ehren sat in the back of the cart. They were talking, but Cavan couldn't hear them. Not until Qalas started to shout.

"Are you sure this is safe?"

"No!" Cavan yelled back.

Not the answer Qalas was looking for, but what did the ex-hunter expect? They were speeding along in a cart not built for speed. They were being propelled by a magical arm's length of silvery disc, trapped behind the cart and desperately trying to get to Cavan.

That was the brilliance of his idea.

The spell was one that every apprentice learned. Nester's Platter. Most had to use it to serve at their masters' parties, or to carry books and trade goods.

So far as Cavan knew, no one before him had ever made use of this particular feature.

The disc was designed to stay within ten feet of its master. It could travel at whatever speed it needed to, in order to maintain that maximum distance. That meant that it could ride as swift as a wizard's horse — or in some cases, as fast as a wizard could fly.

So Cavan had summoned the disc back in the courtyard of the baronial manor, loaded his friends onto the cart, then jumped aboard from behind and scrambled to the front of the cart.

The cart was just over ten feet long. The disc zoomed to close the gap, but was barred by the back of the cart.

The cart began to roll, propelled by the force of the spell, because the disc was still trying to reach Cavan.

Thus, did they build up speed.

Tough to steer though. Cavan had to move back and forth, causing the disc to angle its force, while he played little games with other forms of kinetic spells to try to turn the cart.

Fortunately, it was pretty much a straight shot all the way from the township of Juno to the mines. Done so that these carts, when laden with tin, would not have to turn much.

Right now, Cavan was grateful for that little detail.

Still, though he didn't have to steer much, and he felt confident of the techniques he had, he didn't want his friends getting too comfortable.

Just in case something did go wrong.

Oh, Amra wouldn't listen, but Amra never listened.

Of course, it helped that she was confident in her ability to dive and roll safely from any moving cart or horse.

Cavan had never asked *exactly* why she had that skill. Or how she developed it...

The farms and trees and camps and ranches sped past. Cavan kept up his spellwork, keeping the cart as swift as he could manage.

They were only perhaps a mile from the mine entrance when it all went wrong.

The cart began going up the slope of the mountainside. Cavan had thought the slope would be gradual enough that he could adjust for it.

He was wrong.

Right at the bottom, the initial grade was a *hair* too steep. The cart hit a bump as it began its ascent. And it hit that bump *hard*.

The cart tipped. Cavan tried to correct. Used too much force.

The disc slipped free and winged its way to float in the air beside Cavan.

Cavan, alas, was now tumbling through the air.

He was still in the air when he heard the cart crash. Wood cracked, maybe splintered. Somewhere behind him, he thought, but he couldn't be sure.

Then it was Cavan's turn to crash.

He was spinning when he hit, which would have been good if he'd hit at the right angle to roll.

He didn't. He hit the ground harder than the cart hit that bump.

Jarred him. The world spun. Or maybe he was still spinning.

His head hurt. His sides hurt. His back hurt worst of all.

And he *was* spinning. He was rolling after all, and sliding through the bluish dirt down the mountainside. Right up until a hand grabbed one of his flailing limbs.

His ankle, as it turned out.

The grasping hand wrenched Cavan to a standstill. Not that stopping felt any better.

"Ohhh," Cavan groaned.

Amra laughed. She was the one holding his ankle. Her skin and most of her leathers were coated with blue dust, but she otherwise looked none the worse for their little spill.

"Honestly," she said. "It was your spell, and you were the only one who couldn't land?"

"I was too busy trying to keep us from going over."

"Didn't work," Qalas said, stepping up beside Amra, his halberd in hand. Qalas was just as dirty, but he also looked to have been scraped up a little bit, which made Cavan feel a little better.

Not that he wanted Qalas to get hurt. He just didn't want to be the only one who got his bell rung. And he already knew what he'd see when he saw Ehren.

"Truly, not your best work there," Ehren said, walking over to stand beside Amra.

Sure enough. Ehren was spotless. From the crown of his golden hair to the soles of his doeskin boots, if he'd landed on that mountainside, there was no evidence to prove it.

"Yes, well," Cavan said, as Qalas helped him to his feet, "are any of you going to complain? You can't say I didn't get us here quickly."

"We're not quite there yet," Amra said, looking up the mountainside, then turning to the north. "No sign of the duke's men so far. So that's something."

"Can't go the rest of the way on that thing," Qalas said, pointing to the cart, which had lost half its wheels and cracked its frame.

"So we walk," Amra said, then lifted an eyebrow. "If our future lord here can make it."

"I can make it. I can make it," Cavan said through a grimace as he stretched and twisted his bumps and bruises. "Let's go already."

7

AMONG THE MEMBERS OF THE ORDER OF THE FALSE DAWN, THERE WAS a good deal of debate about what skill or quality was most important to an assassin.

Some said speed. Others said timing. Still others insisted poison, as though any member of their order could be deficient in that skill. Others said that the proper physique was what mattered.

Those who said that would have considered Dane to have the perfect build. Lean enough to look skinny, when dressed properly, but strong enough to do whatever needed doing. No visible scars, but an uninteresting face that could be forgotten even by a barmaid who'd just been given a generous tip.

His blood red hair might have caught attention, if he didn't shave his head and pretend to be bald. Shaving his blood red eyebrows might have caught attention, though, but they were narrow anyway. Narrow enough that most passersby didn't notice their color.

No, the only thing that would distinguish Dane from any ordinary peasant was the thin purple mustache that was the sign of the Order of the False Dawn. Every member wore it — both the men and the women — but its arcane nature was such that it was only visible when an assassin was either meeting with clients, or ready to kill.

No, build was not the most important quality in an assassin.

But Dane knew what was.

The most important quality for an assassin was patience.

Those who rushed, failed. He had seen it time and again.

So though Dane had been given his assignment — the death of Cavan Oltblood — while this Cavan was still in Nolarr, he had waited.

Nolarr was not friendly territory. Cavan would be on his guard.

Dane had ridden to the closest town to the so-called Street of Death — Street of Maiming would have been a better name, what what Dane had read about it — and waited there until he saw Cavan's distinctive horse, at the front of his little group.

A blue roan hobby. Not many like that in this part of the world. Not many like it in any part of the world.

Then and only then had Dane ridden close enough to see his quarry.

And Dane had ridden a plain horse. Not even of the quality used by messengers or the post. Only the sort that carried townsfolk from here to there and back again. Cheap, and unnoticeable.

Going unnoticed might have taken second place in Dane's assessment of the critical skills of an assassin. But it was most certainly second to patience.

An impatient man might have gone after Cavan during that duel his companion Amra fought with the Nolarrite champion.

Foolish man. He'd underestimated Amra from the moment he'd seen her. Clearly he hadn't been around enough to know that while all women were deadly, two types of women were the most deadly.

The beautiful women were deadly because most men sighed when they saw them. Wanted to trust them. Wanted to believe that a beauty could truly like them for who they were. Easy way to get inside a man's guard.

The plain women were deadly because most men took less notice of them. Opportunities to exploit that inattention abounded for plain women.

Ugly women *could* be dangerous, but it seemed that they always had to *look* dangerous when they were. Beauties could go underestimated, and the plain ones could go unnoticed. But when ugly women were dangerous, most men would notice.

And so this "champion" underestimated Amra. He didn't see how she stood. How she moved. The fell blade she carried.

She made short work of him, as she should have.

Still, Dane learned an important lesson from that fight — Cavan traveled with dangerous friends.

Amra, of course. Her reputation preceded her, and she appeared to live up to it.

Dane knew how he would kill Amra, if she had been his target. Poison blow dart, preferably as she drank in a tavern. Tricky, though. He'd have to be sure to strike one of the three spots that could lead to instant death. Otherwise her priest friend *might* save her.

Of course, priests of Zatafa relied on the dawn for their best healing. With the right poison, the priest might not be enough to save her.

That priest friend was Ehren, a follower of Zatafa, and dedicated enough to try to heal an enemy, even when pressed for time.

What was more, this Ehren, he looked *pristine* every time Dane had seen him. And Dane had contrived to see that little group no less than four times before they reached the Nolarr border.

Every time Dane had seen Ehren, that priest of Zatafa's white clothing had been spotless. Not so much as a mote of dust.

The truest sign of a priest in good standing with his sun god.

Dangerous.

Most thought of Zatafa only for healing, purification. They did not seem to remember how the sun could blind and burn. Zatafa's best priests could be as potent in a battle as out of one.

Worse, priests of Zatafa, when in good standing with their god, were notoriously hard to harm. It was said that all who dwelt under Zatafa were loath to strike her priests.

Dane had never tested that, but if Ehren had been his target, Dane would have assumed it to be true. Safer that way. A gaseous, choking poison, delivered at night, would have been Dane's solution.

Qalas had been the easiest to assess. His records were available, for he had served the duke. Not much in the records, but they pointed to a clever hunter and a fierce fighter.

A poison blow dart would work for him, as well as for Amra. In fact, an arrow might prove sufficient to slay Qalas, if aimed and timed right.

Speaking of arrows, odd that Qalas had no bow with him. The records had made it clear that Qalas was a competent shot. Dane had not known many competent archers to go without their weapons. A halberd was hardly a fit replacement, however good the man was at hand-to-hand combat.

And Cavan himself, of course. Dangerous with sword and spell, by all accounts. Beat the duke in a fair duel, but then, the duke should never have let himself get drawn into a fair duel.

The sign of a man who rushed.

Dane had ideas about how to kill Cavan, but these could not stay theoretical. And as dangerous as his group was, Dane knew he might get only one attempt.

And so Dane had followed Cavan's crew through the pass. Not down the Street of Death itself, of course. They might have seen him. No, Dane had ridden the military trails on the currently unmanned south side of the pass.

Slower, but speed was not what he needed.

Dane had followed at a safe distance as Cavan and his group rode hard for his future manor.

Easy enough to tell Cavan cared about the people here. Was that for the people themselves though? Or their future value to him? Reports said the former, but Dane would not judge. Not until he'd gotten more of the man's measure.

And that would happen before the end. It always did. By the time Dane killed Cavan, he would know everything important there was to know about Cavan Oltblood.

While Cavan had spent time at his manor, Dane had ridden the town. Gotten a sense of it. Changed horses.

The people here did not speak of Cavan. They spoke of Olivart, the majordomo.

Interesting.

And then Cavan and his crew had come out, riding hard on a horseless cart. Powered by some kind of magical disc, by the look of it.

The *unstable* look of it.

So Cavan *was* a man who took chances. So the report had said, and now Dane had confirmed it.

Good to know.

That cart was bound straight for the mine entrance.

That, Dane greeted with a sigh.

Mines were no good. Too many passages. Too many echoes, even among that blue stone. No, the mine was no fit place for an assassination.

Of course, if the word Dane had heard around town was true, then his services might not properly be needed. The stablehand who had changed horses for Dane had spoken of some kind of monster in the mines.

No doubt that was what Cavan aimed to kill.

Well, perhaps he would. If so, he would likely be wounded when he came out. Or at least exhausted. He had been wounded last night, after all, refreshed only by the blessings of Zatafa.

He'd been awake a long time. Most of a day. Riding, and now working demanding magic on that cart, to get such speed. He certainly appeared to be heading into a mine and to battle.

Would he do that though?

Cavan appeared to be rash enough to risk facing an unknown monster when he was not fresh and prepared. But Amra did not seem so rash, nor Ehren or Qalas.

Perhaps they had some pressing reason to take that risk?

Perhaps.

More likely they would enter, explore for some distance, and return to the safety of the mine's mouth to make their camp.

Well.

If they did *that*, Dane would be waiting for them. Great time to kill someone, while they're making other plans.

And if they did not return tonight? If they were foolish enough to proceed without making camp?

Then Dane would wait. If anything of Cavan made it out of those mines, Dane would be fulfill his contract.

And if not, well, Cavan would be dead, and within the allotted time frame. In that case, Dane would have his pay, or Inari Flintblack, seneschal to the duke of Nolarr, would die screaming.

Dane smiled and set his horse to trot that path after the speeding cart.

One way or another, Dane would be paid and Cavan would die.

8

The hike from the crashed cart to the mine entrance was only about a mile, but it seemed to take forever. Cavan tried to reassure himself that this was a good sort of delay. He'd stiffened up, holding himself steady on that long, bumpy cart ride, and the long walk up the gradual slope had given him the chance to stretch his legs.

It only *felt* as though it took hours. Cavan was sure of that. The air had barely cooled, and the sun, though dimming, had not yet set in the sky behind him.

There was no sky in front of him, of course. Any hope of that was blocked by the mighty Ice Dagger itself, jutting up so high in the sky that — at this distance — Cavan couldn't see the peak. When he looked up, though, he could see the sky above him, only just beginning to darken to its nighttime shade.

When he looked back down, he could spot the ends of the wooden rails, used by smaller carts to shuttle ore from within the mine to the surface, where it could be transferred to the larger carts for transport.

Several carts of both sizes waited near the mine entrance for the next day's work. Though when that next day would come had yet to be determined. The work tables nearby were abandoned, as were several small wooden buildings that likely served as tool storage, dining hall and office space.

All vacant right now. Thank the gods.

Cavan felt some relief that there had been only the one death so far. That none of the campers nearest the mine — mine guards, some twenty minutes behind Cavan now — had heard nor seen anything unusual since the mine's closure.

Here, at the entrance at last, all seemed quiet. No noise but the wind, almost ceaseless this close to the mountains, and chill, but not strong.

The mine began somewhere inside the cavern ahead of him. That cavern looked to have been natural. A scar, in the side of the Ice Dagger's hilt. Perhaps thirty yards across, but tapering to a height of some hundred yards up.

The cave, of course, looked black as pitch already.

Cavan stopped the procession and sniffed the air. Dust. And tin, he thought. But not much more than that. No smell of blood, nor anything to indicate some kind of foul beast or abomination.

He hadn't expected anything, but if the Dunaian Underworld was involved — and Cavan refused to rule that possibility out — he couldn't discount anything. He might even have smelled sulfur.

But no. Normal mining smells.

"Kerchiefs," he said, pulling one from his own pouch and tying it to cover his mouth. "Best to be safe."

"Won't last once the fighting starts," Amra said.

"They'll help in the meantime," Cavan said.

"No need," Ehren said, looking at Qalas as he spoke. "We're not mining, so we won't need them."

Sounded reasonable to Cavan, who found himself glancing at Qalas while putting his kerchief away.

Qalas was staring straight up.

"First mountain?" Ehren asked.

"No," Qalas said, shaking his head slowly. "But ... so many crystal deposits. It glitters more like glass than snow. Still, I would have called it the Icicle."

"Not as impressive sounding," Cavan said with a chuckle. "Ehren, if you would do the honors?"

The wind took its only pause while Ehren prayed to Zatafa, soft words Cavan could not quite make out.

And just like that, it seemed that the sun shone brightly, all around them.

Cavan could now see the first part of that empty cavern ahead of him, bright as daylight.

"How do you get used to this?" Qalas asked. "There are no shadows. Anywhere."

"You don't, really," Cavan said. "You just enjoy it."

Ehren smiled, his usual smile when confronted with something anyone considered remarkable about the blessings of Zatafa. Pleased, but humble.

Amra, for her part, only grinned and drew her sword.

Qalas readied his halberd. Ehren already held his staff at the ready.

Cavan drew his new sword, amazed that its reddish-yellow hues seemed to glimmer in the sunlight, even though there was no real sunlight on them. This particular blessing of Zatafa cast no light. Instead it allowed the faithful to see as though wherever they stood were midday under a cloudless sky.

Cavan led the way into the cavern.

Jagged it was, above them, with small things scurrying about among the stalactites. Bats, perhaps. Cavan couldn't smell them, but he could see signs of their leavings on the uneven cavern floor around him.

The cavern itself had no crystal deposits. It was all pure blue-gray stone, varying only in shade.

No quarry here, which surprised Cavan. He knew that the locals quarried stone from these mountains. And it would have made sense to him if they'd begun their quarry in a naturally large opening like this one. But either they had a better option, or they could not quarry and mine so close together.

Cavan made a mental note to ask Olivart about it later. Just another thing he would need to know and understand, if he ever did become the baron of Juno.

And then he put such thoughts from his mind.

Somewhere ahead of him lay the thing that killed Kaethe. And when they took care of that, there was still the matter of the remaining gemstones. And all before the duke could arrive with his men.

THOUGHTS OF THE DUKE'S SOLDIERS MADE CAVAN PAUSE RIGHT AT THE entrance to the mine itself. Bad enough he was heading into a mine to fight one or more unknown monsters. The last thing he needed would be enemies at his back.

He held up one hand to halt his friends.

Cavan looked around the mine entrance proper. Wide enough for three stout carts, side-by-side. Probably to allow plenty of movement on foot even when a load was coming up on the rails. Arched to a good height above. Not so tall as wide, but that didn't matter.

"What?" Qalas said.

Amra hushed him. Ehren whispered, "Cavan's looking for magic."

"Not for," Cavan said, voice as distant as his thoughts. "Checking the lay of things."

He turned to his friends. "Into the mine, but not more than a dozen steps. I have to ward it."

"Keeping the creature in or the duke's soldiers out?" Ehren asked.

"Both," Cavan said, as he nodded. Yes. The height was proportional to the width. Two to three.

A good ratio for a ward. Not ideal. Worse, Cavan couldn't get to the top to engrave anything, but there were ways he could cheat at least that factor.

He dug around the edges of the cavern until he found three small stones. Each about the right size to fill his palm.

From his belt, Cavan drew one of two spelled daggers he carried.

The one in his boot was for combat, when needed. The one from his belt, however, was for occasions like this.

Cavan placed the three stones on the ground, forming a triangle half-again as wide across the bottom as it was tall.

Cavan tapped the tip of his dagger to his forehead, then behind each ear, then finally at the base of his stomach, all the while murmuring the right words of power to pull together what he would need for this spell.

"*Krisst*," Cavan hissed, as he touched the rightmost stone, etching the letter K.

"*Haasst*," Cavan hissed for the leftmost, etching the letter H.

Finally, for the top, he hissed, "*Nosst*," as he touched it with the tip of his dagger, etching the letter N into this last stone.

He could see the flow of energies between the three rocks now. Barely visible, and only that because he had as much wizardly training as he did, but visible enough to reassure him that he'd worked his spells right so far.

He set down his dagger and picked up the three stones, the topmost in his mouth, the other two in their appropriate hands. All the while, maintaining that perfect, proportional distance between them.

Cavan carried the rightmost stone to the place where the edge of the mine's true entrance met the wall. He placed it there, hissing words of power around the dry taste of the topmost stone, clenched between his teeth by its edge.

More words of power then, forcing Cavan's tongue to work double-time around the stone in his mouth. And awkward way to work a spell, but necessary since he could not reach the keystone location at the top of the mine shaft.

Fighting resistance, the pull of the rightmost stone which was now locked in place, Cavan fought to carry the other two stones across to the left side of the entrance.

Facing the left side helped, but it meant that the one stone was now trying to get past Cavan's teeth into his mouth.

Yes, this was the least comfortable way to cast he'd found so far.

He could only hope it got no worse.

He was sweating with effort and gritting against pain by the time he finally placed the leftmost stone. Still, he managed to get the right words out. Though they came out more sibilant than the spell called for, Cavan would have to hope he came close enough.

The moment the leftmost stone was in place, Cavan grabbed the topmost stone in both hands and wrenched it from his mouth.

He lost a moment, just working his sore jaw to try to bring feeling back to it. He hoped he hadn't cracked any teeth in the process.

Now, with two stones in place, the force wrenching at Cavan for the third was almost enough to bear him to the ground. He stumbled to the center of the mine opening, which helped, but the stone was desperately trying to yank itself down, into line with the other two.

At last, Cavan stood in the right place. Now he could properly finish the spell.

Gripping the stone tightly with both hands, Cavan hissed out the next words of the spell through his sore jaw and dry tongue.

But those words did their work.

The stone sprang from Cavan's hand, flying straight up to lock itself into place at the top of the mine — exactly in the correct, proportional spot to where Cavan had first placed it when beginning the spell.

The three holders of the ward were now in place.

Cavan retrieved his spelled dagger. Put it back in his belt.

He walked past the porous field generated by the magical tension of the three stones. Still a triangular field, which was the first order of business.

The moment Cavan was inside the field, he turned and raised both arms.

He spun his hand in a circle in the air in front of him as he chanted the right words to shift the way the stones' magic connected. Instead of a direct link between the stones, the connection now ran along the edges of the mine's opening, filling the opening completely with the porous energies that flowed between them.

Cavan scooped up a handful of blue-gray dust, and mixed it with some iron shavings from his spell pouch. He gathered power in the center of his being, then tossed that handful into the air blew power across it as he hissed out the final words of the spell.

"Kressa, nil esk hass crissindass."

The dust and shavings spread across the field of power, that was no longer porous.

"There," Cavan said, turning to his friends and wiping his brow with the sleeve of his tunic. "Test—"

A thrown rock flew from Amra's hand, past Cavan's head, and bounced off the ward.

"—it," Cavan finished.

"Good enough," Amra said. "How long will it hold?"

"Until daylight next touches it," Cavan said, drawing his sword. "Given its location, I'd say it'll hold until Ehren does something to dismiss it."

"I don't like that," Ehren said with a rare frown. "It's fell magic that recoils before Zatafa's brilliance."

"Not fell," Cavan objected. "Dark."

"As I said," Ehren said, raising an eyebrow, "fell."

"Will it work?" Amra said, stepping between Cavan and Ehren.

"Should," Cavan said. "The entrance is wide enough that if they hit it hard enough in enough places at the same time it may come down, but—"

"Then it'll do," Amra insisted.

Ehren gave a stiff nod.

Cavan, grumbling about ingratitude, turned to take the lead again.

DANE SIGHED AS HE INSPECTED THE TWO OF THE THREE KEYSTONES THAT held the ward in place. In the dimness of dusk, the power of the ward limned a blue-purple light to his well-trained eyes.

"Interesting place for a ward, I suppose," he muttered, "but it does mean you're not coming out to camp. Doesn't it, Cavan?"

Dane frowned. Glanced behind him over his shoulder.

The ward meant more than that. It meant Cavan was expecting company.

That seneschal, Inari, she had said nothing about Nolarr invading Juno. But Dane couldn't believe Cavan was worried about anyone from Juno following him into the mines. Not with the locally beloved Olivart closing that mine.

Could it mean that Dane had tipped his presence?

No. He couldn't believe that. He'd been too careful. He'd stayed out of view.

Besides, there were four of them and one of him. Not to mention that one of those four was a priest of Zatafa, and two had excellent reputations as warriors.

No. If Cavan suspected that Dane was on his tail, those four would have lain in wait to ambush him. Question him, perhaps. Otherwise kill him.

They would not have taken the time and effort for a ward that might stop soldiers, but could never stop a competent assassin.

That meant the ward had to be there for those Nolarrite soldiers that had been mustering near the border.

Dane frowned deeper. A complication. And competition. Letting some monster kill Cavan was one thing. That might as well have been natural causes, which would appear that Dane had arranged the death to not look suspicious. A respectable outcome.

However. If a soldier did Cavan in, when an agent of the Order of the False Dawn had been contracted to kill him, the shame would be unbearable.

Not to mention that Inari would not have to pay.

No, the cost — in both money and honor — would have to be paid by Dane.

That would not happen.

Dane slipped grippers onto his hands, specially prepared gloves that, when worn, connected with his high, soft boots, to let Dane climb any surface as easily as he might a tree with low-hanging branches.

In no time at all, Dane had reached the third of the keystones.

Looked as though the letter N had been scarred into it. Much like the H and K below.

Simple enough ward then. Intended to keep out force. Perhaps to keep it in, as well. Cavan seemed the type to worry about the monster getting past him.

Dane smiled as he scrabbled back down to the cavern floor and took off his grippers, slipped them back into his belt.

A ward intended to stop force was the easiest to slip.

He moved to the leftmost edge.

And there, Dane began the Litany of Vanishing, a simple chant that had nothing to do with invisibility. That was a point of professional pride for the Order of the False Dawn. Let lesser assassins lean on invisibility. That led to mistakes, like forgetting noise, or smells, or footprints.

No, a member of the False Dawn was always perfectly visible, yet was only seen when he wanted to be seen. Only detected, when he wanted to be detected.

And when he wished otherwise, the Litany of Vanishing made it seem as though he did not even exist.

As Dane finished the Litany, he stilled.

No breath.

No heartbeat.

Not so much as a speck of thought flitting through his mind.

Empty. Absent. Vanished.

Dane stepped through the ward, which could no more stop him than it could stop the air, a sound, or an idea.

Once through the ward, Dane shook himself. Checked his weapons. Long, thin sword, a dozen daggers, wire, poisons, and more. Everything still in place, and only the sword noticeable to onlookers.

Now the hunt truly began.

THE MINE DIDN'T DRINK SOUND. NOT AS MUCH AS CAVAN EXPECTED.

The sound of their boots on the stone was almost completely normal. Perhaps the stone itself did less to consume the sound than Cavan had thought.

It seemed that only the crystals did so much to mute their surroundings.

And Cavan could not help his mind wandering to such trivialities. The mine just seemed that quiet.

They had been following it for some time now. It had narrowed from the entrance. Now it was only wide enough for four to walk abreast on either side of the tracks, and only then if the four were friendly.

Cavan and his friends did not test this. Cavan walked in the lead down the center of the tracks, with Amra on his righthand side, a few steps back, and Qalas the same, on his left.

Ehren trailed the group by a few paces, walking down the center of the tracks, as Cavan did.

All four had been alert to any possible problems for the first ... oh, Cavan wasn't quite sure how long they'd been walking. Cavan had traveled in mines before, and usually he'd gotten used to tracking time by the burn on the torches he'd carried.

But traveling with Ehren meant no torches. Only that sunlit brightness that allowed now a single shadow.

Great for visibility. Terrible for tracking time.

Either way, so far they'd seen nothing but two carts of debris.

There'd been only a few branches so far, and Cavan hadn't done more than poke his head down them. He knew that the branch he sought was blocked off, and these weren't.

Then they came to the chasm.

This was unexpected.

All of a sudden, the shaft ended in a wooden bridge that arched slightly in the center and continued through mid-air about a hundred feet before it reached the shaft on the other side.

"Looks solid enough," Qalas said, leaning over the side farther than Cavan could have done comfortably.

"How far down does it go?" Amra said, looking over the side.

"I can't..."

She turned accusing eyes on Ehren. "I can't see the bottom. Why can't I see the bottom?"

Cavan looked over the side. Ehren did as well.

Sure enough, it vanished into darkness somewhere down there. The same was true when Cavan looked up.

"I didn't know the blessing had limits," Ehren said, shaking his head, then bowing it. "I am sorry, my friends. Zatafa has no limits, which means that the fault is with me. My imperfections as a person, and as her priest."

Cavan cleared his throat to stop what might have been a long list of things that Cavan would not have considered faults. He'd heard it before.

"So there are limits. So what?" Cavan shook Ehren by the shoulder. "That's more than an arrow's flight. How much farther do we need to see?"

"My bow," Qalas said suddenly. "I never replaced it in Juno."

"So we go without," Amra said. "What are the chances we'll need it?"

A screech echoed wrongly through the cavern. The sound was high and piercing, but ... off. A quick glance told Cavan that there were enough crystal deposits along the chasm walls to eat some of the sound, kill some of the echo, but worse than that, to give it shape it shouldn't have had.

Amra whipped her head about, looking for the source of the sound, though Cavan had never known her to fail to pinpoint a sound within moments.

The screech came again, but none of them could see the creature that made it.

"Tell me again how we won't need my bow," Qalas said softly.

"We should rush across," Ehren said. "One at a time, so—"

Amra covered Ehren's mouth. "No arrows, remember? And I'm not sure Cavan's trick with sunflower seeds could hurt whatever made that sound."

The screech came again.

"Let's go," Cavan said, and hunching forward, started a quick march across the bridge. Amra and Qalas practically on his heels, but Ehren a few steps farther back.

They were at the middle of the bridge when it struck.

It looked for all the world like a bat. If the bat were larger than a horse, with fur and wings the color of yellow river mud.

It swooped down at Ehren.

Ehren swung his staff.

Too late. Too slow. The bat slammed into him. Ehren's staff flew from his hands as he tumbled backward off of the bridge and into the mine behind the others.

What was a bat doing slamming into someone?

The bat continued its course as though it had not even noticed Ehren. Ehren, still spotless — for all his complaints about flaws — picked up his fallen staff and crouched there at the mouth of the tunnel.

"Come on," Cavan said.

"No," Ehren said. "It wants me. I'll draw it here."

"Ridiculous," Amra said.

Ehren stepped onto the bridge again.

The bat came swooping back down. Now Cavan could see that it had legs. And all four of its legs had claws up, ready to shred and slice.

Amra was there first. She cut a foreleg off the bat. It screeched a complaint that made Cavan's ears ring.

Qalas' thrust with his halberd. Struck the side of the creature. A stab that brought blood, but not much and not deep.

Cavan was a step behind, but his swift new sword cut through the webbing of one wing.

The bat — or whatever it was — spun as it flew, spiraling down into the darkness of the chasm below.

But Cavan did not hear it hit.

Then came more screeches. Dozens of screeches. Hundreds maybe. And at the edge of what Cavan could see looking up, he was sure he could see movement.

Lots and lots of movement.

"Move!" he yelled.

The four of them rushed across the bridge as the screeching got louder and closer.

Cavan panted and whipped around the moment he had stone under his boots again.

Amra hung back, to make sure Ehren made it.

Good thing she did. The first four giant bats had gone straight after Ehren.

They met her blade instead.

More screeching, and Amra was spattered with blood as she backed into the second part of the mine shaft.

"How are we going to get back past those things?" Qalas asked.

"I'm more worried about where they came from. There's never been a report of anything like that in the mine before. Olivart would have said."

"Questions for later," Amra said, pointing with her sword.

But she wasn't pointing at the scores and scores of giant bats that zoomed and screeched around the chasm.

She was pointing at the four bat creatures that had landed on the bridge.

ALL THOSE GIANT BAT CREATURES FLYING AROUND, AND FOUR HAD landed on the bridge.

Cavan backed his friends up, Qalas guarding the rear, until they were all safely inside the mine again. Yes, that would not stop the four bat creatures from closing, but it might mean they could fight without drawing more.

"I'll take the two in the middle," Amra began as the four bat creatures entered the mine with a kind of crawling walk, each on four legs that didn't look nearly as awkward as Cavan thought they ought to be.

But she stopped because the two bats on the outside of their line hopped onto the two bats in the middle.

And merged.

Two bat creatures in the mine now. They didn't look any bigger, but they looked ... thicker. Denser, maybe. Their mud yellow fur and wings darkened a shade, and Cavan could smell them now. A foul stench, not even like normal bat guano or rodentish musk.

No, this was not a smell that belonged in this world. It didn't have any sulfur to it, but it might as well have. Acidic, the stench was, but with a sickly sweet undercurrent.

And outside on the bridge, more bat creatures were landing. And combining.

That gave Cavan an idea.

Cavan started digging in his pouch of spells.

"Kill one," he yelled. "But not the other. Not yet."

Amra charged without a word. Her boots ticked on the stone with every step.

She swung.

The leftmost bat creature caught her blade in its foreclaws. She ripped. Sheared through one of the claws, but the other gripped tighter. Clutching it.

Qalas charged the other, using his halberd like a lance, and roaring out a challenge that might just have drawn every single crea-ture in the mines, loud as it sounded in Cavan's ears.

He struck true, but his halberd failed to penetrate the furry muscles. He clung tight to his weapon, keeping himself just outside the reach of its flailing claws.

"How?" he called back to Cavan. "*How* are we supposed to kill one?"

"Hah," Amra cried, slipping her blade free and taking part of a claw with it. She spun in place, parrying that damaged claw as it came in to strike.

Then the bat creature's jaws struck just as fast.

Amra leapt sideways, narrowly avoiding the snapping jaws. She stabbed straight into the ear hole. Twisted her blade as she thrust.

The creature screeched so loud Cavan's eardrums burst in a flood of pain that squeezed his eyes and jaws shut.

That creature fell in place. But Amra fell forward with it, trying to reclaim her sword.

Wait. *Amra's* sword got stuck?

Cavan shook himself. Resumed his digging.

The other bat creature knocked Qalas' halberd aside and closed with him. Qalas swung the blade end and handle fast as he could, parrying its striking claws. All the while, giving ground under the power of its strikes.

Ehren knelt. Praying, far as Cavan could tell.

Out on the bridge, Cavan could see more and more of the bat creatures combining themselves together.

Perfect. Just as Cavan thought.

Amra only needed one more stab to kill her wounded bat creature. Qalas, however, was having a difficult time keeping the claws of the other at bay. It seemed to strike as fast as it could fly. It drove Qalas back with each strike.

Soon he might trip over Ehren.

But by then, Cavan had gathered the ingredients he needed. Just the right combination of ground roots and leaves, added to a little of the dust from the mine floor. All the right elements. All the right connections.

Cavan sprinkled the mixture along the blade of his new sword while he chanted the words that would bind his next strike to reach the core of his enemy. The truth of his enemy.

As Cavan mouthed the final words — words he could not hear — the spell came alive.

More alive than Cavan expected.

He'd expected a soft, greenish glow.

What he got was a spout of cold blue flame, all along the length of his sword. On the handle, the three gemstones glittered.

He looked up. Amra and Qalas were struggling with the remaining bat creature, which seemed faster and stronger now than it had been only a moment ago.

Of course it was. Everything was making sense to Cavan now.

He roared, hoping his friends had hearing enough to heed his warning as he charged, flaming blue sword in hand.

Amra and Qalas only jumped aside at the last moment. They hadn't heard him any more than he heard them. Still, they managed to knock the creature's forelegs aside, giving Cavan one open shot.

Cavan thrust his sword straight into the jaws of the bat creature before him. Stabbed into the roof of its mouth.

Ice spread from the wound, even as he cut deeper.

He cut straight through the creature's skull and into its brain. A strike that slew the bat creature instantly.

And not only the one.

Out on the bridge, all the bat creatures began to fall and lie still.

Dead, one and all.

Cavan was still puffing with the effort of what he'd just done, having withdrawn his still-flaming sword, when sound returned to his world again.

A fact that Cavan only knew because Ehren said, "Better?"

He nodded.

"Exactly what did you just do?" Qalas said, gawking at the dozens of dead bat creatures visible on the bridge, and the dozens of others plummeting even now.

"Those weren't a thousand bat creatures," Cavan said, leaning back against the wall of the mine shaft. "They were one bat creature, that could split itself a thousand times."

"Brilliant," Ehren said softly. "You attached your strike through their own link. When you stabbed the one, you were stabbing them all."

"Did he just call me brilliant?" Cavan asked Amra, who changed the topic.

"I'm more interested in why your sword is burning, and why the flames are cold."

"Now," Cavan said, holding up one hand. "Let's not gloss over this 'brilliant' thing."

"Oh, let's," Qalas said. "Talk about the flames."

Qalas held a hand close to those flames, then jerked it back. "Like frostbite."

"Not sure," Cavan said, gazing with some wonder at the flames himself. "As soon as I shunted a spell along its length, it's like I awoke some connection between the blade and the gemstones."

"That wasn't deliberate?" Ehren asked.

Cavan shook his head. "Not that part."

"I take back my 'brilliant,'" Ehren said, shaking his head in disbelief. "The idea was a good one, but the execution might have been accidental for all we know."

"The spell was perfect! Anyway, it's too late to take it back," Cavan said. "I'm brilliant."

He bit the inside of his cheek for luck, then sheathed the sword.

The flames seemed to go out.

"See?" he said. "Knew exactly what I was doing."

"Guesswork," Ehren said. "Pure guesswork."

"Look," Cavan said, "did I just take care of the problem or not?"

"Let's go," Ehren said, turning and starting down the mine shaft. "Before he finds some other excuse to experiment."

"Hang on," Qalas said, pointing at the corpse of the nearest bat creature. "Where did that come from?"

"Not sure," Cavan said. "Olivart never mentioned—"

"No," Amra said, smacking herself in the forehead. "He's right. Juno's been mining here a long time, and this is the first anyone's seen of those things? So where did it come from?"

A cold feeling swept over Cavan. He locked eyes with Ehren, who looked to have paled at whatever he was thinking. And for Ehren, getting more pale was a trick.

"You think there *is* a portal to the Underworld down here," Ehren said.

Cavan nodded.

"Well, good," Amra said with a grim smile.

Cavan looked a question at her.

Her smile widened. "I was worried there wouldn't be enough to kill."

Somehow, Cavan didn't think that would be a problem.

9

———————

Perhaps Olivart was trying to get him killed.

That was all Ser Ranus could think as he took up his position.

Not that he could imagine why Olivart would want him to die. After all, it wasn't as though Juno had another knight to replace him. And besides, Ranus had served this barony faithfully as the commander of its forces for a good thirty years.

And they'd been a *good* thirty years. Only two times had Ranus had to muster the farmers, miners, crafters and traders of the barony and drill them into something like a fighting force before marching them off in the service of King Draven.

And both times he'd brought almost all of them home alive.

Far more often, Ranus rode against bandits with a unit of the small standing baronial guard. And Ranus had done that as adroitly as he'd commanded his troops in real battles.

Juno had seen little banditry in at least five summers now. All because of Ranus' work.

Nevertheless, as Ranus looked out across the green, grassy field that lay between the hills his men stood on and the Royal Road, he could not help feeling as though he'd been set up.

Politics. It made for terrible warfare.

Here he sat, in the dying light of the summer sun, the only one with real plate armor among all twenty guards here with him. The rest in chain and leather. And none of them accustomed to fighting on horseback, so only Ranus was ahorse.

Well, Ranus and his squire, anyway. Roll. A good lad. Not a drop of noble blood, and not yet old enough to shave, but a good lad nonetheless. Roll wore leathers, as appropriate for a standard bearer. And with no proper force around Ranus, he needed *someone* to bear the standard.

Only two ahorse.

These others were all skilled with their crossbows, at least. That was something. And if it came to a melee, they'd acquit themselves well.

Still, twenty guards, and one aging knight.

Against the standing army maintained by Duke Falstaff of Nolarr.

Suicide.

Yes, Olivart had put out the call. Yes, not long after dawn tomorrow the reinforcements would arrive. The levies, properly said, which meant no more true soldiers than he had around him right now. Not without leaving the baronial manor undefended, and Olivart would never do that.

Morning would be too late. Morning would...

Ranus stopped his deliberations.

He could hear them. He could hear the drums. The distant sound of marching boots as well. And given how close he was to those bloody blue peaks and their sound-eating crystal deposits, that meant they were far closer than he wanted.

They had to be coming through the Street of Death.

Damn it all. And damn politics.

Those soldiers were coming, and they were going to kill, just as surely as Ranus had wolfed down a quick meal of eggs and cheese before riding out here.

Ranus knew it. Olivart knew it.

The sensible thing would have been to position Ranus' twenty on the passes above the Street of Death. Rain down arrows and hot oil and rocks.

From those positions, twenty men could stand against an army and do some real damage.

But no. Olivart had been clear as daylight.

No meeting them outside Juno, which meant not on the Royal Road and certainly not from the passes above the Street of Death.

No striking the first blow. Not unless they set foot on Juno soil and refused to leave.

Ranus sighed. Too late for the Street of Death anyway.

"Come on, Roll," he said. "Let's get this over with." Louder, to the rest of the men had had scattered among the bushes and oak trees, he added, "If they come back without me, start shooting. If we come back pursued, start shooting."

Ranus swore. "Just use your damned heads, and take a few of them with you before they slaughter us."

Ranus kicked his steed forward. Lance, he'd named it. A fine steed. A white charger. The best horse he'd ever owned.

The horse would probably be dead come morning as well.

Ranus set a determined look on his face. Hoped he looked as tough as he used to, with the twin scars on his cheeks that marred even his stubble, and the heavy brow that used to intimidate other knights even at tournaments.

He was still a big man, despite his nearly sixty summers. His arm still strong and quick.

He had to hope he would be enough.

His steed carried his swiftly across the grassy fields, Roll beside him with the baronial standard flapping.

He saw the enemy all too soon.

Two dozen knights, and all of them looked to have horses as fine as Ranus' own. At least three companies of footmen behind them, with spear, shield, and sword.

Yes. A slaughter.

Ranus reined in at the edge of the Royal Road, the very limit of the border of Juno.

"Hail," he called, raising his empty sword hand in salute. "I am Ser Ranus, commander of the forces of Juno. I would ask your business."

One of the knights broke off. Youngish and unscarred. Probably half Ranus' age, with slicked black hair and a slicker black mustache. His plate armor was enameled black, and he wore a two-handed sword across his back.

Had to have been stronger than he looked.

"Hail," the knight said, but he didn't sound happy to be saying it. "I am Ser Sarkin. Is there some law against riding down the King's Road?"

"None," Ranus said, "nor should there be. But you understand that a small barony such as Juno, seeing a force such as yours, might have concerns."

"Valid concerns, Ser," Ser Sarkin said. "I'm afraid that our commander is back aways, but may I give you some advice?"

"Ser, you may," Ranus said, narrowing his eyes.

"Flee," Ser Sarkin said. "Flee across the road into the next county. Or down the road into the county after that. But do not get in our way."

"You mean to enter Juno?"

"We do."

"For what cause?" Ranus shook his head. "Nolarr has no claim on Juno. The king himself is the current baron."

"Duke Falstaff claims that the miners of Juno have dug too deeply into our side of the mountain. That all tin — and anything else — drawn from the mine now is rightfully the property of Nolarr. We are here to enforce his rights."

"Then let us send for a royal surveyor," Ranus said, hope swelling in his chest. "That is the proper approach, and can lead to the only solution that avoids bloodshed."

"I agree, good Ser," Ser Sarkin said, "but the duke believes that, while we wait for the surveyor, he must ensure that nothing of surpassing value is drawn from the mine."

"The mine has been closed for some time now," Ranus said, "by order of the steward."

"Ah," Ser Sarkin said with an oily smile. "Therein lies the problem, you see. The duke takes that as proof that something valuable has been discovered, and accuses Juno of mining those valuables in secret, with the intention of taking what Juno knows rightfully belongs to Nolarr."

Ranus sighed. "There's no way around this, is there?"

"Sorry," Ser Sarkin said, and for just a moment Ranus thought he saw actual feeling in the younger knight's black eyes. "I've heard of you, Ser Ranus. You're a good man. I hate to see you die over this. But you know you're overmatched here. We'll roll right over anything Juno can muster."

"Will your commander accept a challenge to single combat? Me representing Juno, your commander representing Nolarr?"

Ser Sarkin frowned, taken aback. "Do you have the authority for that, good Ser? After all, if you lose—"

"If I lose, Falstaff will try to claim the whole barony, won't he?"

"Would he be wrong?" Ser Sarkin said, softly. "A challenge like that..."

"Very well," Ranus said. "No challenge. We'll have to meet you in the field."

"You'll die."

"Then we'll die."

Ranus then drew himself tall in the saddle, and spoke in his best, carrying battle tones.

"On behalf of the barony of Juno, I, Ser Ranus, commander of the legions of Juno, deny Nolarr's claim as baseless and false. I deny Nolarr access to the lands, farms, and mines of Juno, and warn that any attempt to enter Juno by Nolarr will be treated as invasion, and an act of war, and will be met with force."

Ranus turned Lance then, and rode hard for the meager line his men had drawn, Roll riding just as hard beside him.

The boy was letting the standard droop behind him, in his hurry.

Ranus couldn't blame him.

10

"THIS MUST BE IT," CAVAN SAID.

They'd reached what seemed to be the end of the mine.

It was narrower still, down here. Only wide enough for perhaps six to stand across it. Certainly not enough room for four to fight in a line. With any luck, that wouldn't matter much. They'd seen little opposition since the bats. Only spiders the size of dogs, which went down easily enough to their swords and spells.

None of those in a while, though. And here they'd reached the place where the wooden rails came to a halt, perhaps a dozen paces from the mine's end in solid, blue-gray stone.

And next to that ending, on the right-hand side — likely west, if Cavan had been tracking the gentle twists and turns of the mine correctly — lay another opening, boarded over. Barricaded with sheet boards of raw wood.

Prickling feeling through Cavan's guts, and a little lower, as he looked at that barricade.

He wrote that off to what they *hadn't* found so far.

They'd passed dropped mining equipment and torches (long since burnt out), a clipboard, and carts half-full of tin ore, but there'd been *no bodies*.

Good. Cavan told himself that was good. But still, he felt uneasy. He knew at least one had died down here. Kaethe. And, from what Olivart had said, she'd died somewhere close to this barricaded branch of the mine.

But the boards were in place. And on the stone beneath them, no bodies. No blood.

No sign of a struggle, if he didn't count all the dropped picks, hammers and tools.

"Ready?" Amra asked, her voice betraying some of her excitement, but her tone attempting softness. As though she knew Cavan was thinking about the fallen overseer.

Cavan nodded.

"I should take the lead here," Amra said. "Cavan, you behind me on the right. Qalas, the left. Ehren, in the back, and ready to blind anything that comes at us."

Everyone took positions.

Amra, sword in her right hand, grasped the edge of the main board with her left.

She pulled.

The board didn't give.

Amra frowned. Looked closer.

"No nails on this end," she said.

She pulled again. Then again.

"Need a hand?" Qalas asked, which got him a glare from Amra.

But then she sighed. Sheathed her sword. Qalas leaned his halberd against the side of the mine, while Cavan stood ready, sword in one hand (not burning, but he hadn't tried any more spells with it yet), and a handful of mustard seeds in the other.

Together, Amra and Qalas pulled with all four of their hands. Muscles strained. Cavan could hear them both growling with effort.

The board refused to budge.

"Something's holding it in place," Qalas said.

"How?" Amra demanded. "The edges are on our side. Not even a handful of nails binding it to the stone."

"Why is it closed in the first place?" Ehren asked. "Didn't Olivart say that it was open when Kaethe was killed by ... whatever killed her?"

"Maybe the foreman sealed it," Cavan said, but even he didn't believe it.

"No nails on this side," Amra said, gesturing to the edge of the board she'd been pulled. "And none on the other." She shook her head. "Nothing that should resist like that."

Cavan tried looking closer, seeing if he could detect any spellwork.

That uneasy feeling in his gut grew stronger.

Cavan stood still, blinking in confusion at that. The closer he looked, the more his stomach objected. Not violently, just a growing, gnawing uncertainty, as though each time he looked, Istanlos, the god of death itself, was looking back at him.

And seeing him clearly.

Cavan slipped those seeds back into his spellpouch. Sheathed his sword, which made Amra draw hers as if by reflex. Qalas was only a moment behind her, taking up his halberd.

Cavan held his palms over his eyes. Breathed out *"neela asa"* the words that would sharpen his senses for anything magical...

...and was immediately knocked backward. Only reflex made him duck his head and not smack his skull against the wall of the mine shaft behind him.

"Cavan!" Ehren yelled, stepping closer.

Too close. The priest seemed to glow with coruscating golden fire.

Cavan recoiled, and Ehren stopped.

Still too close. Too bright. Too hot. As though Ehren were Zatafa herself, standing before him.

What was going on? The spell never acted this way before.

Cavan fell to his hands and knees, panting for breath. Sweat drenched his hair, stuck his shirt to his skin.

"What?" Ehren said, but softer now.

Cavan wouldn't look at him. "Need a second here."

He could hear Amra and Qalas shifting about, looking for something — anything — to strike.

"Back away, please, Ehren," Cavan said.

Ehren did. And then a little farther until Cavan held up a hand to tell him the distance would suffice.

Cavan shielded his eyes from Ehren. Looked up at the sealed boards again.

Once more he was thrown backwards.

He was ready this time. Squeezed his eyes against the glare, as well as against the force pushing him back.

Blue-purple energies spiraled around that barricade. In and out. Swirling. Shifting. Colors changing. Becoming lighter, almost sea blue-green now, then verging down toward indigo and darker. Nearly black in spots, before easing back up the spectrum.

Sudden shift toward lighter colors. The change whipped out a wave of energy. Threw Cavan back again, but his back was already braced against the wall. Pressure shoved the air right out of his lungs. Made breathing difficult.

It lessened again, and Cavan panted for air.

"Cavan," Amra said, voice warning, "what's happening?"

Cavan's eyes flicked to her by reflex. And he saw her sword.

Her sword wasn't just black of steel. No. It was solid black. Blacker than any colors shifting and swirling around that board...

It was the blackness of the space between the stars in the midnight sky.

And there was more to it than that.

"You haven't been telling the whole truth about that sword," Cavan said, hearing the tension in his voice.

"What do you mean?" Amra said, voice guarded. "I hardly think this is the time—"

Cavan canceled the spell enhancing his vision.

Relief flooded through him. So much that he slumped down against the side of the mine and, for a moment, forgot about the uneasy feeling still in his stomach.

"Your sword," Cavan said, sounding as though he'd run here from the Redoubt Inn without a moment's pause to rest. "It's forged from the corpse of a demon. Isn't it?"

Amra frowned, but not in a guilty way.

"If it is," she said, looking down at her blade, "that's news to me."

"To me too," Ehren said, and he sounded far more unhappy about it.

"Doesn't matter," Cavan said, getting to his feet. "This..." he gestured to the barricade. "It's being held in place by flux. Some kind of energy I've never encountered before. And there's more. It's messing with my magic. Made Ehren glow with golden fire like Zatafa herself, and made your sword, Amra, look ... empty."

"Empty?" She said, one eyebrow raised in thought. "Well, then."

She turned and slashed right through the boards.

The explosion knocked Cavan unconscious.

***

CAVAN AWOKE SLOWLY. EVERY PART OF HIM HURT. EVEN HIS TEETH AND tongue ached. The bones in his skull. Everything down to the small bones in his hands and feet, even the little bones of his spine, and all of them.

Every single bit of Cavan ached, and he would swear that he could feel each one of those individual aches, crying out for attention over and above all the others.

Groaning seemed like the best course of action.

Cavan tried it.

Sure enough, he felt a little better for a moment, for having done so. Alas, the lessening of his aches didn't last.

"Awake then?" Ehren asked.

Ehren sounded entirely too unharmed. As though ... as though the explosion hadn't touched him at all.

Cavan wedged his eyes open.

He could still see. Which meant that Ehren's blessing from earlier was still in effect. Or perhaps Ehren had renewed it. Either way, Cavan could see the cold, blue-gray stone around him as clearly as though the sun were shining right here in the mine shaft.

He could hear, too. He could hear Amra groaning softly. He could hear the creak of leather that told him either Amra was shifting about on her back, or Qalas was shifting about on his.

Cavan didn't hear Qalas moan.

No. If Ehren looked so ... composed, Cavan had no doubt that Qalas was at least as alive and well as Cavan was, himself.

Sitting up seemed like just about the worst idea since Amra's strike.

Cavan did it anyway.

He got as many internal protests as he expected. Worse that uneasy feeling in his guts yet remained.

He could see Ehren standing over him, looking concerned. He had a poultice in one hand and his staff in the other, as though not sure which he'd need first.

"What happened?" Cavan said.

"I'll tell you what happened," Amra said, sitting up. Her voice sounded more angry than hurt now. "I tried cutting through those boards and they blew up."

"Not quite," Qalas said, sitting up. He sounded more pained than angry. Cavan took some comfort in having someone to share his pain with. "The exact spot you struck exploded. I can still see the spots in my eyes."

"Well," Ehren said. "I can see that Cavan is not the only one attempting foolish experiments."

"Watch it," Amra said, standing on shaky legs. She looked a wreck, worst of the three. The left side of her face was bruised, as was much of the skin Cavan could see. Her hair was matted with sweat and caked with mine dust.

Still, she began to stretch her muscles as though this sort of thing happened every day.

Cavan shook his head, and made his way to his feet about the time that Qalas did. Qalas began to stretch as well, so Cavan joined them.

It felt both awful and wonderful at the same time. But as he continued, the wonderful to awful ratio began to slant the right direction.

It helped that Ehren began to feed them blessed oranges. Orange was the fruit of Zatafa, but Ehren had never handed them out this way before. Each drop of juice and flesh that worked its way down Cavan's throat seemed to lessen his pains and breathe life anew into his limbs.

"Are these..." Qalas started, then swallowed and started again. "Are these *healing* oranges?"

"Oranges are like priests of the fruit world," Ehren said with a smile. "Where you find an orange, there you find Zatafa." He raised a sardonic eyebrow. "Not as good as sunrise for what ails you, but with the right consecrations, these should at least keep you three going. And we can't afford to wait for sunrise."

Ehren let them eat in silence then, and sure enough, as Cavan finished his orange, he felt much, much better. Both Amra and Qalas looked better as well. Still just as dirty, but now significantly less bruised and battered.

"Now," Ehren said, "if I may return to what I was saying."

"How is it you weren't touched?" Qalas said.

"Zatafa's blessing," Ehren said, voice just a hair too smug. But then, in a more normal tone, he continued. "That golden fire Cavan described. It must have shielded me from the energies of the portal. Which brings me to what I had been going to say."

Ehren arched an eyebrow at Amra. "If I may speak without getting my head bitten off."

"Depends what you say," Amra said, fluttering her eyelashes.

"I was *going* to say that you and I should strike the boards *together*. If Zatafa is stronger in me here, strong enough that Cavan could see me glowing with her fire, then I should be able to act as a counter-weight to the ... *demonic*..." — Ehren made that word sound as though it tasted sour — "energies of your sword. It may defend against one or the other well, but both at the same time should prove too much for it."

"Not sure it's demonic," Amra said, over her sword where it lay on the ground, beside where she'd fallen, "no matter what Cavan just saw. But we'll act as though it is, for now, and go over all that when this is over."

She picked up the sword.

"That doesn't trouble you?" Ehren asked.

"This sword has been with me longer than you or Cavan, and it's never harmed me yet." She turned to face the barrier. "Let's give it a go."

"Wait," Cavan said.

He positioned them so that Ehren stood on the right-hand side, and Amra on the left. That seemed to work best with the flow of the blue-purple energies as Cavan had seen them. He couldn't have explained why he thought so, but he was sure of it. It just ... felt right to his gut.

"I worry that I'm not bringing enough magic to this group," Qalas grumbled, but Cavan didn't look away.

He counted them down.

"Three...

"Two...

"One!"

Together, they struck. Amra with her sword, shouting a battle cry. Ehren with his staff, crying the name of his sun goddess.

The boards fell as though nothing had been holding them up at all.

Cavan realized he was holding his breath, waiting for another explosion that didn't come.

He started chuckling. Then Amra joined him. Then Qalas. And finally Ehren, all four of them laughing in relief.

Still, Cavan worried that the uneasiness in his gut had not diminished.

THIS UNEASE IN CAVAN'S STOMACH. HE DIDN'T LIKE IT. HE HAD JUST about convinced himself that it was a reaction to that strange barrier, but if so it should have vanished when the energies dispersed.

And yet, it remained.

It had to be a kind of magical reaction of some sort. The way he could always sense the approach of dusk and dawn, midnight and midday.

But he did not understand the nature of what he was sensing.

He licked his dry lips, tasting dust like licking stone and tin, and only a little of the orange he'd eaten a few minutes ago.

He could try that spell again. See what he could see, now that the barrier was down. Perhaps that would be for the best. He could ask Ehren to move away up the shaft…

"Cavan," Amra said, looking through the opening beside the fallen boards, "I thought you said this was a *small* side branch."

"I did," he said, crossing the shaft to stand beside his three friends, at the entrance to the side branch.

The side branch that could never be described as small.

Oh, it might have started small. It looked as though someone had tunneled no more than two dozen paces this direction, not much more than head-height, and only wide enough to two, if they weren't moving.

Clearly, an exploratory look, of the kind Cavan had seen back farther up the mine. Most of those had gone no farther.

This one though.

There was a spot along the left side of this branch. Almost at the mid-point. There, the side of the shaft just … wasn't there.

It didn't look as though it had been chipped away with hammer and pick. Not like the rest of the mine. Even from a half-dozen steps away, Cavan could see that this new opening didn't have the rough, irregular edges of the rest of the mine.

No, it appeared to have been sheared into the side of the mine shaft. And opened up into something much, much greater.

A rumble came from somewhere below them.

"Did you guys feel that?" Qalas asked. "Tell me you guys felt that."

Cavan nodded. So did Amra. Ehren said, "Yes."

"So," Qalas said. "That was a magic thing, right? One of you is about to explain how Zatafa interacts with some dwarf god, or,

Cavan, you're going to tell me about some flow of energies that does some damn thing?"

"That is not Zatafa's doing," Ehren said, softly, so they could all listen to the rumble.

"If it's magic," Cavan said, "it's magic I don't know."

"So this *might* just be a CAVE IN?" Qalas said. "We need to move, folks."

"No," Cavan said. "Kaethe had heard something like that. And there was no cave-in."

"Not unless a whole bunch of mountain fell away to cause that," Amra said, pointing at the sheared opening with her sword. "I don't think so though."

"What then?" Qalas said.

Amra frowned at him. "We don't have all the answers, you know."

"You guys have a hell of a lot more answers than anyone else *I've* ever met."

"Yeah," Amra turned her frown on Cavan and Ehren, "those two are walking libraries, I'll grant you. But that sound. It's not general enough to be a cave-in. A cave-in would come from all around us. That's definitely below us. And maybe a little forward. Tough to tell."

"You're sure?" Qalas asked, eyes narrowed.

"Bet me," Amra said.

Qalas already knew better than to take that bet.

"Forward then," Cavan said. "But maybe I better take the lead. There's something going on here that I don't like."

"Oh," Qalas said, "you think?"

"No, I mean..." Cavan sighed. "I don't know how to explain it. There's something ... off here. Wrong. Not like anything I've ever sensed before, magically, and I don't know what it means."

"By all means then," Qalas said, "you go first."

"Wrong," Amra said, stepping in front. "The last thing we need is a distracted point-man." She flicked her eyes to Cavan and back to that opening. "You need me to move, you know what to do."

"Right," Cavan said. He didn't like letting Amra take lead here, but he knew he couldn't talk her out of it.

"Same formation," Amra said. "*Now* we move."

Amra stepped in first. Cavan and Qalas were altogether too close in that narrow side branch, but Cavan knew that would only last a moment.

They reached that sheared opening in only a few steps.

Amra whistled.

The stone floor sloped away before them. Up above, the ceiling was too high for them to see. And to the sides, Cavan knew there had to be more walls. He could see the continuation of the blue stone leading off into the distance.

But once more, the limits of Ehren's sight blessing were tested by the size of this place.

"Just like the chasm," Amra said. "Too big to see."

"Makes you wonder," Cavan said, "if the chasm was that big before what happened here recently."

"You're overthinking," Qalas said. "That bridge over that chasm has been there a while. If the chasm had changed, the miners would have said something."

"Focus," Amra said.

"Which way?" Cavan asked.

"Straight," Amra said. "Good as any."

"No," Ehren said. "We should stay to one side. Follow a wall. That way we can't get lost."

"Fine," Amra said, and turned to the right. She moved a few dozen steps away from the wall, so they would all have room for the fight they knew would be coming, but began to follow the gentle downward slope of blue-gray stone.

Which was changing in color as they walked.

Most of the blue-gray stone of the Blue Mountains had a certain amount of variation to it. But it was always within a certain, limited spectrum.

That spectrum broadened as Cavan and his friends continued to follow the gentle slope of a space that seemed too damned big to be real.

The stone was darkening in shade as they continued along.

Slowly, but not so slowly that Cavan failed to notice.

"How big is this place?" Ehren said, after they'd been walking for at least a few hundred paces. Their boots echoed off the stone just as normally as they would have anywhere else. But then, Cavan didn't see any crystal deposits anywhere along here. Not in the wall, not on the floor...

"I don't see any stalagmites," Qalas said. "Shouldn't there be some? I mean, even if the ceiling is arched, it still needs some kind of support. Doesn't it?"

Cavan couldn't answer. Too busy thinking.

There were no crystal deposits here. And he was becoming increasingly aware of the uneasiness in his stomach. It had gone from a suggestion to a disquiet, and now it was fairly roiling, in a way he hadn't felt since he was staring at the ... at the coruscating energies of that barrier.

Something was definitely wrong.

"Stop," Cavan said. He craned his neck looking around. "Do any of you see crystal deposits?"

The others quickly confirmed his suspicions — none around them.

"Do any of you hear the rumbling?"

They shook their heads.

"What?" Ehren said, voice soft.

"Not sure," Cavan said. Then sighed. "I need to open my vision wider. I need..."

Cavan stretched out with his internal sense of time. He knew they had come into the mines not long before sunset. He'd been vaguely aware of the sunset passing, the way he was always at least somewhat aware of it, even when focused on different things.

But right now, Cavan couldn't tell how long ago sunset had been. And he couldn't tell how far away midnight was.

Sweat broke out on his forehead.

"What?" Amra said, voice sharp.

"This place. Either we're caught in something, or we're not in our own world anymore."

CAVAN DROPPED TO HIS KNEES, THERE IN THAT GREAT EXPANSE OF darker and darker blue stone. Even the noise of his doing that sounded so normal, he might have been anyplace else.

Anyplace except in a cavern, deep within the Blue Mountains.

The others gathered around him, keeping two paces back out of habit. They, no doubt, could tell that Cavan intended some spellwork, and knew to give him room to maneuver.

"Get ready," Cavan said to Ehren. "This may blow up in my face."

"Blow up?" Qalas asked, alarmed.

"He means it may knock him out or something," Amra clarified.

"Are you sure? After last time—"

"Sorry," Cavan said, irritated at having to explain himself, even though he knew it was a reasonable question. "I didn't mean an actual explosion. Anywhere outside my head, anyway."

"Let's go back," Qalas said. "There's no reason to do whatever you're doing right here. Let's go back to the opening, where we know at least what one side of that opening is. Do your magic there."

"That would give you more controlled circumstances," Ehren said.

Cavan frowned at the delay, but agreed. He hopped to his feet.

The four of them fell back into formation by reflex, and Amra led them back toward the sheared opening that had led to his huge place.

After a few hundred steps, she stopped.

"We should have found the opening by now. Or at least be close enough to see it. We haven't gone that far."

"She's right," Ehren said.

"The stone," Cavan said, pointing at the stone floor of the cavern. "It's still that dark blue color. Not at all the normal range of colors within the Blue Mountains."

"Are you sure?" Qalas said. "Did you specifically notice the color through here? Maybe this place is just bigger than we thought."

"No," Cavan said, kneeling in place once more. "No, there's something very wrong here. The stone had shifted as we walked, but it never shifted back. And Amra's right, we should have come to that opening by now."

Cavan puffed out a breath. "There's more. My guts have been roiling in a way that's not normal."

"And I suppose hunger isn't a valid answer," Qalas said, wryly.

"Not like this." Cavan said. "This is like it got near that barrier. I'm going to have to try something."

"Let me try first," Ehren said. He held his staff high, and chanted in the tongue of ancient, lost Penthix.

Nothing happened.

Cavan hadn't thought it was possible for Ehren to turn any paler than he already was. But any blood that had been in his neck and face just seemed to vanish. He looked positively ghostly.

"But..." Ehren said, then swallowed and tried again. "But, we can still see. The blessing of Zatafa."

"If we're still seeing anything at all," Cavan said. "Now let me work."

Cavan dug around inside his pouch for salt. Then he scraped mine dust off his skin, then more from Qalas' skin, and Amra's. He blended the dust with the salt, while mumbling just the right words.

Not breathing power. Not yet. This part of the spell relied entirely on the nature of the salt from Cavan's homeland, and the dust of the place they'd just been.

Two blends of the land they'd come from. Two blends of real places.

Cavan chanted words of binding as he sprinkled the mixture in a circle around the four of them. A wide circle, allowing them room to move a bit, and him room to resume his kneeling position.

Cavan dug a candle out of a side pouch. A small, yellowish, beeswax candle that Cavan had made himself. It was about half-burned away, but more than enough of it remained for his purposes.

Cavan drew his only unspelled dagger.

"One drop of blood each," he said, holding the dagger up. "Get the blood on the wick."

Amra was first, pricking her wrist.

Qalas was second, pricking his thumb.

Ehren was third, still that ghostly shade of white, as though he might not have enough blood in him to surrender a drop.

But Ehren pricked his finger, and a drop welled up and fell onto the wick.

Finally, Cavan added a drop of his own, from his left thumb.

A breath of power, and the wick ignited, blood and all.

Swift words then. A song, as much as a chant, pulling power from the core of Cavan's being, and sifting it through the circle of the land they'd come from. The flow of spell power swirled through the circle, three repetitions, then arrowed right back into each of the four heroes.

As one, all four felt their backs lock stiff and arched. Breathing became impossible.

Time itself seemed to stop.

Then the world about them twisted, swirling them down through it like a whirlpool sucking down a leaf.

Dark blue stone and darker, blue-black shadows, spinning together, threading like twists of ribbon around a pole in a folk dance. All other colors stripped away. Light, shadow and darkness, blending and separating. Blending and separating.

The four of them seemed to blend and separate as well. The four of them swirled together like colors, mixing and matching and separating, then unifying again. Cavan couldn't tell where he stopped and Ehren began. Or Qalas. Or Amra.

They were all one. But all separated.

And the spinning got faster and faster.

Cavan's heart sped faster and faster. Like it was spinning too. Or maybe he heard, felt four heartbeats in his own chest. Heard, felt four sets of shallow, rapid breaths. Felt all eight hands clutching, grasping. Four stomachs, all quivering.

All four bodies were Cavan.

But none of them were Cavan. Not really. Not even his own.

Cavan was the darkness now. And the light. And the shadow.

Cavan was the dark blue of the stone. And the lighter blues too.

The blues and the grays. More of them. Swirling through him now. Twisting. Each insisting that it was the most important.

That was new. All was no longer one.

Precedence became the rule. And precedence began to organize. Separate.

Slowly, slowly, Cavan became Cavan again. Became less Ehren. Less Amra. Less Qalas.

He began to feel only one heart, beating fast in his chest. Only one set of lungs working like a bellows as he tried to hold himself together.

Literally. His hands were clutching his ribs and belly as though worried that his body were flying apart.

And for some time out of time there, it had felt as though it was.

But now, Cavan slowly felt like he truly was Cavan once more.

And Cavan was not standing in any great, vast cavern.

CAVAN WAS STANDING JUST INSIDE THE EDGE OF THAT SMALL SIDE tunnel off of the mine shaft. Standing just inside the edge of the sheared entrance to something more. An entrance that the miners said didn't exist.

Amra stood one half-step in front of him. Qalas stood to his left, shoulder to shoulder. Ehren stood a half-step behind the two of them. All four, bunched tighter together than Cavan could remember them ever standing.

Each had weapons in their hands.

Cavan's unspelled dagger, though, that was still in his belt. And from the feel of his thumb — and he was gripping the hilt of his sword with both hands, tight enough to tell this — he had never poked it to draw blood.

"Everyone all right?" Ehren said, voice tight.

"I ... think so?" Cavan replied. And part of him felt as though he should be. His heart was pounding a bit, yes, and his breathing was a bit shallow, and it was true he was drenched in sweat. But he was uninjured. And his stomach's disquiet had settled down to unease.

And he wasn't, in fact, standing in a different world. He was pretty sure of that now.

Which meant that the evening was, in fact, looking up.

And it was still evening. He could sense now that midnight was still a few hours away.

"Good here," Amra said. She wasn't even sweating, which Cavan thought was grossly unfair. She continued, "Little tense, and wondering what the hell just happened, but otherwise good."

"So," Qalas said, voice as tight as his grip on his halberd, "situation normal then? I have no idea what the hell is going on, but I'm uninjured, so it's cool?"

Cavan glanced at Qalas, but decided this wasn't the time to pursue the questions the ex-hunter's words had just provoked in him.

Right now, Cavan was more concerned about what he saw past that sheared opening. And, for that matter, what he heard.

What he saw, was a tunnel. Not a broad, tall mining tunnel, but a narrow channel that looked more as though it existed naturally than as though it had been chiseled out with picks and hammers.

The sides were smooth. It was only wide enough for them to go down single file — which Cavan didn't like at all — and it didn't look wide enough to really fight in, which he liked even less.

That the sides were that smooth though, was even stranger. Cavan had seen his share of mines and tunnels, especially in the north near the Dragon Spikes, when he had spent a summer with a dwarf clan.

Their tunnels were *almost* that smooth. And Cavan had never seen anything underground that got smoother.

He was wondering a little bit about how the footing would be, when the sound recurred.

It was almost like that rumbling from before, but now it had a little more sound to it.

Now, Cavan might have thought it sounded like a roar.

It didn't, of course. He was sure of that. Nothing down here could be roaring loud enough to cause a rumbling sound. This was clearly just some kind of overreaction on his part. Perhaps in response to the illusion he'd just had to break. Making him a little paranoid.

In fact, Cavan breathed out a single word of power that should have noticed any illusions he was not currently caught inside.

Nothing. The tunnel wasn't an illusion, and neither was the bend to the right that it took ahead, as it slowly went deeper into the mountain.

"So, Cavan," Amra said, her eyes still moving over the tunnel as though she expected an attack. "Mind telling us what the hell just happened?"

"Illusion," Cavan said. "Not like anything I've ever seen before. Don't know what school of magic that was from, but it was ... primal. More ... visceral, almost."

That got Cavan three confused stares.

"Sorry," he said. "I know you guys always expect an intellectual answer from me, but the fact is that I just don't know. That wasn't like any other kind of magic I've run across."

"What kinds do you know?" Qalas said.

"Well, I *recognize* forest elf magic, dwarf stone magic, orc magic, and about three more general varieties of arcanology that are practiced by pretty much all the races."

"So how often do you run across magic you *don't* recognize?"

Cavan stopped and thought about that. "Not often. Most recently, the gemstones on this sword."

"Weren't there supposed to be more of those gemstones in this side tunnel?" Ehren asked, looking around. "I don't see any."

The rumbling sound that couldn't have been a roar recurred.

"Oh, and by the way," Qalas said. "ARE WE JUST GOING TO IGNORE THAT?"

"For the moment," Amra said, still watching the tunnel ahead of them. "Focus on the problems at hand. Best way to deal with the unknown."

Her tone was smooth. Confident, but Cavan also thought she was reassuring Qalas as she continued.

"We see a lot of things that don't make sense, at first. Best way to survive is to focus on what you have to deal with right now. Like what just happened. I think we need to know more before we try this tunnel."

"I disagree," Cavan said. "The spell is broken. It won't hit us again."

"You're sure?" she asked.

"Positive."

"Right then," she said. "Next order of business. Where are the rest of the gemstones?"

"I think the answer to that, the illusion, this new tunnel, and that roar are all related," Ehren said.

"It's not a roar," Cavan said. "Just a trick of the way echoes work here."

"Safer to assume it's a roar until we know otherwise," Amra said. "Go on, Ehren."

"One, there are no gemstones here. Two, there's a side channel we weren't expecting. Three, there have been two different magical approaches to keeping us from this side channel, and both of them involved magic that Cavan didn't know."

Ehren looked at Cavan. Cavan nodded. Then realized Ehren expected him to say something.

"I don't think that the barricade was held in place by any kind of proper ward. It was more like a kind of magical tension between two forces. I just don't know what kind, or what they were for."

"Assume they were there to keep people like us out. What would be the purpose?"

Cavan nodded toward the new side channel. "Keep us away from that?"

"Exactly," Ehren said. "As for the missing gemstones, I think they were probably consumed in whatever magic was done to change this place. Create that tension you spoke up. Carve that new channel. Summon whatever guarding we're hearing."

"Guardian?" Qalas said, alarmed at first, but calming quickly. He nodded. "Makes sense. So you think when they pulled those first gemstones out, the three Cavan has, that it provoked a response?"

"I'm worried that it unlocked part of an ancient lock. A lock built on magic that predates anything practiced in the world today. So nothing Cavan would recognize, intellectually, but something his blood might respond to in a very visceral way."

"My blood?" Cavan asked. "You think ... you think I *do* have Dunaian blood, and that this is all Dunaian magic?"

"Sounds like a good working theory," Amra said. "Can you refute it right now?"

Cavan frowned in thought for a moment, but shook his head.

"Then assume it's true until proven otherwise," Amra said. "I'd say we have enough to go on. Let's move."

"Wait," Qalas said. "What do we know about Dunaian magic that might involve the creature making all that racket. Or at least give us something to prepare for?"

"Nothing," Cavan said. "No one knows for sure what kind of magic the Dunaians practiced."

"We know that the legends say that the portal to their Underworld is down here somewhere," Ehren said. "So it may be that they have magical means of sealing it."

Ehren cleared his throat until everyone was watching him, instead of watching the tunnel ahead of them.

"In other words," he said, "No just attacking anything that looks like spellwork. No cutting into carved words around the edges of things, no breaking circles, no trying to read anything aloud, especially if you don't speak the language. Are we all agreed?"

"Fine," Amra said, though Cavan knew she loved breaking enchanted things that were being used against her. And her sword seemed to enjoy cutting through them as well.

Was this the first time Cavan had considered her sword to express an opinion? He might need to remember that.

"Wouldn't dream of it," Qalas said. "I leave that stuff to you guys."

Finally, Cavan realized that Ehren was staring at him as though he were the worst offender in the group.

"I won't," Cavan said. "I promise."

"Now we can go," Ehren said.

THEY HAD TO MOVE SINGLE FILE DOWN THE TUNNEL, WEAPONS STILL OUT and ready.

Amra leading, three good steps ahead of Cavan, who was three steps ahead of Qalas, who was three steps ahead of Ehren. And following Amra's recommendation, they had to keep their boots to the left side of the tunnel. That was where the footing seemed most stable. The rest was smooth enough that it risked getting slippery.

Of course, the side of the tunnel was fine for a short thing like Amra, but Cavan had to hunch to proceed, and that started getting old pretty quickly. Not that walking down the center of the passage would have been all that much better. Cavan wasn't positive, but he was pretty sure the apex of the tunnel wasn't higher than a thumb-span above his head.

The air was colder down here. In fact, it seemed to get colder as soon as they set foot in this small passage. That was disturbing enough that Cavan muttered his spell to detect illusions again, and tried to reassure himself about its accuracy when it failed to detect anything.

So the air really was getting colder.

No smell of tin along here either. Smelled like ... snow on a rocky patch of mountain. Not that Cavan could be sure. Not with the taste of dried beef still on his tongue from the quick snack Ehren had forced on them.

At least there were still crystal deposits along the tunnel walls. After the illusion, Cavan found them reassuring. These, though, had been shaved down as smooth as the rest of the tunnel. And though they all held that little bit of magical resonance that all the Blue Mountain crystals seemed to carry, none of them had the coloring or extra potency of the gemstones affixed to the hilt of Cavan's sword.

Down the passage they went. It seemed to wind downward to the right for a time before curving back to the left. Snake-like, Cavan found it. Still, it continued to go deeper and deeper into the mountain's core.

Every thirty paces or so, Amra stopped to listen. Cavan never heard anything at these pauses, though occasionally Amra's head twitched as though she might have. She didn't say anything though.

The rumble that Cavan didn't want to think of as a roar did recur every so often. Irregular, and not any louder. But whether that was because it wasn't closer, or just an effect of the way the crystals ate sound, Cavan couldn't be sure.

Every time that rumble happened, Qalas said something to himself. Not loud. And not in Rentissi, or any of the other languages Cavan spoke. He suspected that it was a prayer, but it would have been impolite — and impractical — to ask.

Another rumble-not-roar as they came around a bend back to the left, where the tunnel appeared to level off.

And exactly in time with the rumble, Cavan noticed that the gemstones on his sword hilt sparked.

"Hold," Cavan said. Held the sword up higher.

No glow. No lingering effect. He might have thought it a trick of the light, except that the way he was seeing — through the blessing of Zatafa — didn't play those kinds of games. Ehren always said that this was the truth of Zatafa's shine, and the truth of Zatafa played no games.

But the spark had been there. He was sure.

"What?" Amra hissed, without looking back.

Cavan told them in quick, terse words.

"What's it mean?" Amra said.

Cavan didn't know how to answer that.

"Then we move on," Amra said. "Keep an eye on it."

The tunnel, still level, began to curve harder left, then, up ahead, looked to cut quickly to the right.

Amra held up a halting hand.

"Something's different," she said. "I think it's the air."

"Yes," Ehren said after a moment. "It tastes lighter. I was starting to think it might be getting stale down here, but it's definitely been freshened."

"No breeze though," Qalas said. "So how?"

"Answer's up there," Amra said, pointing at that switch-back with her sword. "Hang back. I'm going to have a quick peek."

Cavan didn't like it, but said nothing as Amra moved soundlessly up to that switch-back. Held her sword back. Peeked around the edge.

Yanked her head back and returned quickly, hands calling everyone in.

Cavan and the others crowded around her.

"Cave. Big one. And there's movement."

"I wish I had my bow," Qalas said.

"Too late for that now," Amra said. "Movement ... couldn't be sure without risking being seen, but I think it was big. And maybe alone."

"That's something," Ehren said.

"Maybe," Cavan said. "Why did you think you'd be seen?"

Amra shook her head. "Long as I've done scouting, you pick up instincts for it. Mine said duck back."

"Can we get there unseen?"

Amra frowned as she thought about that. Shook her head.

"Know any spells that could help us?" Qalas asked Cavan.

"Maybe," Cavan said, "but the gemstones spark every time that rumble occurs. I'm not sure what they'll do if I cast."

"So we go without," Ehren said firmly. "And you take care what you cast in a fight."

"Don't I always?" Cavan asked, but then wished he hadn't. He knew what Ehren would say to that.

Ehren said it all with one raised eyebrow.

"Right," Amra said. "Qalas, you're second now. We need to get in there and have fighters between whatever it is and our two casters."

Qalas nodded grimly.

"You two, assess as fast as you can."

Cavan and Ehren both nodded.

Amra led the way, Qalas right on her heels.

11

———

THEY WEREN'T QUITE TO THE LAST SWITCH-BACK IN THAT SMALL, smooth tunnel when the rumble came again. Louder this time.

Much, much louder.

And Cavan could no longer pretend it wasn't a roar.

The sound seemed to shake the tunnel as it rolled over them, and the gemstones on Cavan's sword flared their three shades in time with it. And this time, that glow stayed through the whole roar.

The moment the sound came, Amra gestured the halt and looked back.

Cavan realized all three of his friends were all staring at the gemstones on his sword.

"Can you remove those?" Ehren said quietly, once the roaring stopped. "They might not be working in our favor here."

Qalas nodded.

Cavan shook his head. Whispered, "If there's one thing I've learned, it's don't assume anything about unknown magic. Assuming these gemstones are bad for our situation is just as dangerous as assuming they're the exact help we need."

"But—"

Cavan shook his head, slow and deliberate. "They stay."

He wished he felt as confident as his words, but Ehren accepted Cavan's decision with a sigh.

Amra started forward again.

They made it to the switch-back. Amra held a finger to her lips. As though any of them weren't being just as stealthy as they could possibly be.

She vanished around the switch-back. Then Qalas.

Then it was Cavan's turn to round that final corner.

Up ahead was a cavern all right. Huge. The entrance was only about a dozen more paces away, but Cavan would have felt better if he could have seen the top. Or at least the far wall. He was pretty sure he should have been able to see the far wall.

From where Cavan stood, that cavern was looking all too familiar.

In fact, if it weren't for the fact that the floor of the cavern, from what Cavan could see, was proper shades of blue and gray, he might have thought they'd been trapped in another illusion.

Cavan tried his illusion detecting charm again.

Nothing.

But then, he hadn't expected anything. His stomach still shifted about in its discomfort, but it wasn't roiling the way it had been...

Had been when he was trapped in that illusion...

And the way it had been when he was staring into the coruscating energies that held those boards in place...

The gemstones. This was all about the gemstones. In some basic way. If only Cavan could figure out the keys.

By then his feet had carried Cavan into the huge cavern. And his eyes confirmed that his suspicions were correct — there was no top to this cavern. Or at the very least, it was so big that the top was shrouded in darkness.

The far side wasn't though. Cavan could see it. Only a few hundred paces away.

That was comforting.

Still, something about this place nagged at Cavan as familiar. And it was nothing like the illusory place had been.

The roar came again, and Cavan wondered how he could ever

have pretended it was anything else. Even though it was loud enough that the very walls...

No. The rumbling did accompany the sound, but it wasn't the volume making things rumble. That didn't make sense.

Cavan desperately hoped that would make sense soon. And that, when it did, it wouldn't be for the worst possible reasons.

His head whipped around as his eyes tried to trace the sound. No good. Even here in this cavern, with crystals all over the walls, there were still too many reflections of that sound to...

Amra was pointing to the right.

Cavan's eyes tracked from her blade's tip.

Qalas must have seen it first, because he said, "Dragon."

And from what Cavan saw, he agreed.

It was serpentine, all right. Not more than two score paces long, which was something, but Cavan couldn't be sure of that, because of the way it coiled about itself.

It did look wide though. Wide as that tunnel they'd followed down here.

The head was no wider than the body. Looked like a snake's head, jaws wide and hissing.

The creature did have legs though. Some of them were folded down right now, so he couldn't be sure how many, but it looked to have at least a dozen pairs.

No wings, that was something.

A very small comfort, though, because of the color of this creature.

It was blue. It was all shades of blue, from deepest indigo to that point where blues fade to whites, or on the seas to greens.

All these shades and colors, and more.

And worst of all, the scales of the beast all looked to be gemstones, just like the ones on Cavan's sword.

"Spread out!" Amra yelled, diving and rolling to the creature's left.

Qalas moved forward three steps, halberd high and ready.

Ehren moved along the wall, his staff high and prayers already on his lips.

Cavan merely stood there, sword pointed down. The thing — it might as well be a dragon, though it didn't fit any of the descriptions Cavan had come across in his studies — was staring right back at him. And it had yet to move.

"Wait," Cavan said, desperately trying to remember the smattering of Dragontongue he'd picked up while studying with Master Powys. Master Powys had insisted that dragons knew some of the best, and oldest, spells in the world, and that they would trade when caught in the right mood.

Cavan had never been able to picture himself negotiating with a dragon. Which was a pity, because if he had he might have known what to say right then.

Cavan's friends all did stop what they were doing, though, and turned to look at him.

Cavan could see that only out of his peripheral vision. He didn't take his eyes off of the dragon.

But was it staring at him? Or at the gemstones on the sword still in his hand?

"Did these belong to you?" Cavan asked, in as soothing a tone as he could manage. Unsure of his Dragontongue, he stuck to Rentissi. He had to hope that language was old enough to suit dragons. "Were they your scales?"

The dragon roared. The very ground seemed to rumble beneath Cavan, even though the sound was not even loud enough to hurt his ears.

Or maybe that was an aftereffect of Ehren's earlier healing. Cavan couldn't know for certain.

What he did know was that during that roar the entire dragon flared brightly in all its colors, just as the gemstones on his sword did.

So brightly now that he squeezed his eyes shut tight against the glare, and could still see the flare against the inside of his eyelids.

"There's no reason we have..." Cavan started, then realized that was a lie. There *was* a reason he and this dragon had to fight. There was a very good reason.

Kaethe. An innocent miner, dead for being in the wrong place.

Yes, these gemstones on Cavan's sword might have been plucked from the hide of this beast while it lay dormant, but that was not cause for murder.

Dragons were all supposed to be intelligent. Some of the most intelligent creatures in existence, according to all the scholars. Yes, they tended to live by their own rules. And yes, they tended to consider themselves more evolved and important than anything else in the world.

Cavan didn't consider any of that an excuse.

The way he looked at it, if dragons were intelligent, then dragons should know that murder carried consequences.

"The scales were taken by accident," Cavan said, instead. "We did not know they were part of you. Still, you should not have killed that miner."

The dragon — if it was a dragon — roared again, and this time Cavan would have sworn there was anger in it. Not anger over the scales though. Deeper anger. Stronger.

And this might have been paranoia talking, but Cavan had the distinct impression that the anger was directed at him.

The dragon — Cavan settled on calling it that for now, and researching the creature later — did speak then. It rumbled out what had to have been words and sentences, in a surprisingly sing-song sequence.

But, though Cavan had studied his share of languages over the years, he couldn't make out a single word of that.

"Any of you catch that?" Cavan said.

The others all shook their heads, quickly. Even Ehren, and he was the one Cavan thought had a real chance at it.

The dragon began to slither forward. Not really approaching yet, just uncoiling itself. Shaking out its legs, so they settled beneath it. It looked bigger this way, somehow, which Cavan considered unfair. It was already quite large enough, thank you.

He noticed something else then. The eyes of the dragon. They weren't gemstones. They weren't even blue. They were green. Yes, a shade on the bluish side of the spectrum, but distinctly green. Sea green, the more he thought about it.

"I'm sorry," Cavan said aloud, "but none of us understood that. Could you say it again? In a different tongue, perhaps?"

The dragon did speak again, voice still rising and falling like birdsong. And Cavan thought he did pick one word out of the rest. He hoped he was wrong though.

"Ehren," Cavan said, "did you hear it say—"

"Dunaian?" Ehren said grimly. "Yes. And it definitely means you."

"Lovely," Cavan muttered, then, louder, said, "I'm sorry, but I don't speak Dunaian. And properly speaking, I'm *not* Dunaian myself. Even if I might carry a little of their blood. That race is dead and gone, I'm afraid."

The dragon roared once more, and when the flare-up dimmed again, Amra said, "Look!"

She was pointing with her sword.

Behind the beast was a hole in the distant edge of the cavern.

And beyond that hole lay another world.

"No," Cavan said. "That's..."

"The Dunaian Underworld?" Ehren finished for him, though he made it a question. "Yes, I'd say it is."

"Are you the guardian then?" Cavan said, addressing the dragon.

But the dragon appeared to be past words.

Now that it had uncoiled itself fully, it began speeding straight at Cavan.

CAVAN DOVE TOWARD THE TUNNEL. IF HE COULD GET IN THERE, MAYBE the dragon would be too big to fit.

Cavan was rolling to his feet when he remembered what probably made that tunnel in the first place.

A loud, screeching sound came from the side of the dragon. Amra, slashing it no doubt. No way to tell if she'd had any effect on it.

The head was coming. Right at Cavan. Jaws open wide. Teeth impossibly long and sharp. Breath smelling as though it had been dining on those odd, yellow bat-things from earlier.

Cavan looked for a direction to dive, but he'd trapped himself inside the tunnel.

He dropped low. Sword held in both hands. Needed perfect timing for this.

Down. Down came the head.

Closer and closer.

Legs adjusting the dragon's position now. Perfecting its aim.

Mouth closed just enough to get into the tunnel. Too tight now to bite.

Dragon nose, harder than steel as it slammed into Cavan.

Right as Cavan thrust his sword into the nostril of the creature.

Struck deep. Felt flesh yield. Blue flame flared around the sword, and Cavan could feel it burning away at the creature's insides.

The dragon tried to rear. No room. Not even enough room to slam its head against the top of the tunnel.

More screeching sounds. And Ehren shouting something in Penthix.

The creature roared.

Blinding light, up this close.

And not just light. Blinding power.

Days, Cavan had spent in that inn studying the gemstones. Days spent exploring them. Learning such secrets from them as he could.

He knew their power when he felt it. And in the brightness that accompanied that roar, Cavan felt more power than he'd ever experienced before. Torrents of power. Tidal waves of power, cresting and breaking over him.

And fire seemed to be hurting *this* dragon.

Cavan reached through the gemstones on his sword. The little bits of that power that he knew. Understood, at least somewhat.

Reached into that power. Grabbed it.

Flared his own power through it.

Cavan knew a spell that could call forth primal fire. And if this dragon was harmed by fire, then the logical thing to do would be to hit it with as much fire as he possibly could.

Except...

Except that he knew that the gemstones were some kind of primal ice. Which meant that the dragon might be forged of primal ice.

Hitting primal ice with primal fire. That was how some said the world was made. When primal fire struck primal ice in the nothingness before existence.

Attempting to re-create the spark of existence might be a singularly bad idea.

So instead, Cavan called on the *second* most powerful fire spell he knew.

"*Rassa nis, na afa fela!*" he screamed, releasing the spell through the gemstones, into the sword, and through them into the dragon itself.

The dragon reversed itself faster than Cavan would have believed.

And it carried him with it. His sword, his flaming sword, was burning away at the thing enough that he could see blue flames coming out of the other nostril as well. And he could smell an odor that bore more resemblance to glass heated in a furnace than to charring flesh.

The creature roared.

Cavan grabbed that power. Repeated the spell.

Burned the nose wide open. Bluish blood began gushing out.

The dragon shook its head. Dislodged Cavan, who went soaring through the air.

Cavan wasn't sure what happened behind him then, he was too busy twisting around into proper diving form. He could only pray he wasn't going to slam into the wall.

For what might have been the first time that week — or at least for the first time since he left the Redoubt Inn — Cavan felt luck was on his side. He wasn't heading straight for a wall.

He was soaring through the air at the speed of a good gallop, that would end in a forty foot drop.

Which, all things considered, *was* pretty consistent with Cavan's luck.

He flipped his sword around in his hand, so that it followed the edge of his right arm, instead of leading.

He tucked. Left arm forward to try to turn a long fall into a long roll.

The wind rushed right out of Cavan as he hit. Either the dragon roared again or Cavan he saw stars as he hit.

He did manage to roll instead of landing in a splashy pool of Cavan. That was something. He rolled and rolled and rolled along the unforgiving stone floor, bumping and bruising practically every inch of his body as he went.

Cavan's head kept spinning after his body stopped. Bracing himself on his hands and knees helped the spinning. He took a quick inventory of his pains.

He'd hit hard enough that he knew he'd at least cracked ribs.

In Cavan's experience, there was a difference between the pain of cracked ribs and the pain of broken ribs. In comparison to types of alcohol, cracked ribs had all the strength of overwatered wine, while broken ribs had the kick of the hardest backroom brews. The kind that Ehren insisted were better used as cleaners than intoxicants.

As Cavan eased up to his unsteady feet and tried a deep breath, he learned that the pain from four of his ribs was watered wine, compared to three on the other side.

Some cracked ribs then, and others broken. Plus heavy bruises in his shoulder and hips. Elbow too, by the feel of it. And there were other bruises that couldn't get their voices heard over the clamor of Cavan's pains.

He had no doubt he'd hear from them all too soon.

At least his new sword looked as though it hadn't suffered so much as a ding or notch.

Still, Cavan's pains were bad enough that he could feel blackness trying to seep in around the edges of his vision. Trying to steal his consciousness.

Cavan had no choice then. He had to do something then that he knew Ehren would lecture him for.

Cavan called on his wizard training to shunt the pain behind a door in his mind.

That done, and lock in place, Cavan rushed back to the fight.

The dragon swiped with its tail, while its legs carried it in circles. Its head was staying up high and out of the fight now. Bleeding and burnt, the head looked, with smoke coming out of the nostrils.

But the tail was bad enough. Amra was flying through the air right now, clearly having been struck. Ehren was firing rays of golden fire from the head of his staff, something Cavan had never seen him do before.

Those rays struck the dragon well enough, and each time they scorched the gemstone scales.

Qalas. Where was Qalas? Cavan couldn't see him, and that was more than a little worrying.

Cavan hustled faster. He could feel heat from his ribcage, which was not a good thing. No way the pain should be back already, not unless it was serious.

But he couldn't see Qalas. Amra was rolling right now — and better than Cavan had — but still too far away to protect Ehren.

And the dragon was tired of those bolts of flame.

The dragon didn't roar, though. It hissed. It hissed a soft, yet insistent sound, like late night fog near a lake.

And much the same way, fog seemed to emanate from the dragon. Not from its mouth. Not by breathing. No, the fog seemed to seep out of its very scales.

Worse, Cavan could see ice crystals in the fog.

Cavan was still ten yards distant from the fight. Ehren clutched his staff in both hands now, chanting something that might be able to stave off that cold.

But Cavan couldn't take that chance.

Cavan reached again into the gemstones on his hilt. They'd been part of this dragon...

No. Cavan couldn't be sure of that. He hadn't seen any missing scales.

No tricks that way.

Damnation.

Cavan, his mind still half inside the gemstones, took another approach. After all, what could come out of those gemstones, might be able to go back into them.

He held his sword up by the blade, hilt high. And through those gemstones and their primal cold, he reached for that fog.

Contact. The fog might have been physically nebulous, but it was all one object as far as the gemstones were concerned.

And Cavan began to call that fog into his gemstones.

It started working. The fog began to swirl Cavan's way. Away from Ehren, who cried out, "Yes!" and started chanting something else.

Away from Amra, who was running back to the fight, faster than Cavan had been.

And away from Qalas, whom Cavan could now see had snuck up beside the dragon. He hefted his halberd in both hands.

Thrust.

The dragon must have been clinging to the fog somehow, because instead of slowly swirling toward Cavan, half of it dispersed and the other half whipped right into Cavan's gemstones. They flared brighter.

The dragon roared. Loud and long it roared. But that roar was not the same as before.

The ground did not seem to rumble now. Not this time.

And its scales, they didn't flare bright colors. Nor did the gemstones on Cavan's sword seem to respond to that roar.

And finally, the dragon fell dead to the stone floor of the cavern.

12

THE FALLING DRAGON SHATTERED INTO A THOUSAND GEMSTONES. No deafening clatter though. Not from *these* crystals. They ate just enough of their own sound that as they bounced around they sounded like nothing more than raindrops on distant wooden shingles.

Then silence.

Not the oppressive silence of burst eardrums, which Cavan had grown all too accustomed to, nor the hushed stillness of magical silence, which Cavan knew well from his own spellwork.

This was a momentous silence. As though something tremendous had just happened, and Cavan hadn't quite processed it yet.

Then two things happened at once.

Amra whooped loud enough to wake the dead.

Cavan's pain burst through it's seal.

Hot pain. Twice as intense from being held back.

Cavan gritted his teeth and fell to his knees, keening a sound that he hated to hear, much less make. He was able to stop it quickly, but that it had come out at all would be grist for teasing from Amra for months.

But Ehren was there, as though summoned by the sound of pain.

Ehren, peeling an orange and stuffing slices against Cavan's gritted teeth. Juice seeped past immediately, and Cavan relaxed his jaw to start chewing on slices just as fast as Ehren could feed them to him.

By the time the orange was gone, Cavan felt a bit better, but still not as good as he should have.

"Broken," Ehren said, gently touching Cavan's ribs in a way that, only a moment ago, would have triggered fiery pain all through Cavan's ribs. Instead, the pain felt muted. Dull. But still all too present.

"Three of them," Ehren said. "Four others are cracked. And Zatafa only knows how many bruises you have."

"I think..." Cavan said slowly, only just getting his breath back, "that it's all one big bruise. Pointless to differentiate."

"Honestly, Cavan," Amra said as she strolled up, one hand holding her sword and the other on Qalas' shoulder as he walked beside her. The two of them were grinning like children caught at something. "Here Qalas has a fantastic moment on the battlefield, and you have to go and ruin it by getting hurt."

"Did you even *see* the strike?" Qalas said. "It was beautiful. My halberd could never penetrate those gemstone scales, but then I remembered you had three of them. And I figured that miners wouldn't pluck three distant from each other. They'd get a set. And that meant..."

Qalas continued, but Cavan was too busy with breathing exercises to try to get himself under control again. The orange had helped, but it wasn't nearly enough. Anything hitting him in the ribs again would cause serious damage. Maybe more than Ehren could heal, even by the first rays of the sun.

Hell, even swinging his sword would hurt. But Cavan wasn't foolish to think it wouldn't be necessary.

He might, though, have felt guilty about not hearing the details of Qalas' great strike, if only he and Amra hadn't been grinning at Cavan like that.

Finally, after the tale of the strike that felled the beast, Ehren helped Cavan strip off his shirt, and bandaged up Cavan's ribs. He included some kind of paste that smelled like swamp muck, but went on cool to the touch.

And once Cavan's ribs were wrapped around that muck, he felt as though he could put his own shirt back on. Might even be able to fight.

He smiled at Ehren.

"I know that smile," Ehren said. "Don't be an idiot. You're still hurt. I won't be able to do anything serious about those ribs until dawn. So for the love that Zatafa bears us all, try not to get hit again before then."

"In other words," Amra said, "stay out of melee. You're half a wizard. Lean on that half for a while."

Then she turned and clapped Qalas on the shoulder again, and Qalas grinned.

Cavan sighed softly. He'd have to ask Qalas for the details of the blow later. He was a good man, and proving to be a good friend, but this was probably the first time he felt really useful in one of their fights.

And Cavan had managed to miss it.

That wouldn't do.

But first, there were more pressing matters at hand.

Apparently Ehren knew *that* look on Cavan's face as well, because he spoke first.

"Gemstones or portal?"

"Gemstones," Cavan said. "We might need them for the portal."

"Not sure they'll be much good," Qalas said, voice serious once more, and more confident than he'd sounded all day. "The ones I saw looked blackened and blasted, not blue."

Nevertheless, the four of them searched out a thousand or so scattered bits of dragon. And sure enough, every one of them looked blasted and useless. They didn't even carry the simple magical resonance that most Blue Mountain crystals did. These husks barely even ate any sound.

They were dead. Useless. All of them.

Cavan checked the gemstones on his sword three times. Each time reassured him that the three he had were still their proper shades of blue. Still carried their power inside.

"Looks like you have the only three that still work," Ehren said.

"Yes," Cavan agreed, then smiled. "Let's gather up the rest of them. Can you fit them in your bag?"

"Yes," Ehren said slowly, frowning. "I'm sure I can. But why?"

"Oh," Cavan said, his smile widening a bit. And it was a smile he knew that all three of the others would recognize. "Let's just say I have an idea."

TOOK A WHILE TO GET ALL THOSE BLASTED GEMSTONES TOGETHER. AND once they'd been gathered, Ehren refused to let any of the others watch him put the gemstones into his amazing brown leather backpack.

He pointedly waited until all three of them looked away before he started ... whatever it was he actually did. Cavan was sure he could hear Ehren mumbling something as he worked, but he couldn't make out what.

Instead, Cavan used that time to look over toward what looked for all the world like a portal to another place.

It could have been a teleportation circle. Cavan had heard that such things existed. Usually they were set into the floor of a castle or wizard's tower, not onto the side of a mountain cavern, but still. They existed.

Of course, those usually had glowing words of power inscribed around the outside.

Cavan was a few hundred feet from the gateway, but he was sure if there were glowing words, he would have seen them.

Instead, through the gate, he saw a world that looked like nothing he'd expected.

Cavan had been to the Borderlands. That place that bordered this world and the next. The Borderlands had been a dead place. Gray, everywhere. Even the trees that had looked like giant evergreens might as well have been evergrays. It was a place where the dead didn't stay dead, and giant spiders had tried to demand a sacrifice to allow others to pass.

It was a place where travel followed intention more than pure movement.

Yes, Cavan remembered it. And sometimes when he remembered it in dreams, he woke up in a cold sweat. Sure he was back there. Sure he'd never made back through the portal and into his own world.

Yes, Cavan would remember the Borderlands until the day he died.

But what Cavan saw through that yawning portal in the wall of the cavern looked nothing like the Borderlands.

If anything, it looked like a beach.

Cavan could see golden sand, and tall trees that only had leaves up at their tops. And those leaves looked ... wrong. They looked long, and tapered like daggers. For that matter, the trunks of those trees looked odd. They seemed to have grown backwards, with bark that came in large sections, and pointed up instead of down.

The trees also looked to bear nuts, up near those leaves. Nuts that grew in clusters, each the size of a helm, if that helm had been made for a small child.

Strange.

The sand of the beach, though, looked rich and golden. Smooth, even where it looked loose, and it did look to pack down as it neared a body of water, where a boat stood waiting.

An odd kind of boat, too. It looked as though someone had taken a typical riverboat, but built it twice as long and half as wide. But to balance it, someone had carved down a small log, and attached it to one side of the boat using bent pieces of wood.

This was a boat the like of which Cavan had never seen before.

He did recognize the net dangling from one side of the boat — a fishing net.

The water, though. Even from where he stood, hundreds of paces away, Cavan could tell that the water didn't look quite right either. It looked more purple than blue. Even though the sky above it looked on the gray side of pale blue. As though, on the other side of that portal, dawn was only just breaking, and the sun had not yet come out.

But if that was so, shouldn't the water have been almost black? Why did it look that rich shade of purple that King Draven used for his royal, fur-trimmed cloak on formal occasions?

Then Cavan had a thought.

"Do you guys see a beach? And four odd trees? And a strange-looking boat on purple water?"

"Well, it's a canoe," Qalas said, "and those are palm trees, but I see the rest just fine."

Amra shrugged and nodded.

"It's a what?" Cavan asked.

"Canoe. A kind of boat they sail on the Rentazzo Sea."

"Fishing?"

"Yes, but personal transportation too. Use them like horses on the water."

"Then why there?" Cavan pointed to that canoe with his sword. "Whose canoe could that be?"

"That destroyer god of the Dunaians," Amra said, with a shrug.

Ehren, apparently able to get those blasted gemstones into his bag far faster than the four friends had been able to gather them, stepped up to join Cavan and the others.

"That's the boat that carries souls to the different lands of the dead," Ehren said. "It's a fishing boat for cosmological reasons."

Cavan opened his mouth to ask a question, but Amra held up a warning hand and said, "Don't."

She then turned to Ehren. "Tell me, does a lecture on the Dunaian Underworld *actually* help us close that gate?"

"Are we sure we want to close it?"

"Yes," Cavan, Qalas and Amra said at once.

"But," Ehren said, "if we went through. Even just a little ways. We could learn *so much*."

"Ehren," Cavan said, "the duke of Nolarr is riding through Juno with his troops. *Right now.* We've recovered the gemstones. That was point one. We've ended the immediate threat to miners. That was point two. Now we have a damned *gateway* to deal with."

"He's right," Amra said. "We need to seal that thing and get back to the surface. Unless you think the mighty forces of Juno can repel the duke's soldiers on their own?"

Ehren turned a pleading look to Qalas.

"One question," Qalas said. "Those bat creatures. And those huge spiders. They came through that gateway, right?"

"Probably, yes," Ehren said with a sigh.

"Close that damned thing," Qalas said.

Ehren sighed again, but relented.

The four of them, side by side, approached the gate.

THEY STOPPED ABOUT THIRTY PACES FROM THE HOLE IN SPACE.

"Thought it was bigger than that," Amra said.

"Trick of perspective," Cavan said, not entirely sure he understood the phenomenon. "It's there and not there at the same time, and how it interacts with our world isn't ... entirely reliable, in the way we're used to thinking."

"Stop," Amra said, holding up a hand. "You've answered the question. It's not bigger than that then."

"It is," Cavan said, waggling a hand back and forth, "and it isn't."

Cavan had to admit, though, that he too had been surprised. From way back there along the bottom of this vast, but narrow cavern of blue-gray rock, the hole in space had looked to be hundreds of feet across.

Up close now, Cavan judged its diameter at not more than ten paces.

No breeze blew through it, no matter how one on the other side made those strange palm trees sway, and drop some of their long, dagger-like leaves.

No smells seemed to come through it at all. Not the sand, nor the purple water.

No sounds either. Not the surf, nor any unseen birds or bats or other creatures.

This behavior was consistent with a gateway, from what little Cavan knew about them, but it was also consistent with a teleportation circle or a permanent scrying circle.

Of course, Cavan would have expected either of the latter two to be located in a castle or keep or tower. Probably enclosed in spellwork both visible and perceptible magically.

This ... this hole in the world, it didn't feel like magic. Or at least, not any kind of magic Cavan could recognize.

He was loath, though, to try using a spell to enhance his magical senses. Not with his gut already roiling like he was back at those odd, coruscating energies that locked those boards into place.

Cavan still did not understand the nature or purpose of that barrier. It had seemed more incidental than deliberate, and yet, something about it had driven part of him wild.

A primal part of him. Something he felt only through his guts.

And his guts were screaming at him now.

Run, they begged him. *Run away from this place. Death. This place is death.*

And so on.

To be honest, on any other day, Cavan would probably have written that reaction off to some very good instincts, and wanted to leave and come back with more information.

But this was not the first time today that his guts had been roiling. And, he wasn't sure this could wait. Not with the mines closed and the duke moving in.

This needed to be resolved now.

Which meant Cavan had to ignore the cold sweat breaking out all over his body. The clammy feeling of his skin.

And, of course, his unhappy guts.

"You don't look good," Ehren said softly. "How're the ribs holding up?"

"The ribs are fine. But all my instincts are telling me to run."

"Your Dunaian blood. Has to be."

Cavan started to scoff, but Ehren said, "Amra, Qalas, are you guys feeling any physical effects of being this close to the gateway?"

Each took a quick self-assessment, and said, "No."

Ehren turned back to Cavan. "I'm not either. Part of *you* recognizes this as the Underworld, but you're still alive, so you know you're not supposed to go through."

"And he won't," Amra said, decisively. "We don't have time for games. How do we shut this thing down?"

"I'll have to get closer," Cavan said, doing his best to give her a sardonic raised eyebrow, but he didn't think he was pulling it off. "With your kind permission."

"Just, just don't do anything without talking to us first."

Wow. Amra sounded worried. That was more alarming than everything his guts had done today, all combined.

"Promise," Cavan said.

She nodded.

Cavan stepped slowly up to the hole, Qalas one step behind him.

Cavan stopped. Turned to Qalas with a questioning eyebrow raised.

"For all we know," Qalas said, "anyone who gets too close gets sucked in. Figure I'll have a chance to grab you, if that happens."

"Rope's better," Ehren said, pulling a length of silk rope out of his backpack.

"Not fast enough," Qalas said.

"And if you get yanked through too?" Amra said.

"Well," Qalas said, "if there's enough force to do that, it'll do it through a rope too."

"Would you guys calm down?" Cavan shook his head. "Look. Can any of you smell that sea?"

"It's not a sea," Ehren said, "properly speaking."

"Well, can you smell the water? The sand? Can you feel the breeze? Can you hear the surf? Anything?"

They all paused and smelled. Cavan knew they smelled only the cold air of the mines — dust and hints of tin.

He waited for them to shake their heads.

"Then the connection isn't open that way. It might suck me in if I touch it — which I won't — but it won't pull me in from a distance. I know that much for sure."

Cavan didn't wait for a response this time. Just turned and kept walking, and hoped he remembered that right.

Qalas stayed with him anyway, but Cavan was glad of the company. He could feel the jitters spreading from this stomach all through his system.

Cavan approached the righthand edge of the hole...

That couldn't be.

He looked up, then down, then up again.

He was right. It wasn't a hole in the rock. It ... floated in mid-air.

Cavan had never seen anything like that before. The closest he could think of was the hole that Iresk the Hawkspeaker had opened for Cavan, Ehren and Amra, to get them a shortcut to Oltoss through the Borderlands.

But that hole had been attached to flames on the ground. Cut into the air by the sword of the Hawkspeaker, with full ritual.

And Cavan knew for certain that the hole cut by the Hawkspeaker sealed behind them.

This hole floated, unanchored by spell or stone or mage.

And it was open. He was sure of that, even without touching it...

But could he trust his education there? His reading on gateways was far from complete. In truth, he was never supposed to have studied gateways at all. They were advanced magic, and Master Powys had said, on the day Cavan had asked, that Cavan would not be allowed to study them for five more years.

But patience had never been Cavan's longest suit. He'd snuck into the library when he was supposed to be sleeping and studied what he could learn.

Not nearly enough, before Master Powys thundered in, yanked the books back to their shelves with a single gesture, and proceeded to lecture Cavan all night on not only patience, but upon building a solid foundation in the basics of magic before progressing to its upper echelons.

And gateways were definitely one of the upper echelons.

Cavan couldn't help whistling as he looked back and forth around the edge of this portal into another world. It hung perhaps the width of his thumb in front of the solid rock behind it. And no matter how far up or down Cavan looked, he could see no magical connection to the stone of the wall or floor. No magical connection at all.

"I swear," Cavan said, loud enough for all three others to hear him, "this looks like it's naturally occurring."

"Which means..." Amra said, even more impatient than Cavan at his studies.

"Which means there may not be a way to seal it. If it's magic, then usually there's a magical solution. But if it's simply part of the universe, well, closing it might be a bad thing."

"Why?" Qalas asked, not loud enough for Amra to hear the question.

Cavan answered at full volume anyway. They all needed to hear this.

"If this is a natural portal between worlds, then its existence helps maintain the equilibrium *among* the worlds. Closing it will create tension in the fabric of reality, and the results could be—"

"Catastrophic," Ehren said.

"So what do we do?" Amra said. "We can't just leave it open."

"I have an idea," Cavan said. "We'll need to—"

Cavan broke off speaking when Qalas tackled him to the hard stone floor. Cavan's ribs screamed pain all through his torso, up his neck, and into his teeth, it hurt so much.

Cavan craned his aching neck to look up, to ask why Qalas had done that, when he saw his reason.

Something had come through the gateway.

It wasn't as big as the dragon, which was just about its only saving grace.

It looked like a hedgehog, with scales instead of quills. If the hedgehog were fifteen feet long, and eight feet wide, with claws that scored the stone floor of the cavern as it landed.

Lightning sparked blue-white all along those scales.

Cavan found himself longing to get away from his blue-gray mine and back to nice green grass, and trees that were brown and green. And...

Before Cavan's longings could go their natural direction, another great scaly beast leapt through the portal. This one looked much like the first, but the lightning sparking along its scales looked red.

Cavan sighed, wondering which god was granting his request for a change of color in the worst possible way. Ehren would probably know.

Part of Cavan did recognize those creatures though. His guts. But rather than roiling in fear or general dismay, they tightened up. Cavan could feel the urge to kill flooding through him.

Cavan was on his feet, sword in his hands and flaming, before Qalas had gotten to his dropped halberd or Amra had even closed the gap to these creatures. Cavan was ignoring his pains without a drop of magical effort. They were secondary to the need to rid the world of these creatures.

"Eyes!" Ehren yelled.

Cavan covered his eyes with his arm, just as Ehren shouted, "Zatafa!"

Light flared so bright in the cavern that even through Cavan's arm, he could see a reddish tinge to the inside of his eyelids. He wasn't used to being on the wrong side of that effect. He hoped he never was again.

The creatures shook their heads. Discommoded and, Cavan hoped, blinded.

He jammed the blade of his sword between the sparking red scales of the creature on his left.

"*Ze axa nah*," Cavan hissed, sending power through his sword and its gemstones, to cascade primal fire out from the blade and into the creature.

It howled in pain, its back half collapsed. Cavan withdrew his sword, and black ichor burned away as he did, while more of it dripped out of the wound down onto the stone beneath.

At the other end of the fight, Amra had managed to lodge her blade in the open mouth of the blue-sparking creature, and was carving her way out the long way.

The blue-sparking creature looked to be trying to get its claws at her, but Amra slid her body underneath it, getting herself drenched in black ichor, but keeping herself clear of those claws.

Qalas slashed at the left foreleg of Cavan's creature, but the blade bounced off its scales, and his body seized as a jolt of blue lightning followed the strike up his halberd.

Then the sparking on both creatures dimmed, and flared out all at once.

Bolts of lightning sprang out in all directions.

Two slammed in Ehren, knocking him backwards, out of Cavan's line of sight.

Another missed Qalas only because the ex-hunter had managed to dive aside at the last moment.

None of them had come near Cavan. It seemed they were still too blind to target yet — or in too much pain — and he'd been luckier than Ehren.

But the lightning sparks were dimmer than before. As though the creatures needed time before they could do that again.

Cavan had no intention of giving them that time.

Cavan took a hint from Amra and slid under the front half of his creature, which had begun keening with pain and slashing out wildly with its left foreclaw.

Under the front part of the creature now, Cavan repeated his attack and spell, withdrawing the sword as fast as he could and rolling away toward safety.

He knew what was happening inside the creature though. Primal fire from the front was burning its way toward the primal fire in the back. Together, they would burn the creature out from the inside. Possibly leaving its shell. Cavan couldn't be sure.

And he wasn't waiting to watch. He turned to the other creature.

Which was already collapsing dead on the ground, cut nearly in two by Amra, who was even now getting to her feet. She was covered head to toe in foul-smelling black ichor, but didn't seem to notice.

"Ehren!" she cried. Running toward the priest, maybe.

Cavan didn't. He turned toward the gateway. Looked for the next one of these creatures. They had to travel in packs, didn't they? They seemed like pack hunters. Yes. Another would be along anytime now. Then he could kill it too. Kill any of them that dared to show their faces in the real world, instead of the Underworld, where they belonged.

Cavan would be ready for them. Aches and pains all through his body notwithstanding. No, he could not die now. Not while *these* were nearby. He had to kill them. He had to kill them all.

Qalas slapped Cavan so hard Cavan's ears rang and the world spun.

No. Cavan spun. In place. One full revolution.

He rubbed his jaw and looked at Qalas.

"You in there?" Qalas said, hand raised to repeat the strike, if needed.

"I'm here," Cavan said, raising one hand in surrender. "Nice shot."

"Seen that look before, but never on you. Bloodlust isn't a good look for you. Get it often?"

"Never before," Cavan said, shaking his head. "But I think I need to understand more about my apparent Dunaian heritage, because part of me just needed to—"

"I know what you needed to do," Qalas said, grabbing Cavan by the shoulder and shaking him.

Probably not necessary, but Cavan couldn't blame him. Cavan just nodded...

Then realized Ehren had gone down.

"Ehren!" Cavan yelled, spinning around, but Qalas caught him by the shoulder again.

"I'm all right," Ehren's weak voice said.

"Alive," Qalas confirmed quietly, "but let the rest of us get him back on his feet. You need to figure out how to close that gateway."

"I'm not sure there *is* a way to close it," Cavan said, keeping his voice just as quiet. "Not safely."

"Well, think of something," Qalas said. "Otherwise the next thing that comes through is likely to finish us."

Cavan grimaced through a painful sigh, and turned to regard the gateway.

There had to be a way to close it.

"No," Cavan said, smiling now as he looked at that strange Underworld shore, with its boat waiting for the souls of the Dunaian dead. Souls it might never again ferry to their proper shores in that world, as the Dunaians were dead and gone.

Properly speaking, anyway.

But they didn't matter. Not right now.

"No, there's..." Cavan started, turning, but stopped when he saw his friends.

Amra had managed to wipe her face clean of that rank black ichor, but apart from her blade and her face, the rest of her remained drenched.

Qalas looked unharmed, more-or-less.

Ehren, though. Ehren looked both perfect and near death at the same time, and the contrast was disconcerting.

Ehren looked perfect, in that every inch of his long blond hair was clean and fresh. As were his white clothes and deerskin boots. As was his goldenwood staff, on which he was leaning heavily for the first time that Cavan could recall. And Ehren's skin, it looked *ashen*. Looked...

...looked as though Ehren were barely holding himself together.

His jaw was clenched, and his clear blue eyes were narrowed by pain into little slits.

Cavan forgot what he was going to say.

"Ehren," he said, closing the gap to his oldest friend. "You look like death walking."

"You don't ... look much better," Ehren said, and the words sounded pained. "Sooner we're done here, the better."

"Well," Cavan said, frowning, "I have an idea, but you're not going to like it."

"Do I ever?" Ehren managed a smile, and it looked so pained that it hurt Cavan to see it.

Cavan felt a ghost of his own smile answer Ehren's intentions.

"Well," Cavan said again, "not as often as I'd like, but there are moments."

"And this won't be one of them, I'm sure." Amra twirled an ichor-covered hand to get Cavan to hurry it up.

"No." Cavan took a deep breath that made him grit his teeth against the pain. "Look. We can't afford to close this permanently, even if we figure out how. Not until we know what the larger effect would be on the cosmos. We could be causing all kinds of—"

"Fire from the sky," Amra said, voice clipped, "squirrels riding raccoons into battle against farm animals. We get it. What *can* we do?"

Cavan lost a moment, picturing squirrels riding racoons into battle, but shook away the image.

"The way I see it, we have two options. One," — he held up a finger — "we can try to cause a cave-in or something to bury this gateway in stone."

"Won't work," Qalas said. "Olivart was saying that cave-ins just don't happen here. Something to do with the nature of the rock. We might be able to take some picks and dig out a big enough boulder, if we had the time, but we'd still be stuck trying to figure out how to get it here."

"True," Cavan said, "And I suspect that the nature of the rock is related to this gateway. Its presence and nature probably keeps it from getting buried. After all, this is the gateway to the Dunaian Underworld. What good would it be, if souls couldn't get through it?"

"I doubt," Ehren said, voice a bit strained, "that souls have to pass through a physical gateway, but I see your point. That it's here at all probably helps keep it from being blocked. So we can't."

"Ah," Cavan said, smiling. "Not quite. You see, we can't block anything from our world from passing through to that Underworld. It's the nature of things. I might be able to try, with a ward or something, but there's nothing on this side to lock a ward on. And any ward trying to keep anything from moving the natural direction would be likely to fail."

Ehren sighed. "You're going to say we have to close it from the other side."

Cavan nodded.

"Oh, great wizard," Amra said, voice dripping with even more sarcasm than her body was dripping with ichor, "has it occurred to you that if we seal it from the *other* side, that we'll be stuck there?"

"Not if it's *my* magic sealing it. I can write us into the ward. Give us exemption."

"Still means we have to pass through," Qalas said. "The one thing you agreed we weren't going to do."

"And I don't want to do it," Cavan lied, "but I honestly don't see any other way to keep the nasty things on that side from wandering into this side and raising hell."

Amra groaned at the inadvertent pun.

Good. The pun was a distraction. He did have one or two ideas that might work to close it from this side, but frankly, they were less likely to work and they were more time intensive.

And right now, Cavan wanted to get Ehren to safety even more than he wanted to close the gateway. That meant speed. And *that* meant extreme measures.

"So," he said, "you guys with me or not?"

As if he had to ask.

13

———

Lightningbeasts.

Dane didn't know what those creatures were properly called, but lightningbeasts worked well enough in his own head. And he was grateful for their appearance.

This had been his first opportunity to truly see this little band of heroes in action. They had just fought something else. He knew that. Probably everyone within a hundred miles of these mines knew that. It was a thing that thundered when it roared.

Dane could not guess what it had been though. Something demonic, most likely. Something that had vanished when it died, for Dane could see no corpse left behind.

He'd arrived only in time to see Cavan get his ribs bandaged. He looked rough. His friends still looked more or less intact, when Dane arrived, at least.

Now, though, that could no longer be said.

Amra had gotten herself coated in some sticky black substance that the lightningbeasts used for blood or other organs. No way of knowing what effect that would have on her. If they'd been native to this world, Dane would have assumed it to be just ichor. But he had seen the lightningbeasts come through that gateway.

They were of another world. The longer their ... whatever stayed in touch with Amra, the more likely it was to have some sort of otherworldly effect.

Dane could only hope it would slow that she-devil. Strong, as well as fast, and fearless enough to carve one of the lightningbeasts open from the inside.

Qalas seemed more-or-less unharmed. But Dane considered him the least dangerous of the four. He had no magic, and no special weapon.

Cavan had *licha* now, and that was bad. He hadn't had it when he left Nolarr.

But then, Dane had no intention of letting matters come down to melee. Not with this group.

No, after Amra, the most dangerous of the four — for Dane's purposes — was this Ehren. A priest of Zatafa. And Zatafa's healing was second only to Nilasah.

Good thing he wasn't a priest of Nilasah. He would have had to die, just to ensure he didn't manage to snatch Cavan back from the jaws of death. Some said a priest of Nilasah could revive a headless man, who would then stand up, confused as to why anyone had ever thought he was dead.

Worse, the man's head would appear on his shoulders, by the grace of Nilasah herself.

Fortunately, Zatafa could not accomplish so much.

Zatafa's best work was done by the rising sun. If Cavan didn't live to see the sunrise, then Dane could neutralize most of what Ehren could do to prevent Cavan's death.

In the middle of the night, Zatafa's priests were weakest.

Dane reached for his blowgun.

Yes, perhaps now would be...

Wait...

Were these idiots preparing to go *through that gate*?

Cavan was wounded. So was Ehren, who took not one, but two blasts from the lightningbeasts.

And now they want to go through a gateway?

Well, that was fine with Dane. He had food. He had water. And if they went through a gateway, he had time.

Oh, they'd probably survive whatever they met on the other side of that gate. Their kind always did.

But they'd expect time to lick their wounds once they came back through.

Dane smiled, and started looking for the best vantage point for a blow dart. A blow dart laced with a good, virulent poison. That should do the trick. Cavan would be long dead before the first rays of morning light could heal him.

And as long as Dane had some time, he might as well prepare his escape route.

Yes, he could be ready to collect the balance of his payment by morning...

14

Cavan insisted on being the first one through the portal, and was surprised that Amra agreed. If grudgingly.

"You *are* half a wizard at least," she said. "You might notice something we need to know. Maybe enough to give us a warning I couldn't."

Cavan didn't press the point. Normally, he might have clapped her on the shoulder, but the ichor that covered her had turned sticky, and she *shlucked* with every movement.

Cavan wasn't sure he'd have gotten his hand back.

He stepped up to the edge of the barrier. Took one shallow breath, and stepped through.

The transition felt like ... like ... the transition felt like every little bit of Cavan was getting judged and weighed, sliced apart out of him, jostled around, and put back together without too awful much care.

It was all over in an instant, but he came through shaking. Had to pat himself all over, just to make sure he'd come through intact.

He was standing on loose sand, his tall, leather boots sinking only as deep as his heels, and the sand didn't resist any more than normal sand as he turned about to get his surroundings.

He could hear the surf now, as he watched the purple waves

kissing the golden sand, down by that strange boat. That *canoe*, with its fishing net dangling over the side.

Where was the ferryman? Weren't boats like that supposed to have ferrymen, seeing that everyone got exactly where they were supposed to go?

Cavan shook his head. Kept checking the lay of the land.

Those palm trees bobbed lightly in the cool, early evening breeze. Or perhaps it was pre-dawn. Cavan couldn't tell, and that was almost as disconcerting as his entrance to his place. The sky, though, was a dark shade of gray, though Cavan didn't think it had changed at all since he'd been here.

Wait. Was it a lighter gray before?

He couldn't be sure. Besides, it might have been a trick of the portal, the way its size had seemed to change as Cavan and his friends had gotten closer.

He drew a shallow breath, sniffing the air without breathing deep enough to hurt his poor ribs any worse than they already were. The pain had gained a sharp, fiery twinge again, after his fight with those sparking creatures, but Cavan couldn't bring himself to mention it to Ehren. Not in Ehren's current state.

The breeze came in across the waves of the surf, and it smelled like blood.

Cavan stretched out with his magical senses then. His guts had settled, which wasn't comforting under the circumstances, but he could sense no magical threats. No magic at all, except for the gateway itself, which he could perceive from this side even without looking at it.

No immediate threat, then. No reason to keep the others from following him.

So Cavan turned and waved them over while he took a look at the gateway from this side.

Here, it was more the way Cavan would have expected a gateway to look.

It was rimmed by a vertical stone ring, a dozen paces across on this side. The stones alternated between black and gleaming, and dull blue-white. Onyx, and Blue Mountain stone, if Cavan had to guess. Each had its own rune engraved into it, in pale gold tinged with red. Cavan didn't recognize any of the runes.

"Yeesh," Qalas said, shaking all over as he found his footing on the loose sand. "I feel like, like..."

"Yeah," Amra said, beside him, though she hadn't done more than shiver once.

Cavan blinked at her. The ichor was gone. All of it. Every drop.

Why?

Cavan cocked his head as he thought, while the other three exclaimed about Amra's nigh-cleanliness. The ichor must not have been part of Amra, or the way she thought of herself. That was the only explanation he could come up with. The rest of them came with their armor and weapons and possessions, all the things they had chosen to make part of themselves in their travels. All things they would miss if they vanished.

Only Amra had carried something she had not chosen to carry — the ichor.

Cavan looked down at his hands and arms. None of the dust and dirt from the mine was on him now.

"I think we really were judged," Cavan said.

"Of course," Ehren said. "There's no way to enter *any* Underworld without being judged."

"Less talk," Amra said, "more casting."

"Have to make sure I know what I'm looking at," Cavan said. "Have to make sure it will work."

"Then do your thing," Qalas said, hefting his halberd. "We'll guard your back."

And Cavan returned to his studies.

True, he had not studied nearly enough of gateways. Not enough to create one of his own, nor enough to change the endpoint of this one. And certainly not enough to do anything else to meddle with the magic of this gateway.

But after several minutes of study, Cavan was able to smile. Because he knew he was right about what he *could* do.

It was so simple.

Cavan chuckled as he thought about Master Powys, who had always said that the best magical solutions were always the simplest. And that any complicated solution ... meant the wizard had failed to find the simple answer.

Cavan wondered what Master Powys would think of him now.

But he wondered only for a moment. Then he began to scrounge through the sand for three stones, all round, that would fit, more or less, in the palms of his hands...

CAVAN FOUND THE ROCKS HE NEEDED WITHOUT TOO MUCH TROUBLE. And from there, it was a simple matter of casting the same kind of ward on the gate that he'd cast back at the mine entrance.

Oh, he knew it wouldn't keep out anything too much more powerful than himself. Not if it were intelligent and free-willed. But those bat creatures sure weren't, and he wasn't sure that dragon was.

And the lightning creatures were beneath contempt.

The lightning creatures...

They came from this side...

Despite his pains, and despite his hurry, Cavan found himself turning to look up and down the beach to make sure none of those lightning creatures were nearby.

They weren't, but he did spot another pack of the gray-black spiders they'd fought in the mines earlier. Big as hunting dogs, these spiders were, and they traveled in a pack of at least a dozen.

And they were all coming this way.

Cavan drew his sword. The gemstones flared to life immediately, calling forth the fire of his blade, even without Cavan's seeking it.

"What are you doing?" Qalas yelled at him. "Get back to your casting. If we need you, we'll tell you."

"I knew I liked you for a reason," Amra said, grinning at Qalas, as Cavan sheathed his sword and returned to his casting.

He ignored the sounds of fighting behind him. He focused

instead on the spells that engraved the right runes, bound the rocks together. Then came the spells that bound each rock to its keystone location. And after that, the spell that linked them so that their warding covered exactly the area of the gate opening. No more, and no less.

When he finished, Cavan turned back to see the beach littered with dead spiders, and his friends breathing hard. Amra was smiling. Qalas too. Ehren was leaning on his staff, his breathing labored.

"Done?" Ehren managed.

"Yes," Cavan said. "That should keep out the nasties, at least. But if the Dunaians had demons, then—"

"Oh, they did of course," said a voice smooth as velvet.

CAVAN TURNED AWAY FROM THE GATEWAY TO SEE A MAN. AT LEAST, HE looked like a man. A man a full head-and-a-half taller than Cavan, at the least. He was built like a warrior, and wore a toga of royal red, trimmed with gold. It suited the deep, reddish hue of his skin.

His hair was black as the onyx of the gateway, and worn in a topknot that came most of the way down his back. He had eyes as blue as summer skies, and they held more laughter than threat.

Cavan didn't trust that for a moment.

At his side, the man wore a simple sword, of a style long out of fashion. Heavy, and short, and made of what looked like gold, though edged in something that glittered.

"The Dunaians," the man continued in perfect Rentissi, "knew many demons. Thousands. But I'm surprised *you*" — his eyes focused on Cavan — "don't know that. Has the lore of your ancestors truly been lost then?"

"Not all of it," Ehren said. "We know of Juno, and the tale of her love for you."

"Ah," the man said. "Then you know me?"

"You can only be Yeenach, the Destroyer," Ehren said.

"And *you*," Yeenach said, focusing on Ehren in a way that made

Cavan feel the absence of his gaze like a release of tension, "worship that new sun god?" He shook his head. "She has risen to prominence, and I am merely a tavern tale."

"Yours," Ehren said, voice more respectful than Cavan expected, "is a tale told by scholars. And known to those who care for history, and understand that all gods have their place and role in our cosmos."

"Spoken like a true priest," Yeenach said, turning his gaze next to Amra. "*You* I like even more. Tell me, girl, does that blade answer your call?"

"It answers no one else's," Amra said, though Cavan wasn't sure she truly understood the question.

"Impressive," Yeenach said. "That blade was known in the days I last walked your world. I imagine there must be those who try to take it from you weekly." He smiled even wider. "And I can just imagine you slaying them each in turn, a smile on your face and a song on your full lips."

His voice grew more intimate. "A song I should love to hear."

"Most lore of that sword," Ehren said, "is lost to common knowledge."

"Truly?" Yeenach laughed, a long, rolling sound. And as he laughed the seas rose and fell in greater waves, that crept up the beach and fell just shy of kissing their boots.

But then the tide settled back as Yeenach turned to regard Qalas, whose jaw was set. And if Cavan wasn't mistaken, he saw dread in Qalas' dark blue eyes.

"Interesting," Yeenach said. "Very interesting. Tell me, are you of the line of—"

"Yes," Qalas said quickly. "But my family does not talk about that."

"No?" Yeenach nodded, thoughtful, but with a hint of sadness around the edges of his lips. "Times have truly changed then. Once every man, woman and child knew the Blood of the Godkiller."

Qalas hissed in a breath, and for a moment Cavan thought the ex-hunter was going to attack. But the moment passed as Yeenach turned back to Cavan.

And once more, Cavan felt the weight of the Destroyer's regard, as though it pressed in at him from all sides.

"As fascinating a group as has entered my lands in centuries." The ancient god smiled. "Now. Let's just talk about what you've done to my gate, shall we?"

Something about that smile was sending waves of fear all through Cavan. But training in both war and wizardry had done more than enough to keep him fully functional, even in a state of heightened fear.

"Well," Cavan said, "your creatures had begun coming through and killing our people. I had to put a stop to it."

"Truly?" Yeenach nodded. "*You* did?"

"We did," Cavan said. "But I take it more personally, because I stand to inherit the land that holds the other end of this gate. Assuming nothing changes before the current holder dies."

"Who is this current holder?" Yeenach said.

"King Draven of Oltoss."

Yeenach's black eyebrows rose the barest fraction. "You stand to inherit a kingdom, and yet you risked entering the Underworld to save your people?"

"Not the kingdom," Cavan said. "Only one barony in the kingdom." Then Cavan frowned, and the familiarity of the topic, by now, did him some good, in terms of calming his nerves. "I am a bastard son of a king. By the laws of succession of this land, all the king's titles are divided among his offspring, in descending order of precedence. I won't inherit the kingdom. Only a single title, the meanest. As things stand, this barony."

"So you're telling me that my gate stands within the least holding of this King Draven?"

"Yes," Cavan said. "But you must remember. Most people think the gate is nothing more than a legend. We might not have found the gate at all if tin hadn't been discovered in the mountains."

Yeenach's smile quirked up lopsided on the left-hand side.

"And you, a bastard, not even certain that you would inherit this land and its people, yet led your friends into hazard to save these strangers?"

Cavan nodded. "It's ... well ... it's what we do."

"Honorable. Respectable. Worthy of your bloodline."

But before Cavan could think of something to say to that, the Destroyer god continued.

"However, it does not give you license to enter *my* lands and muck about with *my* gate. Tell me, boy, do you truly believe you know better how a god should conduct his business than he does?"

Ehren drew breath to answer that, but Cavan stilled him with a raised hand. He was in this now, all the way to his neck. So far, Yeenach the Destroyer had decided that they were here and doing what they were doing solely with Cavan to blame. Letting Ehren speak now might disperse that blame among his friends.

And if this god was going to mete out punishment for what they'd done, Cavan would see to it that he alone suffered the consequences.

"I do not, nor would I," Cavan said. "However, the mine had been in operation for some time without problems. Not until a certain rare type of crystal gemstone had been discovered. A few were mined, and they appeared to have awoken something. It resembled a dragon made from these."

Cavan held up his sword, hilt first, turning it to show the three blue gemstones set into the hilt.

"Whatever that creature was, it slew a miner. The mine was closed. But the barony needs the mine, so I led my friends down here to find and kill the creature. But while down here we discovered yellowish bat creatures, and spiders like those."

Cavan pointed with his sword at the bodies of the dead spiders, slain by the others while Cavan cast his ward.

He sheathed his sword.

"We cannot let creatures from this realm freely enter our world. Someone had to put a stop to it. This was the least intrusive way I could think of."

"You others," Yeenach said. "Do you agree with your leader's account of events?"

"We make decisions about such things as a group," Ehren said, giving Cavan a dark look for trying to take all the blame himself. "But otherwise, his account is right enough."

Amra and Qalas nodded. Qalas added, "Frankly, in a fight, we listen to Amra here first."

Amra and Ehren nodded, and Cavan grimaced, but nodded as well.

"Truly?" Yeenach said, looking over Amra again. "A tactician as well?"

"Believe it," she said.

If she felt at all awed or cowed by the regard of a god, Cavan couldn't tell.

"Well," Yeenach said. "A fine story, however..."

He snapped his fingers, and Cavan felt his ward collapse. He heard the stones he'd enchanted fall to the sand behind him.

"I can't have mortals wandering in and ensorcelling my gates," Yeenach said. "Doesn't look right, and I won't stand for the implications."

"Then I'll have to try to close it from the other side. Dangerous. Could be worse for both our worlds."

"Which is why you won't do it," Yeenach said with a smile. "No, I think the gate shall stay open, both ways."

"Then," Cavan said, drawing a deep breath and savoring the hot pain that reminded him he was, for the moment at least, alive, "as the foster son of the current steward of the Barony of Juno, and as the likely future lord of Juno, I charge you to stop all hostile incursions into our realm."

"And if I refuse?"

"If you refuse, I have no choice but to force the issue."

Cavan adjusted his grip on his sword.

Was it possible to kill a god?

"WAIT!" EHREN YELLED, HOLDING HIS HANDS HIGH — STAFF STILL IN one hand — and running to interpose himself between Cavan and Yeenach. He looked as though he were holding himself together by an act of will alone, wounded as he was, but his hands and voice were steady.

Yeenach gave Ehren an amused, enquiring glance. Cavan had his hand on the hilt of his sword, but the Destroyer had not yet made any movement toward that short, heavy sword he wore.

"Great Yeenach, counterweight to Nuwin the Creator," Ehren began, "you two are the poles of the universe. Should one die, the universe might well fly apart into nothingness."

"Well," Yeenach said slowly, one eyebrow high, "you've done enough homework to at least *say* the right things."

"Please," Ehren said, planting his staff in the sand with a quick movement, then holding up his empty hands in a gesture of beseechment. "Do not let this come to violence."

"I have been offered violence," Yeenach said, as though discussing his dessert options in a high class tavern. "Why should I refuse it?"

"Please," Ehren said again, "may I ask a question before any actions are taken?"

Yeenach nodded.

"Great Yeenach, Destroyer, presider over the souls of the dead, and the lands that lie below, the mine in Cavan's future lands has been open for years, and there have been no creatures coming through the gate on your side. Please, if you would, could you explain to this poor mortal what changed?"

"Do you not know *all* the lore of the Dunaians then?" Yeenach said.

"Some, but far from all. My ignorance shames me."

From anyone else, that comment might have been too much. But Cavan had no doubt that for Ehren, failing to know the finer mythic points of a lost civilization *was* worthy of shame.

Yeenach pointed to the gemstones on Cavan's sword.

"The old magics flared up again. The first time they'd been used on that side of the portal in hundreds, perhaps thousands of years. I daresay this has produced more than a few odd effects, if you've encountered them."

Cavan remembered the coruscating energies that held those boards in place. The ward that wasn't a ward, guarding what was not there to guard.

"The old magics," Yeenach continued, "but not the sacrifices. Not the old rituals and rites."

"The imbalance," Ehren said, voice full of more reverent awe than he held when anytime previously in this conversation. Which was saying something. "That imbalance had to be righted. So creatures from this side felt compelled to explore the other side."

"Very good," Yeenach said. "If you ever wish to branch out from your sun goddess, you could do well in serving me."

Cavan didn't want Ehren to answer that one. So he interrupted quickly.

"If I offer up these three gems in sacrifice," Cavan said, "will that be sufficient to redress the imbalance and halt the incursions?"

"You offered me violence," Yeenach said.

"I saw no other choice."

"Those gemstones are power. I can tell that you've touched that power, but believe me, you have yet to explore their depths. To learn what they can truly do for you."

"Even so," Cavan said, voice firm despite the crying out of his wizardly nature, "I will sacrifice them to redress the imbalance."

"This is too much pain," Yeenach said, voice soothing, and for a moment, Cavan could see only the god. His dark red skin, his royal red toga trimmed in gold, his onyx hair and blue eyes. Even the sights of the beach and the sky faded.

Cavan could not hear the surf now, only the voice of Yeenach.

"Too great a sacrifice. Close one branch of the mine. What is the harm? You'd leave a place ripe for would-be adventurers to test their mettle, while still pulling forth all the tin you could wish for. Other metals, as well. I could tell you where to find them all."

Cavan found himself wondering, would that work? But the Destroyer continued talking.

"And I could show you some of the secrets of those gemstones. Teach you ways to draw more from them than ice. Hints of what real power could be. Power such that even Master Powys would bow to you. Admit that he erred in sending you away. That he'd failed to realize your greatness."

Respect from Master Powys...

Oh, maybe he *could*—

"No!" Cavan yelled from not only his lungs and diaphragm, but from deep within the wells of his soul.

"I want power," he said. "I won't deny it. But the price is too high. So far only smallish creatures have come through. What happens when the greater creatures come through? What happens when they devour one barony and spread beyond?"

"You exaggerate," Yeenach said, but his voice, though still smooth, was no longer driving away the sounds of the surf, the breeze, his friends, shifting about behind him.

Cavan could see the beach now. Could see Ehren, watching Cavan carefully, even as Yeenach continued.

"There would be some who died, yes, but many die every day."

"No," Cavan said, shaking his head firmly. "Not for my power. Not for me. I choose to sacrifice the gemstones instead."

"You are certain?" Yeenach raised an onyx eyebrow.

Cavan nodded, not sure he wanted to trust himself to speak.

Turning his back on power would never be easy.

"Very well," Yeenach turned to the others. "He would surrender the gemstones. Any of you could take them. Even without a wizard's training, there are many ways to tap into their power."

"Never," Ehren said.

"Tempting," Qalas said, "but I'm going to take a pass."

"If I can't get what I want in life without *that* kind of power," Amra said, "just kill me now."

While the others were talking, Cavan set about removing the gemstones from his sword. This was both easier and harder that prying gems out of any other sword, because they hadn't been set in the normal way, but held in place by the enchantments that allowed

Cavan's new sword to function as a staff or wand, a true conduit for his magic.

And Cavan had to admit, he would miss that. He hadn't had it long, and he could already see the true advantages of it.

But this was necessary.

That didn't mean he had to like it, though.

Most wizards never dismantled their staves and wands. Either they kept them throughout their lives, or they destroyed them in a suicidal gesture, releasing any stored magic along with every bit of magic they could muster, in one massive strike against … well, against whatever made it necessary.

Cavan wasn't sure any wizard actually did that. It was a device used by singers and storytellers in taverns and inns, but Cavan had never read of it happening in any serious histories, nor heard any other wizards mentioning it.

No, Cavan did know of a few wizards who had dismantled staves or wands, but only because they'd been built with flaws, back when they were apprentices.

Conduits of power, when made properly, only improved with use. And wizards were never the types to walk away from power.

Not even Cavan.

Which he had to remind himself, when he realized he'd managed to hold off what he needed to do long enough that everyone was now staring at him.

"You don't have to," Yeenach said, softly. "You can still change your mind."

Cavan drew a deep breath to flare pain all through himself. Remind himself that he was mortal, that all the people in danger were mortal. That if Cavan failed them now, many would suffer wounds much worse than his own broken ribs.

Cavan holding his sword in both hands, by the blade, he looked deeply into the gemstones and chanted the charm of unmaking.

The three gemstones fell to the sand.

Cavan sheathed his sword. Picked up the gemstones.

"I'll take those," Yeenach said, stepping forward.

"They have to be destroyed, to ... sacrifice them ... properly..." Cavan said, words petering out as he remembered the title of the god he addressed.

"Sacrifices in your world must be destroyed in the offering," Yeenach said. "But this is my realm, and I make the rules. Offer them to me properly, and place them in my hand."

Cavan took a knee, held the gemstones up in both hands.

"Great Yeenach. Destroyer. Foe and Friend of Nuwin, the Creator. Half of the perfection of the universe. I offer up to you these gems of power, drawn forth by those of my land, offered to me by my foster father. I have plumbed their depths to the best of my abilities. I have fashioned a conduit from them. I have wielded them in battle against my foes."

He stretched his hands a little higher.

"I offer you their power. I offer you their beauty. I offer you their victories in battle."

"And I, Yeenach, ancient when the gods you know were children, accept your offering." He plucked the gemstones from Cavan's hands. "And as a gesture of thanks for a mighty offering freely given, I permit the four of you to leave to leave my realm."

Cold sweat broke out on Cavan's forehead. He hadn't thought about that side of things.

Cavan stood. Said in tones that sounded all too nervous in his own ears. "We should be going then. Thank you for your ... hospitality, great Yeenach."

"Yes, yes," Yeenach said, giving a dismissive wave with one hand as he studied the gemstones. "Heartstones of a *krintax*. Quite rare, even here."

Cavan hustled his friends back through the gateway. Wounded Ehren first, then Qalas, then Amra, who gave Yeenach one last appraising gaze.

Cavan was the last through, but just before he entered the gateway, he heard Yeenach speak.

"Farewell, Cavan Oltblood. We *will* meet again."

15

The trip back through the gate felt like walking through a waterfall. A moment of drenching cold, and then it was over. Cavan half expected to be soaking wet when he stepped into complete darkness.

Complete darkness that lasted only a moment before Ehren, in a shaky voice, renewed the blessing that let the four of them see as though the cavern were in bright sunlight.

All three of the others were sitting on the cold blue-gray stone floor of the cavern. Cavan wanted to join them. Wanted to sit. No. Wanted to *sleep*. Wanted to sleep away the rest of the night and let Ehren heal them all by the first rays of the sun, before he went on to face the next crisis.

But there was no time.

"We need to move," Cavan said. "It's near midnight. The duke's forces are going to be at my ward soon, if they aren't already."

"Sit," Ehren said, and it was unfair that sitting there, looking barely this side of the grave, he should be able to put such firm command into his voice. "The duke will wait a few minutes. We all need to sit, and eat."

"But—"

"Sit," Amra said, in her command voice.

Cavan sat before he knew he'd done it.

"Now get him to roll over," Qalas said, and all three of them burst into laughter. Though, admittedly, Ehren's was weak as he dug in his backpack.

"Ha, ha," Cavan said. "Mocking battle reflexes, shame on you, Qalas."

Qalas grinned, completely unashamed.

Ehren handed out apples, hunks of a good, strong cheese, and bits of roast turkey. And as the four of them tucked in, Cavan realized that at least some of the roiling of his stomach had been hunger after all.

Then he realized, the *only* roiling in his stomach at the moment was hunger. The rest of his discomfort appeared to have abated.

"The imbalance," he said, and though his mouth was full, he'd been traveling with the others long enough to know they'd understand him. Still, he swallowed before he continued. "Was that what was upsetting my guts before?"

"Might be," Ehren said. "You're the only one of us with the right bloodline." His eyes flicked to Qalas and back. "The right bloodline for *that*, I mean."

"Not now," Qalas said softly. "I'll tell you all. I will. Just ... not now. Okay?"

Amra nodded as though she never expected him to say anything else.

Ehren and Cavan nodded a moment later.

Qalas nodded his thanks at the others, and tucked back into his food.

For several minutes, there was nothing but the enjoyment of good food, and fresh spring water.

When the last of them finished, Cavan got slowly to his feet, trying to give his poor, complaining ribs a rest. But Ehren saw him wince.

"Let me change those before we move on," he said.

Cavan nodded, and stripped off his shirt.

Ehren pulled out fresh poultices, fresh bandages, and even an extra waterskin, in case it was needed.

Cavan was amazed once more of all that Ehren could keep in that backpack. And still, somehow, he'd had room for all those blasted gemstones.

Ehren was in the middle of winding the bandage around Cavan's ribs, with Cavan's arms over his head, when something pricked Cavan's throat. Right at the jugular vein.

Pain roared right out from that wound. Deep pain. Throbbing pain. Too intense to bear.

Blackness. Edging in past the light. Narrowing Cavan's world to a tube. A tube that narrowed with each rapid, fluttering beat of Cavan's heart.

Roaring in his ears. His blood, or maybe his body itself roaring. Maybe that was Cavan's voice roaring. Wordlessly, if so. The sound made no sense, but it was all he could hear.

Pain, though, was all he could feel. All he could taste, even. No turkey on his tongue now. No cheese.

Only pain. Sharp pain, that tasted juicy, like persimmons.

That was the last thing Cavan thought as he collapsed.

Cavan awoke ... sometimes later. He wasn't sure when. Not immediately. No, the first thing he noticed were his eyelids.

He wanted to open them. That was how he knew he was awake. He wanted to open his eyes. But the lids were too heavy. Too much effort involved, trying to open his eyes.

Hell, breathing alone was a labor unto itself. Slow. In. Out. Each breath painful.

Why was each breath painful?

Oh, yeah. The dragon thing. Yeenach had called it something else. Not a dragon thing then. Whatever it was, it threw Cavan. Long,

long fall. Long, long roll. Rolling and rolling and rolling. Bruising and breaking, cracking and creaking.

Oh, so many pains. And now one more.

How was that fair? How should Cavan have had to suffer one more pain? Just when he'd had to sacrifice power — real *power* — for other people.

And then, more pain? Just when he was eating?

No, this was not fair. Just not fair at all.

And Cavan intended to tell Ehren that. He would tell Ehren all about that. Just as soon as he opened his eyes.

Just before Cavan passed out again, he realized he could hear someone screaming. Someone who wasn't him.

Wasn't Ehren. That was good. Wasn't Amra, either. Or Qalas.

Wait. Was it Qalas? Cavan had never heard Qalas in enough pain to be able to guess what he'd sound like screaming.

Well, he'd never heard Amra scream either, but this voice was definitely male.

He hoped it wasn't Qalas...

⸻

THE NEXT TIME CAVAN AWOKE, HIS EYELIDS WEREN'T NEARLY SO HEAVY.

Oh, the pain in his ribs was, if anything, worse than before Ehren had changed his poultice, and that pain in his neck was still a soreness that had settled in to linger. And he could still taste a hint of persimmons, but he tasted something ... chalky, too. Like someone had squeezed all the juice out a blueberry, dried it in the sun for three days, then smeared it on his tongue.

Still, at least Cavan could flutter his eyes open.

He knew that, because he did it.

He was still in that cavern. Right below the gateway.

Why was he still here?

Oh. Yeah. That pain in the neck.

No one was screaming now. He could hear talking though.

Sounded like Amra and Ehren, talking in low voices. Cavan couldn't quite hear what they were saying.

Still, he didn't hear Qalas.

"Is..." Cavan cleared his throat. "Is Qalas all right?"

Cavan didn't like how weak he sounded.

"Right here," Qalas said, getting to Cavan even faster than Ehren. But then, Ehren still looked about like Cavan felt. Qalas looked healthy enough to be worried about Cavan. "What do you need?"

"Good," Cavan said. He sat up. Not as hard as he thought it would be. And his voice sounded stronger, now that he was using it. His mouth was even producing enough saliva to chase away the worst of that chalky taste.

Better and better, though dawn was still hours away.

"Heard someone screaming earlier," Cavan said. "Afraid it was—"

"Oh, *that*," Amra said, smiling as she sauntered over. "That would be our guest there."

She pointed. Cavan saw a man who'd been trussed up like a hog, for the slaughter.

The man didn't look remarkable. Slender enough to be fast. Boring features. Head shaved bald...

...and a thin, purple mustache.

"An assassin," Cavan said, not naming the Order of the False Dawn out of respect for Ehren.

"*Your* assassin, to be precise," Amra said, sounding as though she were enjoying this. "Caught you in the neck with a blow dart and had the gall to try to escape."

"As if we'd let that happen," Qalas said, and Cavan could hear the anger in the ex-hunter's voice, as much as see it in his eyes. "We brought him down before he'd gotten too far."

"Put up a decent fight," Amra said, "for one man, anyway. Sorry you missed it."

"I'm just glad he didn't kill me."

"He underestimated the skills and preparedness of our dear Ehren."

Ehren hadn't spoken yet. He looked like death walking. Even his smile looked ghostly.

"Is there anything we can do for *you*?" Cavan asked.

Ehren shook his head. "The dawn is what I need. Keep me alive 'til then."

"We will," Amra said. "Especially if this guy's the best they can do."

She turned to the trussed-up assassin. "Honestly. I'd expected better from a group with your reputation."

"We're assassins, not fighters," the assassin said, in a bored voice. "You shouldn't have gotten past my rock trap."

"Please," she said. "In *this* place? Saw it coming a curve away."

"What was the poison?" Cavan asked.

"Myrranese," Ehren said. "Fairly obscure. You're lucky I carry a broad selection of anti-venoms."

Cavan found himself offering Zatafa a quick prayer of thanks, as well as whoever had made that marvelous backpack Ehren carried.

"What was the screaming then?" Cavan said.

"Oh, that," Amra said. "I just thought if I leaned on an open wound or two, answers might magically pop out of his mouth."

"We do *not* torture," Ehren said firmly. "I put a stop to that at once. Must have woken you."

"Didn't get the answers anyway. What should we do with him?"

"Throw him through the gateway," Qalas said. "Just like he is. See how he does in the Underworld."

"*An* Underworld," Ehren corrected. "There are several."

"No," Cavan said. "We'll take him along. I think we might be able to use him against the duke."

"Tell me you're not thinking of hiring this man," Ehren said.

"Yeah," Amra said, just as irritated. "Not like we need help killing."

"That's not what I mean," Ehren said.

"Well—" Amra started, but Cavan cut in, pleased that his voice was capable of volume.

"I *mean*," Cavan said, "the duke either sent him or knows who did."

"Fair enough," Amra said, and began adjusting the assassin's ropes.

"Much better," Ehren said, leaning on his staff.

"Are you okay to make it back?" Cavan said.

"I want the open sky and the first rays of dawn," Ehren said. "And woe to anyone who stands between me and them."

"Then let's go."

Cavan stood. His knees were a little shaky, but he had to hope they'd settle in as he hiked.

Then he realized Amra had set the assassin up to be dragged.

"We're not dragging him," Cavan said.

"You and Ehren are wounded. Qalas and I need our hands free to fight, if we need to. Dragging him makes more sense than carrying. Tactically speaking."

"He's wounded," Ehren said.

"His own fault for trying to kill Cavan," Amra said with a shrug. "Carrying him risks Qalas or me being too tired if a big fight comes."

"Do you have a better idea?" Qalas said.

"Well, no," Ehren said, "but—"

"I've got this," Cavan said with a smile.

Before today he hadn't cast Nester's Platter since he'd been an apprentice with Master Powys. Now he'd found an excuse to use it twice since the last dawn.

And this time, he was even using it for its proper purpose.

THE HIKE BACK UP THE TUNNELS FELT AS THOUGH IT TOOK MOST OF THE night, but Cavan knew better. He could sense the approach of the cardinal times again, and he kept checking them to assure himself that he was still conscious, still alive, still in this world and still not bound inside another illusion.

Yes, this had been one hell of a day.

Still, nothing crossed their path as they made their way up the long and winding side tunnel, back into the main mine shaft itself, back across the bridge over the chasm — which might have been over the cavern at the bottom, Cavan couldn't be sure — and finally all the way back to the entrance of the mine itself, until there was only one last cave between Cavan and the open air.

Well, that wasn't quite true.

There was a big cave, and an enemy army.

16

Cavan stopped walking just inside the mine entrance. Just inside his own ward as well, which he was grateful to see was still intact.

On the other side of that ward though, sat the duke's army. Or at least a portion of it.

It looked as though there were a dozen knights in full plate armor, with banners and sigils that Cavan didn't recognize and didn't want to waste time worrying about.

Only the duke mattered here.

The knights looked to have set up camp, complete with at least three campfires, and torches set all around the cave, providing more than enough light, since Cavan doubted any of *them* were currently blessed by Zatafa.

The knights were all still in full suits plate armor, and they didn't look happy about it. They looked as though they'd been too tired for this hours ago. Not one of them was sitting, as though they might fall asleep if they tried it. They were all pacing about, snapping at each other.

Their squires, wearing chainmail instead of plate, looked just as haggard, but even more stressed out. As though they blamed themselves for their knights' foul moods.

Other men at arms milled about in the background, along with cooks and other servants, keeping busy and very much out of the way.

No sign of the duke.

And no one had noticed Cavan as yet.

He cleared his throat.

Nothing.

"Hey, you lot!" Amra yelled in a ringing voice.

Every face turned their way.

Amra bowed, and gestured for Cavan to take over.

"I could have done that," Cavan said.

"Yes, but not with as much style," Amra said, grinning.

The knights came over in a bunch, each trying to be the first on the scene. Perhaps the first to cross swords.

Certainly they were all drawing their swords, though a few favored maces or hammers. Some of them called for their shields, their helmets, or both. One, holding a two-handed sword, stepped to the fore, shouldering past others to get there.

This one wore black armor, that suited his hair and mustache, and he didn't look to be much older than Cavan.

"I am Ser Sarkin," he identified himself. "And you would be Cavan Oltblood?"

"I am," Cavan said.

"Then I must inform you that you are my prisoner. Surrender yourself and your friends immediately, or face the consequences."

Cavan frowned at him. Turned back to his friends. "You think he expects that to work?"

Ehren shook his head.

Qalas shrugged.

"If he does," Amra said, "then he even stupider than the fool who made his sword. Just look at that crosspiece. Terrible workmanship."

The man's face went red like magic.

"How dare you!" he challenged. "I—"

"Won't do a damned thing," Cavan finished for him. "Look, Ser Sarkin. I'm not your prisoner. You should know better than to make pronouncements you can't back up." Cavan pointed to the edges of the mine entrance. "If you hadn't figured this out, you're standing on the wrong side of this ward to try to hurt me."

Ser Sarkin frowned. "You would hide behind a wizard's trick?"

"I'm the wizard who cast it, and I'm not *hiding* behind anything. I *demand* to speak to my uncle, the duke. Go get him." Cavan raised a hand, as though Ser Sarkin had been about to turn and do Cavan's bidding. "And while you're at it, fetch Ser Ranus. I won't do anything until I've gotten a full report I can trust."

"I am no hound, to fetch for you, boy."

"And I am no prisoner, but your liege's nephew."

"Bastard nephew," Ser Sarkin added.

"True enough, but I'm also the heir to the land you're standing on. Now." Cavan gave this Ser Sarkin the best glare he could, with his ribs paining him as they were. "Get my uncle, or I'll send for him by magic. And then you can tell your liege why he had to wait to speak to me."

That was a gamble. Cavan wasn't sure Falstaff would be angry with Ser Sarkin for not fetching him at once.

And unfortunately, Ser Sarkin didn't think so.

"Surrender yourself," Ser Sarkin said, "and you may speak to the duke as my prisoner. Otherwise," — he glanced around as though he could see the ward, which Cavan doubted — "we'll see what it takes to bring down that ward."

"Try it," Cavan said. And just then he saw one of the knights issue an order to his squire, who turned and began to run.

Cavan smiled. "Then again, maybe you don't have so much time as you hope."

Ser Sarkin swung at the ward.

His blow *clanged* off harmlessly.

Cavan smiled wider.

Amra clucked her tongue. "Who is training these people?"

"Yeah," Qalas said, "look at his footwork."

Cavan didn't see anything wrong with Ser Sarkin's footwork, but Amra and Qalas might have been tweaking his beard.

The blows came faster then. Just as noisy, but with no more success.

"If you think you're impressing anyone," Ehren said gently, "we'd be a lot more impressed with noble treatment."

"Oh, just let me kill him and be done with it," Amra said, "then whoever's next in line can fetch the duke for us."

"There'll be no need for that." Falstaff's ringing voice, carrying over the clatter of Ser Sarkin's sword failing one last time to penetrate Cavan's ward. "And stop that, Sarkin, you look even more the fool than I already think you."

Falstaff stepped up then, tall in his dark blue enameled armor, armor that Cavan knew had been enchanted to make the duke a little stronger, a little tougher, and a little harder to hurt. Once more, he had forsaken his helm for the time being, and Cavan saw reflected his own strong chin and nose, though the resemblance ended there. Falstaff's hair was golden, like the king's, though Falstaff kept his cropped short.

He did look every inch a noble. Cavan had to give him that.

"Uncle," Cavan said by way of a greeting. "I'd say it's been too long, but under the circumstances..."

"Yes, I know." Falstaff sighed. "Terrible business. Still, I had my rights to think of."

"Rights?"

"Yes. Of course. Juno's miners dug too deep this time, and veered across into my part of the mountain. Anything they found, well, it's mine by right."

"Including any gemstones? Is that it?"

"Whatever," Falstaff said with a smile.

"Well," Ehren said, "you must know that the proper response is to call for a royal surveyor."

"Yes," Falstaff said, "and I have. But that takes *time*, and who knows what Juno's miners might have pulled out of there and never mentioned to me. No, that would never do."

"The mine was closed," Cavan said.

"Was it." Falstaff made that a statement. "And I'm to believe, then, that those jewels, rarer than sapphires, were simply left alone down there?"

"You broke your word, uncle," Cavan said, quietly enough that the knights would not hear.

"I did no such thing," the duke said.

"Cavan—" Ehren said.

"You swore you would leave Juno alone."

"I swore no such thing," the duke said.

"Cavan!" More urgency in Ehren's voice now. Enough to make Cavan turn and look. "He could not have. Even if he wanted to. Zatafa ensured it."

That meant the assassin wasn't his then. Cavan resolved to hold that question back, for the time being.

"Quite right," the duke said, giving Cavan a smile that Cavan didn't like at all. "I never agreed to have Zatafa guarantee my word, but your ... enthusiastic friend there saw to it anyway."

Cavan got as far as opening his mouth to voice a sarcastic comment when Falstaff spoke over him.

"Your error," the duke said, "was in assuming my promise freed Juno. No, you made me swear off any claim to your inheritance, whatever it turned out to be. Juno is not yet your inheritance, and after word of those gemstones gets out, it never will be. And we both know it. I can think of counties that Draven holds that would be valued at less than this tiny barony. Once those gemstones are known."

Cavan's turn to smile. "No, uncle. You're wrong. In fact, I'd say those gemstones have *guaranteed* that this will be my inheritance."

"A meaningless distinction," the duke said, "for it's not your inheritance *now*." The duke shook his head. "Honestly, Cavan, you have no head for politics. You really ought to just sell your birthright. If not to me, then to someone else. You'll be doing everyone a favor."

"You had no right to invade Juno."

"I had *every* right," the duke said with a sigh. "And this is growing tiresome. Set down this ward of yours and let my miners in."

Cavan smiled wider. When he spoke again, his voice was barely a whisper.

"Difficult, isn't it? Facing a ward in the field. Maybe you could unweave it. Maybe you couldn't. Even failing would teach you *so much*. But you can't risk it. There's no way to try without telling every witness that you're studying magic."

"Don't make this personal, Cavan. It won't end well for you."

"What will it take to make you leave?" Cavan said, louder. "Do you need a personal challenge? Is that it?"

"You're not in a position to issue one."

"He is!" A voice declared. A voice Cavan knew well. "As major-domo I declare Cavan Juno's champion, until such time as the steward or the baron assigns the post to someone else."

Olivart approached then, his step sprightly, his "walking" stick moving in his hands like a baton leading a parade. Around him were a small company of baronial guards.

"Where's Ranus?" Cavan asked. "Were any lives lost in the invasion?"

"A dozen or so," Olivart said, stepping up beside the duke. "Ser Ranus was taken hostage, as were another dozen or so guards, and his squire."

"Yes," the duke said. "He lead an ill-advised aggressive action against my men before they even set foot on Juno soil."

Ser Sarkin, still close at hand, looked angry enough at that statement to have bitten right through his own sword. He aggressively shoved the blade back into the scabbard he wore on his back, and stomped off toward a tent.

"I doubt that very much," Cavan said, "but now I have standing and you cannot ignore me. Do you agree?"

The duke sighed, long and slow though his nose. But finally, he nodded.

"Then as champion of Juno, I challenge you."

"Withdraw it," the duke said. "You'll never win by surprising me with a trick again, and you aren't warrior enough to beat me."

"Find out," Cavan said.

"At issue are the mines," the duke said. "And so the stakes of the duel must be the mines. Winner claims all mining rights in the Blue

Mountains that lie along the border between Nolarr and Juno, and anything drawn from those mines — or the profits therefrom if those materials have been sold previously — for the past, say, six months?"

Cavan looked at Olivart.

"It's a fair offer," the old majordomo said. "I hope you know what you're doing. We need those mines."

"I do," Cavan said. "And I repeat my challenge, agreeing to those as the stakes."

"Fine," the duke said. "Take down that ward and let's get this over with."

"There's no need for any improper hurry," Cavan said, loud enough for his voice to carry all through the cavern outside the proper mine entrance. "Let the duel take place in the morning. Let us both be rested and refreshed, that the duel be as fair as possible."

The duke gnashed his teeth. No doubt he could see the way Cavan stood. The obvious pain still in his ribs. And probably bruising on his neck, as well.

But with at least a dozen of his own vassal knights looking on, the duke could only nod agreement.

"And the mine is to be left empty until this duel is resolved," Cavan said. "Agreed?"

"Fine, fine." The duke turned to his assemblage. "Clear the cavern. We'll have Nolarr and Juno guards both at the entrance to keep the cavern and mine clear until after the duel is resolved."

Only then did Cavan agree to take down the ward.

⁂

Olivart had tents, which was a blessing.

Apparently, after Ser Ranus' surrender, the duke became almost magnanimous. He didn't allow his men to forage from the nearby farms and villages, and the whole army came straight to the mine and set up camp.

The duke even sent troops to summon Olivart, but allowed Olivart his own guards and servants, and made no pretense of imprisoning Olivart. The duke even went so far as promising to release all prisoners without ransom, once this matter was settled.

Cavan couldn't help but wonder if the promise to forgo ransom on prisoners was part of what had left the duke's knights out of sorts.

Still, Olivart made it clear that he had, and continued to, categorically deny all the duke's claims, and refused to even acknowledge what, if anything, other than tin had ever been drawn from those mines.

All to the good, as far as Cavan was concerned.

What he was most concerned about, though, was sleep. He even shortcut his explanation about the assassin to the barest facts, before sending the Platter straight up ten feet for the night. Though he did first allow Amra to redo the man's bonds, at Ehren's insistence, to avoid permanent harm.

When Cavan crawled into his bedroll at last — in a tent large enough to sleep all four of Cavan and his friends, comfortably — the pleasure was almost obscene.

Sleep was snatches of pure bliss between rude awakenings by his ribs. What sleep Cavan got was so deep he wasn't sure he dreamed anything at all.

He did arise with broken fragments of dreams still in his head, though. Little wisps that taunted him as he awoke. Suggestions of sailing on a vast series of purple channels, and of a red-skinned man in a toga, laughing at Cavan.

That laughter may or may not have been in Cavan's ears when he awoke, minutes before the dawn, as he intended.

When he awoke though, he was sure he heard *real* laughter. Amra's laughter, from somewhere outside the tent.

Amra laughed easily, that was true. But Cavan knew her well enough to know when her laughter was sincere amusement, and when it was mocking amusement.

And this was mocking laughter.

Cavan wrestled his pained way into clothing fast enough that he was panting for breath when he stepped out into the pre-dawn gloom.

Amra was surrounded by the duke's knights. She was clad in her black leathers, but at least she hadn't drawn her sword.

Yet.

A quick assessment of their positions and expressions indicated that they had … unwisely assessed her skills in light of her appearance.

Cavan wasn't sure how she had disavowed them of their initial impressions — no one looked dead, or even seriously injured — but they were all looking at her with considerable respect.

In fact, as he approached, Cavan was sure he heard one of them mutter, "Luck thing she's not the one fighting Falstaff."

And if Cavan heard that, he knew for certain that Amra heard it too. She let it go though, turning to Cavan and giving him a quick once over.

"Did the sleep help at all?" she said.

"Not much." Cavan yawned and shook his head. "Felt wonderful while I was sleeping, but my ribs must have woken me a dozen times."

"Get ready," Ehren said, stepping out of the tent. He still looked ghastly and half-asleep, in complete contrast to the pure spotlessness of his clothes, skin and hair. How anyone could look so clean and so close to death at the same time, Cavan wasn't sure.

"Ready when you are," Cavan said, then bit his lip.

Ehren only smiled though. Both knew that Ehren would be ready when Zatafa graced the world with Her first rays of the day.

Qalas stepped up then, already fully decked out in his studded leather armor and carrying his halberd.

"Prisoner's all right," he said, "considering how long he's been bound up. Must know tricks for keeping his muscles loose, even when bound tightly. How long is that spell of yours going to keep going?"

"Hours yet," Cavan said. "One of its benefits." Then Cavan blinked. "Wait." He looked up into the air, where he'd left Nester's Platter overnight, with its passenger. "How did you—"

Qalas smiled mischievously. "I have my ways."

Cavan smiled and clapped him on the shoulder.

"Time," Ehren said.

Cavan hustled over and grimaced as he knelt beside the white-frocked priest. Qalas knelt on Ehren's other side. Amra merely hung back and watched.

Two of the duke's knights approached. Older men, graying at the temples, and perhaps with their best fighting years behind them.

"Lord priest," one said, with strain in his voice. "May we share in Zatafa's blessing? The conflict yesterday left the two of us ... a bit strained."

Amra opened her mouth to say something, but Ehren spoke first, and louder.

"All are welcome to share in Zatafa's bounty. Let any come to me who need healing, and Zatafa shall cleanse and bind their wounds with her love and light."

Three other men at arms approached and knelt.

Ehren stood, facing east.

Sweat broke out on Cavan's forehead. This wasn't going to work...

The Blue Mountains were in the way. Cavan could feel the approach of dawn, yes, but with those peaks so close, there was no way the light of the sun would reach them for hours yet.

Hours. They were too early, Cavan realized. They were all there, and all ready, and they were hours too early.

And Cavan knew from experience that the difference *did* matter. The last time they had ridden through Juno before the first rays of the sun had hit them, Ehren had been just as listless and exhausted as he always was when they rode late at night. That Cavan had sensed the sunrise hours previously had made no difference.

The rays of the sun were what mattered. And those were hours away.

The duke would not wait. No one would expect him to wait. Cavan had gotten his night's sleep. He would break his fast. That would be all the readiness the duke would require, and his knights would uphold that view.

He was going to have to fight the duke as he was.

And Cavan could not win. Not as he was. One good blow to the chest might kill him.

But Ehren held up his staff all the same. And Ehren sang his prayers, loud and clear in ancient Penthix...

Wait...

Cavan spoke no Penthix, but he had been traveling with Ehren for years now. And in those years, Cavan had heard Ehren's morning prayer of healing many, many times. Hell, he'd been healed by those prayers on at least fifteen occasions that Cavan could think of without trying.

But the prayers that Ehren sang this morning, they were different prayers.

What did that mean?

Ehren's prayers got louder. Louder than his voice ever seemed to get on its own. Louder than he seemed capable of.

Louder and louder he sang.

And then, just at the moment that Cavan sensed the dawn, a single, huge shaft of light shone straight down out of the sky.

The sun was nowhere to be seen. The sun was still tucked away behind the Blue Mountains.

And yet that single, bright shaft of sunlight sizzled down out of the clouds. Exactly big enough to engulf the singing priest.

The shaft of sunlight faded. The sky remained all pre-dawn gloom.

But Ehren, Ehren glowed with golden sunlight, from the tip of his upraised staff, to the soles of his doeskin boots.

And in an instant, Ehren was healed. He looked stronger. Fitter. Cavan hadn't been entirely what injuries Ehren had suffered when those twin blasts of lightning struck him, but whatever they were, they were no more.

And then Ehren began to touch the supplicant with the head of his staff, while continuing to pray in nonstop Penthix. Words now, not song, but still he sounded better and stronger than he had in nearly a day.

And each person Ehren touched was momentarily engulfed in

the same golden glow. But the golden glow around the supplicants faded quickly, while the glow around Ehren remained.

First he healed the men at arms. Then he healed the two old knights. Then he stepped over to Cavan, but did not reach for him. Instead, he extended the staff above his head and touched Nester's Platter, and the silver disc began to glow gold. A moan of relief came from the bound assassin.

Qalas was next, and though Cavan had seen no wounds on the ex-hunter, Qalas sat straighter and smiled broader as the glow faded.

Finally, finally it was Cavan's turn.

Ehren touched the tip of his goldenwood staff to Cavan's forehead.

Wondrous relief, starting from his scalp and spreading all the way through Cavan's system. Faster than usual. Usually Ehren's morning healing flowed like sweet molasses through Cavan's system. But this morning, this healing swept over him like a wave.

And just like that, Cavan was awake, refreshed, healed, and ready to fight. He even felt as though he'd eaten a full meal, though he doubted that feeling would last.

He jumped to his feet, as the glow around Ehren slowly faded.

"Now," Cavan said. "Where's the duke?"

"Over here, of course," the duke called.

Cavan turned from the men and arms and old knights who were still gushing their thanks to Ehren, and saw that the duke's men had cleared a circle twelve paces across. Leveled the dirt, and surrounded it with knights, in armor, their shields forming a wall to keep the duelists inside, once the struggle began.

"You're ready then?" the duke said. "No more prancing about and singing? I still haven't seen a dance routine from your friends, and I imagine they know some marvelous steps."

"If I showed you steps," Amra said, fluttering her eyelashes, "you wouldn't survive to see the finale."

"Enough," Cavan said. "You tried baiting me last time, uncle. In fact, last time you tried positioning me in slick blood, and seizing every other advantage you could name. I still beat you."

"And if you expect the same outcome this time," the duke said, donning his dark blue enameled helm with its great bat wings and full visor, which was still up. "You're in for a rude awakening."

"Oh," Cavan said, drawing his new sword. "I think you'll find I have a few surprises myself."

"*Licha*," the duke said, astonished. "Where did *you* get your hands on *licha*? You've barely been out of my duchy a full day, and I know for a fact you didn't have it when you left."

"Sorry, uncle," Cavan said with a smile. "My secret."

"Fine," the duke said. "Is my word enough for you? Or must you insult me by having your priest ensure the outcome again?"

"Well, you did violate the spirit of the last agreement anyway," Cavan said, as though he were thinking it over. "And there *is* the small matter of an assassin..."

"Assassin? What are you blathering about?"

Cavan had been watching the duke closely, and if his uncle was lying, Cavan couldn't tell. But then, his uncle *was* an experienced politician.

"I know he's not yours," Cavan said, with more certainty than he felt, "but I have every reason to believe you know who sent him."

"Oh, save your accusations," the duke said. "I won't bandy gossip. You have more than enough enemies without running down the list of anyone you offended while in my lands."

"Very well, then."

The duke lowered his visor. Drew his great sword of war, with its long, golden hilt. He nodded at Ser Sarkin, who drew breath to call the cry to begin...

But before he could, dazzling red light filled the area. Everything Cavan could see was bathed in red. It was magic, he could tell that much, but that was all he could tell.

He turned quickly to look at Ehren, but Ehren shrugged helplessly.

"THERE WILL BE NO DUEL," a loud voice thundered.

"Amra?" Cavan said, turning to look at her.

Amra bit her lip, her head cocked to one side. Then she turned and pointed.

Just as she did, Cavan began to hear the sound of thundering hooves.

A *lot* of thundering hooves.

Cavan quickly looked the direction Amra was pointing, and now he could see the dust of many, many approaching horses.

And he could see a standard, borne high and clear above those horses.

The sigil it bore: twin rivers crossing at a heart, on a background of pale blue.

The standard of Draven, King of Oltoss.

THE DUKE'S KNIGHTS QUICKLY FORMED INTO RANKS, AND AS ONE TOOK A knee. As did their squires. And the men at arms. The servants.

Soon everyone around Cavan was kneeling except the duke, and Cavan's friends, all of whom were looking to Cavan's lead.

Cavan turned to face the approaching force, and knelt. He didn't look behind him. He knew Ehren and Qalas would kneel, though he wasn't sure about Amra...

The duke remained standing. Still, he did sheathe his sword, and remove his helm.

The king himself rode in the lead, resplendent in gold enameled plate armor, with his sigil engraved onto the left shoulder and enameled separately. He rode a brilliant white destrier, and carried a hand-and-a-half sword at his belt.

Cavan's father looked every inch the warrior king. Strong and proud, with the chin, nose and eyes that Cavan had inherited, though beneath his diamond-studded crown, he had flowing locks of golden hair.

Just behind the king rode Larindra, his Royal Wizard, on a

palomino destrier. She looked to be the same age as the king, somewhere between her fortieth and fiftieth summer, but she was a wizard. Her appearance might mean everything and nothing. Despite the beauty of her face and slender form, she might have been hundreds of years old.

And if half the tales told about her were true, she would have to be.

No doubt the red glow — that faded as the king's company approached — was her work. Though Cavan was still not sure what it did. If it did anything other than demand attention.

She carried a gnarled oaken staff, with various red-gold runes burned into it, and gemstones studded here and there.

Behind her rode a portion of the king's army. It looked to be scores of knights, followed by hundreds of men at arms.

Not so many as the duke brought. Then again, the king brought his Royal Wizard, who outstripped everyone else here in terms of pure power.

Well, everyone except possibly Ehren. Cavan was never entirely sure about where the limits of Ehren's power lay.

In any event, Cavan suspected that the king had brought enough of a force to make the duke hesitate, at the very least.

The king reined in a dozen paces away from the assemblage of kneelers, and slid straight out of his saddle. Larindra followed him, one step behind, muttering something that Cavan did not doubt the king heard, even though he showed no sign.

Right now, the king's brown eyes looked as hard and angry as Cavan's own ever got. And all of that anger was directed straight at the duke.

The duke, who had not knelt. The duke, who still had his helm in his hands, and who looked very much as though he wanted to don it right now.

"Brother," the duke said, "there was no need to trouble yourself so."

The king walked straight up to the duke and slapped him hard across the cheek. With his gauntleted hand.

Duke Falstaff faltered back a step, but did not fall.

"Just what in hell did you think you were doing, Falstaff?" The king thundered. "Bringing an army into *my* barony? Assaulting *my* people? Did you think I would stand for it?"

"Brother, this matter is quite ready to resolve without your royal hand. The champion of Juno and I stand ready to—"

"Champion of Juno? There is no champion of Juno."

"I beg to differ. Juno's majordomo, Olivart, named Cavan champion only last night."

"And I unname him," the king said. He turned to Cavan. "As baron of Juno, I strip you of your post as champion. Furthermore," — here he turned to Olivart, who looked quite uncomfortable on his knees, and gentled his tone for a moment — "stand old friend."

Olivart stood, using his walking stick to help.

"Hear this," the king said, tone firm once more. "Cavan Oltblood is never to stand as champion of Juno, whatever the cause, without my permission. Is that understood?"

"Understood, your majesty," Olivart said.

"And you?" the king turned to Cavan. "Do you understand this as well?"

"I understand, your majesty," Cavan grumbled.

"Good." The king raised his voice. "All may rise, but I charge all to stand as witness to what I say next."

Everyone stood, and Cavan couldn't help feeling contradicting feelings here. On the one hand, he had really been looking forward to personally punishing the duke for needlessly hurting the people of Juno and for getting around the spirit of his promise.

On the other hand, even though he had plenty of mixed feelings about his father the king, he did like the idea of seeing the duke formally taken down for what he'd done.

"Duke Falstaff of Nolarr," the king said, and the duke's eyes widened at being so formally addressed. "You have conspired to steal lands not your own. You have conspired to steal property you have no right to. And worst of all, you have conspired against your king."

"I—" the duke began, but the king silenced him by slashing one hand through the air.

"When I wish you to speak, I will tell you," the king said. "You had no right to make attempts on the life of Juno's heir. You had no right to make claims on Juno's mines, and most of all, you had no right to bring your troops into Juno to press your false claim."

"I'll have a court decide that," the duke said.

"Silence," the king said. "One more word out of you, and I'll have your title."

The duke blanched, but held his tongue.

"You would have had your day in court," the king said with a malicious smile. "I've had good people assembling a case ever since Kent first got word to me about your hunters chasing Cavan, as well as about those gemstones, and what you planned to do when you got them. Since then I've had agents in your duchy supplying me with a *wealth* of information."

The king paused a moment, as though daring the duke to speak. But Falstaff held his tongue.

"But instead you went and pressed the issue. You attacked Juno." The king's smile widened. "Didn't think I knew you initiated the attack, did you? Thought it would be your word against whoever was left alive. No doubt some lowborn man at arms, whose word you knew would never be taken over your own."

So *that* was why the duke was so angry at Ser Sarkin for taking Ser Ranus prisoner. With the commander of Juno's forces as witness, the duke's claim was weakened.

"Fortunately, I've had Mistress Larindra here spying the Royal Road near Juno with her sorcerous agents ever since I heard that you began mustering troops."

Larindra spoke for the first time, her voice high and clear.

"I can testify to what I've seen," she said. "And I can show others just as easily, with a priest of Zisan the Truth to assess the value of what I show."

"And we both know what we'll see, don't we, Falstaff?" The king shook his head. "No more of this, brother. No more. I've been lenient with you for too long, and you've overstepped yourself this time."

The king turned to Cavan.

"Tell me," the king said, "what were the stakes of this duel of yours?"

"All mining rights to the range of Blue Mountains between Juno and Nolarr, as well as the proceeds of all mining over the last six months."

"Not bad," the king said, nodding his head in thought. "But not enough." He raised his voice again. "Hear this. In punishment for this unwarranted act of aggression, Nolarr shall cede to Juno ... all access to the range of Blue Mountains between the Sea of Tormyr and the Royal Road."

The duke had to bite his gauntlet to keep from speaking.

"But that's not all. Nolarr shall furthermore cede the land between the Blue Mountains the nearest branch of the River Rance to Juno."

Cavan could hear one of the duke's teeth crack, he was biting down so hard.

"There," the king said, nodding. "That should be sufficient punishment." He looked over at the duke. "Go ahead, brother, say it before you choke on it."

"You could lose your crown for this," the duke said, voice low and rumbling with menace. "The other dukes will never stand for your blatantly seizing land like that."

"Ah," the king said smiling. "You think so, do you? Well, for the time being, those lands are held by the crown, pending trial."

"Trial?"

"Of course, trial," the king said. "I did say you'd have your day in court." Then all the humor in the king's face died. "But, brother, that day would have been much gentler had you not tried to seize my land by force. And believe me, all the other dukes may need to see what happens when one of their own tries to overextend himself."

"So," the duke said, voice still angry, but restrained. "You'll take my title, will you? Give it to one of your courtiers?"

"Not at all," the king said. "Once your guilt is proven, and the other dukes see why I have done what I've done, I'll restore you to your lands. Or, what remains of them, anyway."

The king started to turn toward Cavan, then stopped himself, and turned back.

Cavan was sure that move was calculated.

"Oh," the king said. "Two other minor issues. First, I hereby dissolve your standing army, and forbid you to ever assemble another. You have abused the privilege. I'll have my men break the news to your company commanders. And the second" — he turned to the duke's own knights — "you are sworn to the duke, and you are sworn to me. Tell me, knights, where does the greater duty lie?"

"To you, your majesty," they said with one voice.

"Excellent," the king said. "Well spoken. Then please, seize the duke. Form a party of your six senior knights, to accompany me back to the palace and act as his guards until he can be properly jailed. I'll trust you on your honor to do this."

Cavan half-expected the duke to bolt, but he didn't. He grimaced, but he held his head high as his own knights took him into custody.

Then the king turned to Cavan.

"I've heard it said that you led your group of friends into the mines to face down an unknown monster. Did you kill it?"

Cavan quickly, and in as understated a fashion as he could, recounted their adventure of the past day.

"Then that gate *is* down there," the king said, softly. "I've always wondered."

"It is," Cavan said, "but it shouldn't interfere with the mining operations, once the miners get their orders to steer clear."

"Yes," the king said with a chuckle. "Few men *seek* the Underworld." He shook his head. "And *all* the gemstones are ruined?"

Cavan nodded. "We brought them along. I was going to present them to my uncle."

"Best not, for now," the king said with a smile. "He's had enough for one day." He raised an eyebrow at Cavan. "Perhaps you'll find another use for them?"

Cavan shrugged.

"If there is nothing else, your majesty, may my friends and I have leave to depart?"

"Not yet. Walk with me a moment, Cavan."

Cavan frowned, but fell into step beside the king.

THE KING WAITED UNTIL THEY'D WALKED UP NEAR THE CAVE THAT LED to the mine, before he turned back to face Cavan. The two of them were alone now. Or as alone as they'd ever be, with bustling activity no more than two dozen paces away, and countless eyes watching them without really watching them.

And, of course, Cavan's friends, who made no pretense of doing anything but watching. Hell, Amra could probably hear every word they said.

"That man you have up on your magical disc," the king said. "The False Dawn assassin. Do you know that Falstaff sent him?"

"Actually," Cavan said, "I'm positive he didn't. Not personally, anyway. Someone on his staff might have done it thinking to please his liege, but that's all I can think of."

"That seneschal of his. Inari. She's scheming enough to do it." The king nodded. "Leave that to me. The assassin too. I'll want him in the royal prisons."

"As you say, your majesty."

"It's just the two of us, Cavan. You may call me father."

"I don't know that I can, your majesty."

Cavan frowned, not wanting to speak the words he had to say next, for fear of insulting the king. But he could not bring himself to hold those words back, either.

"Kent is the only father I've ever known."

"Yes," the king said, nodding, his brown eyes distant. "I understand, of course. And I hope *you* understand that I never wanted to set you aside. Had I my choice in this, I would have claimed you formally, and you would have grown up in the castle with your half-brothers and sister."

Cavan doubted that, but said nothing.

"I couldn't, of course," the king said. "The queen would never have stood for it, and neither would her family. Politics can be an ugly game, Cavan."

"So I understand ... father."

The king laughed, a rich, honest sound, and it carried a few tones that Cavan recognized from his own laughter.

"Stop, stop, I yield," the king said, smiling. "Return to calling me 'your majesty,' if that's how you're going to say 'father.'"

"As you wish, your majesty." But Cavan was smiling now too.

"You'll never be free of Falstaff, you know," the king said, his face growing serious again. "I can't strip him of his duchy, not unless he does something truly egregious."

Cavan's mouth opened to object, but the king stilled him with a raised hand.

"I know, I know. This looks truly egregious to you. As I said. Politics."

Cavan almost pressed that point, but another occurred to him. A matter he considered even more pressing.

"What about those troops?" Cavan said. "You're disbanding the duke's standing army, but they're fighting men and you've taken away their steady pay. They'll become mercenaries. Or worse, bandits."

"Won't happen," the king said with a wink. "Not if they join the *royal* standing army." He chuckled. "Falstaff will spit when he realizes I've stolen his men without actually stealing them."

Cavan wasn't sure what to say to that, but the king had more to say anyway.

"And Falstaff, I'm afraid he's likely to be your neighbor long after you're the count here."

"Count?" Cavan said.

"Of course," the king said. "I've added enough land to Juno that it's too big for a barony. Twall will be unhappy to lose a baron, but I'll make it up to her. I'll let her raise another vassal to help her exploit her rich fishing rights. And anyway, none of this is official until after the trial. Still, I assure you, the outcome will not surprise anyone."

"Count?" Cavan said again.

"Yes. Falstaff can still cause trouble for you along the Royal Road though." The king sharpened his tone. "What should be done about that?"

Cavan answered without taking time for thought.

"There are mines on both sides of the mountains, and all the stonemasons swear that tunnel collapses cannot happen here. Dig a tunnel through the mountain, wide enough for trade and troops, but with plenty of gates and murder holes and so forth."

"Perfect," the king said. "And I imagine your friend Amra would have design ideas?"

"She'd love it."

"See to it then," the king said. "Best to get the plans in motion sooner than later."

"*Count?*" Cavan thought his voice sounded almost frantic now. Why didn't the king see his point? "But ... all the added land. The mines. The rents. The..."

"Yes?" the king said, smiling.

"This is too much of an inheritance for a bastard. Your legitimate children will object. One of them should have it."

"None of them have risked their lives more than once for the people of this soon-to-be-county. No, I'll make sure you inherit Juno." The king shook his head. "Three legitimate heirs, and they're all solid politicians, but they have no soul for adventure. You're more like me than any of my other children."

"Forgive me if I doubt that, your majesty."

"Doubt all you like," the king said. "But watch this."

The king turned toward the mine entrance. He raised one gauntlet. Pointed, but Cavan couldn't tell what he was pointing at.

The king began to mumble under his breath.

A moment passed.

Sweat broke out on the king's forehead.

And then a rock rose up from the ground.

Not a big rock. Not bigger than anything Cavan could have hefted with one hand. Still, the king did it by magic, and that was clearly the point.

The king released the rock. It slammed into the ground, kicking up grayish dust.

The king turned a smile on Cavan. "I failed to become a wizard too. Though I daresay you have more talent for it than I do."

Something warmed inside Cavan at that revelation. Something eased in his gut. Something he hadn't even known was tight.

Yes, Cavan had always known he was a royal bastard. Yes, Cavan even saw some of his own features in the royal visage.

But only now, watching Draven the man work so hard to do something Cavan could have done with much less effort. To see Draven the man burst into sweat and have his face go red, merely to impress a bastard son with his meager efforts.

Now, for the first time, Cavan felt as though he truly had a father by blood, and not just by fosterage.

CAVAN AND THE KING SPOKE FOR SOME TIME, THE FEELINGS BETWEEN them more relaxed and casual than Cavan had ever felt before. Cavan told more of his own stories, and his father — no, the king, Kent was still ... oh, Cavan couldn't decide — told stories of the adventures of his own youth.

Perhaps the two of them *were* more alike than Cavan would have believed.

By the time they finished talking, the first rays of true sunlight were just making it past the mountains, finally lifting the paling gray that had been with them since the night sky had first begun to fade.

The day was warmer now, and Cavan could hear larks singing as he walked alone back down the trail through the breaking encampments to his friends. They'd already finished breaking their fast, but they kept food ready for Cavan. He dug in without pausing to say hello, not having realized just how hungry he'd gotten.

And the food they'd left him was just what he would have asked for. Good Oltoss rye, a runny white cheese with whiskey undertones to its flavor, though not nearly enough crispy bacon to suit him.

But then, was there ever enough crispy bacon to suit Cavan? If so, he hoped he never found out.

As he ate, the others packed up the horses that Olivart had brought for them.

Olivart had chosen not to bring their own horses, for fear that the duke might have them stolen or slain. A fair choice, but Cavan knew his friends missed their own horses as much as he missed Dzint.

Fortunately, they were talking about that right now, instead of pestering Cavan with questions. He couldn't tell them what all the king had said. Not yet. Not until he had time to process it himself...

Finally, the horses were loaded, and Cavan had finished filling his belly.

Cavan stood.

"Well," he started, but Amra cut in with a grin.

"A count, eh?"

"Apparently," Cavan said with a sigh.

"Give him a year," Ehren said. "He'll inherit the whole kingdom. See if he doesn't."

Then Ehren's smile got wider, and he added, "May he live a thousand years."

Qalas and Amra laughed as they echoed the traditional blessing for the monarch of Oltoss.

"Bit of an exaggeration, that," Cavan said, when their laughter died down.

"Oh, I don't know," Qalas said with a chuckle. "A man who can cut a deal with an ancient Dunaian god is not a man *I* want to underestimate."

"Am I going to hear about this the whole way to the manor?"

"Yes," Ehren said with smile. "You are."

Cavan sighed again. "Then let's get riding. Oh, and Amra?"

"Yes, your lordship?"

Cavan swallowed his first reply, rather than rising to the bait.

"I was going to offer you the chance to design the defenses of a new tunnel through the mountain, but now I'm not sure..."

"I'll do it!" she said, and whooped, throwing her fist in the air. "We'll need lots of liquid fire..."

Cavan was pleased for the distraction. Listening to Amra plot the brutal deaths of theoretical invading armies was many times better than listening to "Count Cavan" taunts for a whole morning's ride.

17

―――――――

Birds sang songs of lies, in the elm trees that grew in groves around this small, private dock on the Sea of Tormyr. The birds were stellar jays, and none of the corvids could be trusted, but stellar jays least of all.

Stellar jays were like titled nobility. They sang of prowess they did not possess. They sang of lands they did not hold, and victories they had not won.

Yes, stellar jays were liars. But at least they were not hunted. Which gave them one on Inari.

Inari stood on that dock, under the cloudless summer sky that lied like the stellar jays. Tried to tell Inari that the day was beautiful and warm, when her life had turned ugly and cold.

The dock belonged to the Evelyn, the countess of Nask. As the countess was currently with the duke over in Juno — perhaps the only bit of luck in Inari's life right now — there was no one in Nask to say that Inari had no right to be where she was. No one in Nask had the right to search her possessions for the money she had stolen from Nolarr's treasury before fleeing.

Not that Inari would admit to her identity. Not if she didn't have to. Not right now.

Draven was in Juno.

And that meant everything had gone to hell.

Falstaff was too damned showy. Always had been. Every time a matter involved the king, Falstaff had to prove that he was just as smart as his brother. Just as powerful. Just as deserving of the crown.

If only Falstaff had listened to Inari, and sent in a single company, under cover of night, to seize the mine, he might have at least recovered some of those gemstones he nattered on about.

But Falstaff had sent his army. Ridden with it, "defending his rights."

And now Draven was in Juno. Draven wouldn't have gone himself, not unless he knew he'd already beaten his brother again.

Inari did not know for certain that Falstaff had gone and gotten himself arrested, but she would have bet everything she carried on it.

She knew only two things for certain. Her agents had been able to tell her this much: Draven was in Juno, and Cavan Oltblood was still alive.

The first meant that Falstaff was sure to be arrested. Censured. Gods only knew what Draven would do to him for this.

The second meant that her assassin had failed.

Together, the conclusions were clear enough that even Draven would see them. He would look for the money behind the assassin sent for his bastard, and he would remember how Inari once tried to impress him with her cunning. When Draven was a new king, and Inari thought she had the chance to become Royal Seneschal...

Now, Inari would be arrested, tried, and put to death. The conviction was a foregone conclusion. Draven had learned well from his father — his counselors were bloodhounds that could sniff out evidence, no matter how lost or faded, and they argued so well it was said that half the criminals in Oltoss confessed their crimes right there in the courtroom.

The False Dawn wouldn't care about the politics. They had their contract. Either they'd send more assassins until the bastard was dead, or Draven would find a way to cancel that contract.

Either way, the False Dawn would come to Inari for the balance of their payment.

And when she didn't have it, she would die.

Well, let them all try to kill her. They would have to find her first.

Inari had contingencies in place, just in case such a day ever came.

She'd received word shortly after dawn.

Within the hour, her double was seen by all the farmers in the market, loudly buying plenty of food, before boarding a coach heading on the road northwest to Holst, accompanied by guards known to be loyal to Inari.

And Inari herself had slipped away south into Nask. Alone, and laden with nothing more than bags of gold and jewels. Her tracks covered by generous applications of memory bane. She had not even stopped for food, but Inari had long ago learned how to still her stomach when she needed to.

Yes, she was starving. But she could wait to eat until she was safely aboard the first ship to reach these docks today.

She'd already spoken with the harbormaster. Bribed him, rather than admitting who she was. Learned that Evelyn had a shipment of silks from the south due here sometime this morning.

Perfect.

Inari needed little room, and she'd passed the age when sailors would be distracted, looking at her. She'd be just one more old noble-woman, looking for warmer climes in her declining years.

Yes, she had no doubt that she could talk and bribe her way into a berth. Enough of a bribe, and the captain would leave again on the evening tide. A little timely memory bane, and he'd forget he ever saw her.

Yes. Inari would be long gone, by the time anyone came to Nolarr looking for her. And Inari still had friends who would take her in. Shelter her.

Then, and only then, could Inari begin to plot her vengeance on those who had ruined her...

18

———————

By mid-afternoon, Cavan was back in Juno, with Dzint under him again.

Yes, he'd ridden a fair distance from the mines today already, but he'd missed his blue roan hobby enough that he had to gallop a few times around the baronial manor grounds, just to enjoy the reunion.

His friends were doing likewise, with their own horses. Each on a different course, but the grounds inside these walls were broad enough that they would all do so without tripping over one another.

Riding another horse, that had been riding.

To be moving with Dzint again, that was more like flying. Horse and rider knew each other so well that they needed almost no clues to turn, to jump, to speed up or slow down.

Each seemed to know the other's needs and thoughts without any cues that anyone else could see.

It was as though, riding Dzint again, Cavan had recovered some lost part of his own body.

And the reunion was joy.

The late afternoon was warm, with plenty of fluffy white clouds drifting about up above. The guards from the walls yelled down greetings whenever Cavan and Dzint rode close enough, and he waved back smiling acknowledgments each time.

That evening, Cavan knew, he would have to sit with Olivart and go over what Falstaff's little invasion had cost. Yes, the king — father? No, still too strange yet — had promised that Juno would be reimbursed by Nolarr for those costs, but only some of them could really be counted in coins.

Some had lost their lives. Cavan wanted to know who they were. If they had families. What, if anything, he could do for those families personally, before he left Juno once more.

No, he was not the count here. Not yet. But King Draven had made it clear that he would ensure Cavan would become count here one day.

And that meant Cavan would have to return to Juno more often in the interim. Get to know its people and needs, and let them get to know him.

But that would come later.

Right now, the joy of riding.

The joy of Dzint, galloping full speed between groves of pear, apple and cherry trees, with the agility that only a hobby could bring to the cuts and turns as they went. He was tempted to lead Dzint racing along the narrow strips between the series of pools out back, but he didn't know the etiquette.

Those pools had some kind of spiritual significance. He knew that much. That he knew no more only pointed to something else he needed to learn before he one day ruled here.

Cavan. Ruling. Still a strange thought, especially for a man who had all but forgotten he would ever inherit anything.

Finally, though, the reunion of horse and rider felt complete, and Cavan rode over to join his friends near the stables. The manor had stalls enough for a score of horses, but rarely kept more than three of four at any one time. At least they kept plenty of hay and oats in stock.

Amra had already brushed down Caramel's bay coat once, and was feeding him a carrot. Ehren's blond chestnut, Highsun, looked as though he needed brushing as little as Ehren ever needed to bathe, but Ehren was feeding his horse some wonder pulled from his backpack.

And Qalas, Qalas had come to understand the importance of a proper relationship between horse and rider. He was not only giving his buckskin rouncey, Ondiq, a thorough brushing, he was instructing three stable boys in proper brush technique for doing so.

"Any of those brushes still available?" Cavan said as he walked Dzint up to join them.

Ehren reached into his backpack, pulled out a horse brush, and tossed it to Cavan without ever looking away from Highsun.

"So, your lordship," Amra said, and before she could even finish her sentence, Cavan was already sighing. Not that this stopped her. "How long do you need to stay?"

"Just overnight," Cavan said. "And don't tell me you'll complain about a featherbed for a night before we go back on the road."

"And a room to myself that I'm not paying for?" She smiled without a hint of menace. "I'll suffer through it."

"We're heading out that soon?" Qalas asked. "I thought sure you'd need to spend a month here or something."

"Juno has a majordomo, a steward, and a current baron. Or count. Whichever. The point is, Juno doesn't need me getting in the way." Cavan smiled. "And besides, I have an idea or two about what we need to do next."

Cavan waited until all three of his friends were looking before he said, "But first, Dzint needs his brushing and his apple."

And Cavan refused to answer any of their questions until he felt satisfied that Dzint had been thoroughly rubbed down, brushed down, and treated to both an apple and a carrot, before being settled once more into a stable.

Only then did he gather with his friends once more on the thick grass just outside the stable.

"Come on, then," Cavan said, and began walking. A question or two was started and ignored, before his friends fell into step.

Cavan led them over to a small building, near the eastern wall, confident that the sounds and smells would tell them he was leading them to a smithy even before they saw where he led them. Though admittedly, underneath the smells of hot iron and steel, as well as coke and such, Cavan was pretty sure he detected odd sweet and savory scents as well.

As though a baker had set up shop inside a smithy.

But the sounds of hammer and anvil were clear enough.

And besides, his friends' eyes would only do them so much good, in this case. Unlike any other smithy Cavan had been to, this one was not open on the sides. Oh, it didn't have stone walls, but it did have sheets of canvas fixed in place, covering most of the ways heat could escape.

Must be hot as an oven in there.

"Ah," Amra said knowingly, and when Cavan caught her glance at Qalas, he knew she'd already figured out what Cavan had in mind.

"What?" Ehren asked.

"You'll see," Cavan said. "At least, I hope you'll see."

Qalas said nothing. Only glanced thoughtfully at Cavan, then turned his eyes back to the smithy.

The canvas over the entryway was not tacked at the bottom, but still, Cavan could only think of it as a closed door.

"Hail, the smith," he called. "I am Cavan Oltblood. May my friends and I enter?"

"Of course," came the reply. A high voice, but rough, and definitely male.

Cavan led the way inside, and almost stopped after his first step.

It was every bit as oven-hot as Cavan expected. So hot he thought of the three days it once took him to cross a desert in the summertime. Three days that felt more like three months.

But it was what he saw that stopped him.

Six stone tables in this place, and all of them covered with ongoing projects that involved mainly sheets of metal. The furnace, in the center of the room, was unlike any that Cavan had ever seen.

It spiraled, widening in places like a snake that had eaten three meals of different sizes, one almost large enough to burst it. And the whole thing appeared to be fed from the bottom.

Cavan made his feet move, so that his friends could enter as well. And this is when the smith finally turned away from whatever he was working on.

Tall, he was, and a wiry kind of thin. He wore clothes of ochre and blood red, made from some thin material Cavan didn't recognize. The smith had skin as red as Yeenach, but the pointed ears and long, reddish blond hair — currently braided down his back — reminded Cavan he was looking at a dune elf, not a god.

The first dune elf he had ever met, but he knew the descriptions well from his studies with Master Powys. Of course, even without the description, only a dune elf could work in such heat without a drop of perspiration on his forehead.

The dune elf looked back, content for the time being with silence, it seemed.

"I am Cavan Oltblood," Cavan said, and indicating his friends in turn, added, "and my friends are Ehren, Amra, and Qalas." Cavan dipped his head in a quick bow. "Forgive me, but while Olivart told me he'd hired a new smith, he neglected to tell me your name."

"Rechaxo," he said, but he added nothing more than that.

Cavan drew his sword, held it sideways in both hands.

"I am told that this is your work. I cannot thank you enough. It's a masterpiece. The finest sword I have ever held."

The dune elf nodded slowly, as though new to the gesture.

"They're unaccustomed to thanks," Ehren muttered. "They—"

"We consider our work to be its own reward," Rechaxo said. "Forgive me. I am new to human customs, and these are human lands. I believe the proper reply is ... you are well come."

"It's just one word," Amra said, leaning forward with a wink.

From anyone else, it might have sounded condescending. But when Amra said it, even though the Rechaxo's expression never changed, Cavan got the impression that he was smiling. Pleased, somehow.

All he did though was nod his head once, slow and deliberate.

"You should know," Cavan said, "the sword has already served me well against creatures from the Dunaian Underworld."

Rechaxo's ears twitched. He said, "Truly?"

"He doesn't need to lie about his deeds," Qalas said, then added something in a harsh tongue that Cavan didn't follow.

Rechaxo did though. He replied back in kind, with a fluidity of speech he didn't have in Rentissi.

"Sorry," Qalas said. "It seemed easier to explain that way."

"You were doing better than I was," Cavan said with a chuckle, and sheathed his sword.

"Wait," Rechaxo said. He narrowed his eyes. "Unfinished. Olivart said you had gems for it?"

"I did, but I had to sacrifice them."

"Give it here," he said. "I will finish it before morning."

"But—"

"Give it here," Rechaxo said again.

Cavan handed him the sword.

Having Rechaxo volunteer more work made Cavan feel guilty about what he had come here to ask, but he could only forge ahead.

"While it feels ungrateful to ask for another treasure of such distinction," Cavan said, "but Qalas here is in need of a weapon that can harm some of the more powerful creatures we find ourselves fighting. Could you perhaps, make a halberd for him, with *licha*?"

"Would that I had enough deepsand to do the job," Rechaxo said. "But I'm afraid I used the last of it on this."

He stepped lightly through a door in the back, and returned with a package wrapped in simple paper. He presented it to Cavan.

"Your man Olivart said you went about without armor." Rechaxo shook his head. "Foolishness. They all tell me you are a good man. It would be a pity if you died. I regret only that I lacked enough to include a coif and greaves."

Despite the heat, a wave of cold shock swept over Cavan.

"No," he breathed, unbelieving.

He opened the package.

Inside were a sleeved hauberk, and leggings.

Made from *licha.*

Amra whistled. So did Qalas.

Ehren uttered a quick prayer.

Cavan only stared at Rechaxo in slack-jawed amazement.

"You are *welcome,*" Rechaxo said.

No more than an hour past dawn the next day — true dawn, though hours of pre-dawn gloom remained this close to the mountains — Cavan and his friends were in the saddle and riding north for the Royal Road.

Rain clouds were coming in from the south, but Cavan didn't mind. Nothing could dampen his spirits. Not today.

He had a belly full of good hot food — including plenty of crispy bacon — he had his friends by his side, Dzint underneath him, and the open road ahead of him. He had fresh new armor so light he almost felt he wasn't wearing it, and his sword was now encrusted with gemstones. Sapphires carved into likenesses of mountains on the sides of the hilt, and at the base of the pommel, a ruby so finely tuned it could hold spells.

Cavan would never admit this to Kent, but it was some of the finest jewelry work Cavan had ever seen.

Ehren yawned through the words, "Could we not have waited for local sunrise?"

"We have a long way to go," Cavan said.

"You still haven't told us where we're going," Amra said.

"Qalas needs a better weapon," Cavan said. "And I happen to know a dwarf who couldn't make a horseshoe without enchanting it. He's up near the Dragon Spines."

"We don't need to do that," Qalas said, and Cavan thought he was hiding embarrassment.

"Absolutely we do," Amra said. "Terrific idea."

"Terrific idea for later in the day," Ehren said, though he was still smiling at the notion.

"And just how could we pay for it?" Qalas asked.

"Oh," Cavan said, "I'm sure he'll just want us to do him a favor."

"Sounds dangerous," Ehren said.

"Sounds like fun," Amra said.

Qalas started laughing.

"What?" Cavan asked.

"You're all crazy."

"You mean *we're* all crazy," Cavan corrected him.

And together, they set out on the road once more.

SIGN UP FOR STEFON'S NEWSLETTER

Stefon loves to keep in touch with his readers, and loves to keep you reading. The best way for him to do both is for you to sign up for his newsletter.

Sign up at http://www.stefonmears.com/join

If you sign up for Stefon's newsletter, you get...

- Monthly updates about his publishing and travel schedules
- His latest news, in brief, and answers to reader questions
- A free short story for signing up
- List-only offers and occasional specials
- Plus a free short story every month!

ABOUT THE AUTHOR

Stefon Mears is wary of people with purple mustaches. Stefon has more than twenty-five books to his credit, and he never stops writing. He earned his M.F.A. in Creative Writing from N.I.L.A., and his B.A. in Religious Studies (double emphasis in Ritual and Mythology) from U.C. Berkeley. He's a lifelong gamer and fantasy fan. Stefon lives in Portland, Oregon, with his wife and three cats.

Look for Stefon online:
www.stefonmears.com
himself@stefonmears.com